Nothing but Trouble

Elise Noble

Published by Undercover Publishing Limited

v9

ISBN: 978-1-910954-20-1

Edited by Amanda Ann Larson

Cover art by Elise Noble

www.undercover-publishing.com

www.elise-noble.com

For every girl who ever wanted to sit at home on the sofa.

CHAPTER 1

AS I SCURRIED back to my desk, my boss, Barry, blocked the way, tapping his watch.

"Seven minutes, Ellen. You've taken seven minutes. The rule for a bathroom break is five minutes. What have you got to say about that?"

Six months I'd worked there, and he still couldn't get my name right.

I avoided his eyes, and instead focused on a glob of jam clinging to the second of his two chins, a remnant from his eleven o'clock donut. He ate one every morning with a cup of coffee, which was perhaps why he bore more than a passing resemblance to one of the doughy balls. Minus the sugar, of course. There was nothing sweet about Barry.

"I'm sorry, sir," I mumbled. "It won't happen again."

"It had better not. With you swanning off tomorrow morning, we're already going to be behind on our targets this week."

I seethed as I crossed the stained grey carpet to my seat. Swanning off? I was going to a funeral. It wasn't like I'd be enjoying myself.

I slumped into my chair and adjusted my headset, trying to gulp back the tears that threatened to fall. Sue leaned over from the next desk and pressed a tissue into my hand.

"Here you go, love. Keep your chin up."

I was trying, I really was, but when the closest person I'd had to family had just died, it wasn't easy.

Still, I didn't have time to grieve, not when the switchboard was already flashing with another call for me.

"Payright Insurance, how may I help you?"

The voice on the other end launched into a monologue about how he'd driven out of his driveway on his way to work yesterday morning, straight into the path of an oncoming bus. As he was in a Peugeot 106, it didn't take much imagination to work out who won that tussle.

"So how long does it take to claim compensation?" he asked.

"Sir, I'm afraid if the accident's your fault, you can't claim compensation."

"But it wasn't my fault."

"I thought you said the bus was on the main road?"

"Yes, but it was five minutes early." His tone left me under no illusion who he believed was the stupid one in our conversation.

In the end, I just typed everything he said onto the form and sent it off to the claims department. He'd undoubtedly call back when they threw the claim out, but at least I'd bought myself a couple of weeks.

The calls came endlessly, and by lunchtime, my throat burned and my voice was cracking. I scooted off to the break room and unwrapped my sandwiches, grateful to have a few minutes away from Barry's withering gaze.

Sue popped in a few minutes later and flumped

down next to me.

"Was it a full moon last night? It's like the entire population of England decided to go out and drive into something," she said.

"Seems so, doesn't it?"

"Profits'll be down. Barry said if we had another bad month, we'd have to start bringing in our own tea bags."

Great, something else to look forward to.

On the table in front of me, my phone vibrated with an incoming call. A kitten wearing a feather boa popped up on the screen—the picture I'd assigned Jasveer, my best friend and another of Barry's reluctant army of call-centre minions.

She'd had a family emergency today and begged for a few hours off, which was something else that sent Barry stomping along on the warpath. If there was a prize for the least understanding boss ever, Barry would be the undisputed champion.

"How's Stevie?" I asked.

Stevie was Jaz's two-year-old. If I ever thought about having a child of my own, thirty seconds in a room with Stevie was enough to send my uterus running for cover. His hobbies included retuning the television, feeding Lego to the cat and attempting his own version of the Mona Lisa on the living room wall. This morning, he'd got hold of a pair of Jaz's earrings, and she'd had to take him to A&E to have a cubic zirconia removed from his ear canal.

"He'll live." I heard the unspoken "unfortunately" at the end of that sentence. "The doctor gave him a sheet of stickers for being such a brave little soldier, and now they're stuck fast to the headrest. Do you know what gets glue off leather?"

It wasn't a problem I'd ever had with my bicycle. "Sorry, I've got no idea."

"I can't get hold of the childminder and Amir's working, so I've got to stay home. I hate to ask, but could you tell Barry? If I phone him, he'll get in one of his moods, and I might be tempted to tell him what I really think of him."

If she ever did that, you'd have to bleep most of the words out. I'd heard her let fly after a glass or two of wine, and she covered every four-letter word as well as making up a few of her own.

"Okay, I'll do it."

"Thanks, doll. I'll be back in tomorrow for definite." Her voice softened. "You take care of yourself in the morning, okay? Take as much time as you need. I'll keep Barry off your back."

"I really appreciate it."

With us still being a person down, the afternoon was just as busy as the morning, but when the clock finally ticked round to five thirty, I wasn't sure whether to be thrilled or sad. Usually I'd have beaten Usain Bolt out the door, but today the reality of going home to an empty house hit me, and I dithered around as I turned off my computer and tidied my desk.

"How are you holding up?" Sue asked, concern showing in her eyes.

"I'm..." I started to say I was okay, which I'd made my standard response. But Sue had known me for too long, and I knew it wouldn't wash. "I'm all trembly inside. I can't believe she's gone. I keep expecting to get home and find her making a batch of chocolate chip cookies or watching *Top Gear*. And when she isn't, I can't stop the tears."

Sue squeezed my arm. "It's grief, Ella, and there's not much you can do about it. I'm sure Edith wouldn't have wanted you to mope around, though. She's probably up there planning a carnival." Sue pointed skywards. Well, ceiling-wards. The dusty strip light above us glowed yellow, complete with a cluster of desiccated moths destined to spend eternity gracing its plastic cover.

I managed a smile because she was right. Edith had probably convinced the man upstairs to install a disco ball so she could keep busy teaching the angels how to do the Macarena. She never did grow old gracefully.

"I know, but I've never had anybody close to me die before. It was a bit of a shock."

"I bet. If there's anything I can do, you just let me know."

"I will. Thank you."

I said that, but I wouldn't. I never asked for anything, not after being let down so many times. If the care system taught me one thing, it was not to hope, because hoping only resulted in disappointment.

I set off home, dreading the stillness of number seventeen Horsefield Road. When Edith was alive, it had felt like a home. She'd filled it with warmth, laughter, and quite often the dulcet tones of the smoke alarm as she got distracted by online bingo and burned dinner. Now it had all the atmosphere of a morgue, but without the company.

I didn't know what was worse—the fact I was living there on my own, or that I wouldn't be able to stay for much longer. The house had been Edith's, you see, and I only rented a room. Now she'd gone, I was effectively homeless.

It was only a matter of time before I'd have to venture out into the big wide world, and that thought terrified me.

Edith had been like a grandma to me since she first found me at age ten, crying on the pavement outside her house. My foster sister's bike lay next to me, and I wasn't just bawling because I'd scraped my knee. I was panicking because she'd be furious I'd taken her bike without asking.

Edith had helped me into her kitchen and cleaned up my cuts, then walked me home. She even stayed while I fessed up to my foster mother, a woman with all the personality of a dead fish, who didn't care what any of the kids did as long as she got her cheque from the council each month.

Over the years, I spent more time at Edith's house than my own. She always had a plate of cookies waiting, and I could sit and read a book in peace without one of my foster siblings pulling my hair or poking me. When I turned eighteen and my foster family absolved themselves of all responsibility, it was Edith who'd taken me in and made sure I carried on with my education.

Although when I recalled the day I'd just spent at the call centre, I did wonder how much benefit I really got from my three year English degree. I'd have been better off taking a course in how to speak idiot.

I sighed as I opened Edith's front door. Was I destined to spend the rest of my life as a representative of Payright? I shuddered at the thought, but the unknown scared me. I already needed to move to a new home. A new job was a leap too far for the moment. I needed to take things one step at a time.

In the kitchen, I set some spaghetti on to boil then ran through my final checklist for the funeral tomorrow. Helping to organise that had left me in tears countless times over the past week. Edith's friends had rallied round, but I'd done most of the work myself, from choosing the casket to arranging the flowers. I felt I owed her a good send off.

Yes, everything was done. The service would be at the church Edith had attended on Sundays, and she'd be buried in the churchyard afterwards. She'd chosen the plot herself many years ago, right next to her late husband. He'd died in a car crash long before I met her, and she'd never found anyone to take his place.

"There's one true soul mate out there for everyone. I was lucky I found John young and had twenty good years with him," she said.

"What if I never find the one that's meant for me?" I asked.

"If it's meant to be, he'll find you."

Well, he hadn't so far. All I'd managed to do was waste two years of my life with a man who did the dirty on me. And not just with anyone. No, when Terry decided he needed a little excitement in his life, he'd found it with a stripper called Miss Demeanor.

No wonder he'd always been broke, what with most of his money going on lap dances and hotel rooms.

Stupid, stupid me hadn't suspected a thing. It wasn't until Amir went on a stag do and spotted him licking whipped cream off the girl that his indiscretions came to light.

When I confronted him, he'd tried his best to convince me it was nothing.

"I was doing research for my next novel," he told me.

"Last week you said you were writing a modern-day version of Pirates of the Caribbean?"

"Er, yeah, I did, but that was until I thought of this one. It's gonna be a hit, I know it."

"But why did you have to get a lap dance?"

"I'm taking the method acting approach, except with writing. I want to experience everything my characters do."

He could be very convincing, and I might even have believed him if it wasn't for Edith. When I told her what had happened, she poured me a glass of sherry then pulled on her winter coat and got her car keys down from the hook.

"Where are you going?" I asked.

"The Pink Panda."

"You can't just walk into a gentleman's club!"

"Of course I can, dear. I'm almost eighty. Someone will help me up the steps."

And that was exactly what she did. She got back three hours later, covered in glitter and wearing a feather boa.

"That place is something else. Some of those young ladies are ever so bendy. I had a go on one of their poles, and let me tell you, it's not as easy as it looks."

I stifled a groan. Sometimes I thought we'd ended up in the wrong bodies. At twenty-two, I preferred to spend my evenings curled up with a book while Edith partied the night away, taking full advantage of her senior citizens' discount.

"You didn't hurt yourself, did you?" Edith had two hip replacements, and she wasn't quite as sprightly as she liked to think.

"Oh no, one of those hunky young men who opens the door for you helped to hold me up. Anyway, I found the girl that Terry's been playing away with. Demi's really quite sweet. She even did my eyelashes." Edith fluttered her new additions, which were royal blue with silver tips.

"Very nice," I said hollowly.

"Terry told her he was single, and not only that, he claimed to be a best-selling novelist. When he took you to the cinema last week, he said he was meeting his agent about a movie deal for his latest book."

I sat down with a bump. How could I have been so stupid? It had never occurred to me that Terry might be unfaithful. I'd always thought we were so well matched, ever since we met in my second year at university. We'd both wanted to check out the same book from the library—*Lord of the Flies*—and as a compromise, we read it together over a pizza and a bottle of wine at his place.

He was the first man to ask me on a date, and after we'd been out two or three times, we were smitten with each other. At least, I thought so. With hindsight, Terry was perhaps more attracted to the money I earned from my part-time job and my willingness to help edit his dystopian fantasies.

A tear ran down my cheek, and Edith passed me one of her frilly hankies. "Keep your chin up, dearie. You were too good for him, anyway. We'll find you a better one."

She'd tried, bless her. Before I could blink, she'd signed me up on *Plenty of Fish,* and men were sending me photos of parts of their anatomy I really didn't want to see.

"Ooh, look, another one," Edith said, as the third such message popped up on my inbox. She leaned forward and squinted. "I'll need to get my glasses this time."

With her encouragement and a bit of a push from Jaz, I'd been on two dates. The first ended in embarrassment as a waiter swept past and accidentally knocked the man's toupee into his soup. The second guy produced a box of condoms after desert and invited me to pick my favourite flavour.

I put my foot down when Edith tried to set me up a third time.

"I'm not wasting another night out with a weirdo."

"But I worry about you spending so much time in the house. You're only young once. You should be out on the town, not stopping in with an old lady like me."

"You're good company, Edith. I couldn't ask for a better dinner partner."

Those words were the truth. I didn't know what to do with myself now she was gone. She and Jaz were the only people I could truly talk to, and Jaz was so busy dealing with the tornado that followed Stevie around, I only saw her outside of work once a week.

So that night, after a quiet dinner alone, I curled up in an armchair. I only had my book boyfriends for company now.

CHAPTER 2

A RAINBOW OF colour filled the church at Edith's funeral. Red hats, blue skirts, yellow jumpers—I'd requested nobody wore black, and everyone enthusiastically heeded the brief. Edith wouldn't have wanted it to be a sombre affair. The coffin I'd chosen may have been slightly unorthodox, but hot pink had been her favourite colour, and she'd have appreciated the floral tour of the world decorating the lid.

We started off with her favourite hymn, "All Things Bright and Beautiful," then moved onto the readings. Tears ran down my cheeks as I spoke, and by the time I got to the final line of my eulogy, half the church was sniffing. We finished up by singing "Get the Party Started" by Pink, which was the song Edith lived by.

I couldn't believe that this would be the last knees-up she'd ever attend.

The wake started off a bit quiet, but once the band struck up, people began to smile a little. The four-piece came from the old folks' home down the road. Not one of them was under seventy, but they put groups half their age to shame.

I tried to get into the party spirit, but I couldn't manage it. In the end, I hid away in the kitchen of the church hall to block out the celebration of Edith's life coming from the other side of the wall. Things were starting to wind down when one of Edith's bridge buddies, Albert, found me sitting there, staring into a cup of tea as if it held all the answers to life.

"Not coming out to join in the party?" he asked. Albert reminded me of a Bassett hound—he had the same droopy face and always managed to look doleful.

I shook my head. "I don't understand how people can celebrate. I know it's what Edith would have wanted, but I'm not in the mood for fun."

He dragged a chair up beside me and propped an arm on his walking stick as he lowered his behind to the seat. "At our age, we need to take advantage of these opportunities while we can. Nobody's quite sure which one of us will be next."

"I suppose that's one way of looking at it."

He stared into space for a few seconds while he sucked on his dentures. "I've been meaning to come and find you. Do you have time to pop round later for a chat?"

"What about?"

I didn't know Albert very well. We'd bumped into each other over the years, usually when Edith had drunk one too many glasses of sherry and I'd had to give her a hand to get home, but we'd never had more than a casual conversation. I couldn't imagine what he might want to talk to me about.

"It's something Edith asked me to do, if she left this earth before she planned to."

Curiosity nibbled at me, but I could also picture Barry tapping his foot as he watched the second hand sweep around the clock above his desk.

"Okay, but it'll have to be this evening. My boss isn't very understanding about people having a personal life."

"Not planning to go anywhere." He wheezed a little and covered his mouth as he coughed. "I tend to be in bed by nine, though."

"I'll be there before six."

Barry gave me a dirty look when I walked in just after one. I could tell from his glare he was itching to say something, but as he got halfway out of his chair his mother came in with his lunch, and she'd clip him round the ear if she heard him being so insensitive. Thank goodness for small mercies.

Jaz gave me a tight smile as she tried and failed to get a word in edgeways with her caller, and slid a cupcake over as I sat down. She had a habit of turning to food for comfort so it was her way of trying to cheer me up. She knew how much burying Edith would have upset me.

"Thanks," I mouthed, even if I didn't feel like eating.

Hollow inside, I drifted through the afternoon on autopilot. If someone asked me to recall a single conversation I'd had, I would have failed miserably, and I doubted the notes I jotted in the comment boxes on the screen made much sense either.

Tick, tick, tick—as five thirty approached, I was clock-watching more obsessively than Barry. The instant I finished my final call, I was out of the door before he could mention the word "overtime." Jaz hurried along beside me with her heels clicking on the pavement. She hated flats and proudly boasted that even her trainers had platform soles.

"When you're five feet tall, you need all the help you can get," she'd once said.

My wardrobe contained a single pair of stilettos. I'd worn them precisely once. On that occasion, I'd nearly broken my ankle trying to climb a set of stairs, and as I'd flung out my arms in a desperate attempt to save myself, I'd accidentally groped the crotch of a man on his way down. Mortified didn't begin to cover it. Now Satan's favourite footwear languished at the back of my closet, never to see the light of day. I was more of a ballet pump type of girl.

"Are you going to be okay on your own this evening?" Jaz asked.

"Yes." No. "I'll manage."

She laid a hand on my arm. "I can stay with you if you want. Amir can deal with Stevie for a night."

"I'm going to visit a friend of Edith's, then I just want to crawl into bed."

"Have you got wine?"

I nodded. Edith had always kept an emergency supply in the cupboard under the stairs, and I'd say this qualified as an emergency.

"I'll see you tomorrow, then. Maybe we'll get lucky and it'll be Barry's evening to get hit by a bus."

She said that every night. I lived in hope.

Albert lived in a big, old detached house two streets away. It was far too big for one person, but according to

Edith, he couldn't bear to part with the place where he'd brought up his family. He simply shut off half the rooms so it was cheaper to heat and enjoyed the home he'd lived in for more than half a century.

I rang the bell, an old-fashioned one hanging from a long chain, and waited for him to answer. And waited. And waited. Eventually, I heard the shuffle shuffle tap, shuffle shuffle tap of him coming along the hallway. The door creaked as it swung open, and Albert ushered me into the dimly lit vestibule.

"Cup of tea, or something stronger?"

"Do I need something stronger?" I still couldn't fathom what he wanted to talk to me about.

Rather than answer, he headed for the lounge, where he paused in front of an old-fashioned drinks cabinet and poured me a whisky. Four fingers. Neat.

Uh oh.

"How about we talk in my study?"

How about I go home and hibernate for six months or so? "Sure, wherever you want."

He settled himself behind a massive desk and straightened the row of pens sitting on the jotter in front of him. *Come on, speak.* I perched on the edge of the seat opposite him, waiting.

"I don't know how much Edith told you about me?"

"Not a lot," I admitted.

"Did you know I was her lawyer as well as her bridge partner?"

I shook my head, feeling a sudden dread. Was this about me living in her house?

"My son's taken over the firm now, but it still says 'Thomas and Thomas' on the sign." His eyes took on a wistful look as he stared at a spot above my head.

"Those were the days. Standing up in front of the judge, picking apart the prosecution piece by piece. Closest I get to a courtroom nowadays is watching *Judge Judy*. Of course..."

Please, get to the point. My knuckles were already white from gripping the wooden arms of the chair.

"I had to defend some real pieces of scum," he continued. "Always felt secretly pleased when one of them got sent down. As long as my fees got paid, of course." He shook his head and re-focused on me. "So, where were we? Oh yes, Edith."

I barely managed to nod my head in agreement.

"A couple of years ago, Edith asked me to draft her will for her. Did she ever mention it to you?"

"No."

"I thought not." He chuckled. "I'd better tell you what it says, then."

He reached into his desk drawer and came out with a long, cream envelope. My heart beat a crazy tattoo as he slit the envelope open with a letter opener and took out a folded piece of paper and a smaller envelope.

"Edith thought of you as family, you know. She used to talk about you all the time."

"She was family to me, too," I choked out. "I was closer to her than anyone else in my life."

"She said as much. She was so proud when you graduated from university."

I knew that. She'd come to my graduation in a pink cocktail dress, clutching a jeroboam of champagne. It took a bit of convincing to stop her from spraying it everywhere.

"But she worried about you," he continued. "She said you don't get out enough. That you spend most of your spare time with your nose in a book. She wanted you to go places and experience things for yourself, not read about somebody else doing it. But more than anything, she wanted you to meet yourself a nice fellow and settle down."

"She tried to help with that on several occasions."

"I heard. She always said she hoped you'd meet your John. Your soulmate. We used to play badminton together, you know, John and I. Smart man. Made his money by inventing some widget that went in photocopiers. My firm helped with the patents."

Edith had never mentioned photocopiers. She just said he was an engineer. "I think meeting the right person's harder than she thought."

"It is if you don't get out there and try." He unfolded the piece of paper and smoothed it out. "She said if anything ever happened to her, I was to give you a nudge in the right direction."

What did he mean? I held my breath as his eyes scanned the document. Would Edith have left me a keepsake to remember her by?

"Edith left everything to you..." Albert said.

I could barely breathe. Everything? As in, her house? It was huge, five bedrooms, an acre of land, even a swimming pool, although that hadn't been used in years. Surely there had to be a catch?

He continued, "On one condition."

I was right.

"W-w-what's the condition?"

He slid the smaller of the two envelopes over to me. "You have a list of tasks to complete. A bucket list, if you like, albeit one that Edith chose rather than you. You've got a year to finish. If you don't manage it, all her assets get donated to the RSPCA."

I had trouble processing his words. My mouth opened and shut several times, like a fish out of water, which in all honesty was exactly what I was. Far, far, far out of my depth. For years I'd lived in my little bubble, and now Edith was trying to force me out of it from beyond the grave.

Albert saw my discomfort and gave me an encouraging smile. "It's quite a good list, if I may say so. I think you'll have a lot of fun if you accept the challenge."

I didn't have a lot of choice, did I? Edith had made it that way. If I let the opportunity pass me by, I'd be homeless, but if I managed to complete the tasks, I'd get to take an escalator right to the top of the property ladder, something I couldn't dream of on my salary otherwise. Trust Edith to do something like this. She always said she knew I'd get more adventurous, but I didn't realise this was what she had in mind.

"Can I see the list?"

"Only if you accept."

I took a deep breath as I made a life-changing decision. Edith wouldn't have planned something horrible, would she? Maybe it wouldn't be as bad as I feared. "Okay, I'll do it," I said, so quietly I could hardly hear myself.

Albert grinned, which was a little disturbing as his teeth slipped forwards. "I thought you would. I'll also mention that Edith's been keeping the rent and grocery money you paid her over the years aside. You're to use it to help in your quest."

What, all of it? I did some mental calculations. I'd paid a hundred pounds a week, plus fifty pounds for food and bills, for the last three and a half years. When I first moved in, Edith said she didn't want the money, but I'd insisted. If my rusty mental arithmetic was correct, there had to be over twenty-five thousand pounds.

"That's crazy!"

"Not really. Edith needed your company, not your money. There was a fortune to be made in photocopiers, and John hit the market at just the right time. He left Edith very comfortable. You can keep living in the house for the next year, and her estate will settle the utility bills."

I was in a daze as I left Albert's house, clutching the envelope. I still hadn't looked inside. I wanted to, but at the same time, I didn't dare. At least not until I'd opened that bottle of wine...

CHAPTER 3

MY HANDS SHOOK as I set the envelope down on Edith's coffee table. Where was the corkscrew? I hunted through a couple of drawers before I found it hiding behind a spoon.

After knocking back two glasses of white, I was still too scared to find out my fate. Nothing like putting things off, eh? The thin, cream monster taunted me all the way through two episodes of *Grey's Anatomy*, another glass of wine and some movie about vampires.

Darkness greeted me when I woke up. Rain battered the windows, and an eerie glow came from the television set in the corner where an overly perky woman tried to sell me a miracle in mineral make-up. The envelope sat untouched.

I reached towards it, but the throbbing in my head made me sit back again. I gave the empty wine bottle a filthy look Barry himself would have been proud of. The pain was all its fault.

I tried again, and this time I snagged the envelope. When I first put it on the table, Edith's elegant cursive flowed across the outside, but right now it all looked a little blurry. Perhaps this wasn't the best time to try and read it? No, I'd have another try in the morning. I heaved myself up the stairs and passed out once more.

The sun had risen when I rolled out of bed, and it

was bright. Too bright. What time was it?

Oh, look, it was eight forty-five.

Eight forty-five? My shift started at nine!

I scrambled round, wiping my face and throwing my hair into a messy bun so I'd get away without washing it. By some miracle, a bit of sweat, and a lot of rapid pedalling, I made it to my desk by ten past nine.

Barry was waiting.

"What sort of time do you call this?"

"I'm sor—"

"Sorry won't cut it, Ellen. This persistent flouting of the rules is unacceptable. I'll have to give you a formal warning."

As recently as yesterday, his words would have thrown me into a spin. Jobs weren't easy to come by, especially for an English literature graduate who couldn't drive and refused to sleep with the boss for a promotion. But seeing as Albert had already put me through a full wash cycle, I felt strangely calm.

Barry wittered on while I thought about my meeting yesterday evening. Edith had left me that money to complete my challenge. If I was careful, surely I could manage to live on it for a year?

I tuned back in just as Barry gave me a smug grin. "If it happens again, I'll be forced to let you go."

Feeling a lightness that I hadn't known since I was a child, I smiled back at him. "Barry, I quit."

Shock registered on his face. Bullies weren't used to someone else getting their own way.

"What? You can't. We've got calls waiting."

"Why don't you try answering them yourself instead of eating donuts all morning?"

His mouth dropped open as I turned and headed

for the door. Boy, that felt good.

A weight lifted from my shoulders as I walked outside, and I felt like whistling as I hopped back on my bike and pedalled away. Only problem was, I couldn't whistle.

As I put some distance between myself and Payright Insurance, between my old life and my new, a different kind of heaviness settled over me. Who knew a tiny envelope could weigh so much? It felt like the force of an ocean was pressing on my shoulders.

The first thing I'd do when I got home was open it. Or at least, I'd make myself a cup of tea, then open it. Hmmm, had I remembered to water the plants this week?

I was so busy thinking up excuses that I didn't see Jaz's minivan until I almost rode into it. A swift tug on the brakes saved me from crashing, but I couldn't help groaning when I saw Stevie strapped into his car seat. He fiddled with the buckle, trying to get out in order to continue his reign of terror.

"What the hell did you do?" asked Jaz, walking around the bonnet. "Sue called me and said you quit?"

"I don't quite know what came over me. I just couldn't stand the sight of Barry any more."

"Goodness, girl, I wish I had the guts to do that. I suppose you'll be job-hunting now?"

"Not exactly…" It all came tumbling out, Edith's challenge and the year I had to complete it.

"So what precisely is it you've got to do?"

"I don't know yet."

"How can you not have opened the envelope?"

I shrugged, not wanting to admit that I was a complete chicken.

Jaz grabbed the house keys out of my hand and marched towards the front door. "We're going to find out, right now."

I looked back at the car. "What about Stevie?"

It was her turn to groan. "Oh, yeah. Stevie."

She turned back to the car and released him. The sun chose that moment to go behind a cloud, signalling the arrival of the Prince of Darkness and the havoc that he brought. I kept a careful watch as she carried him into the house. The last time Jaz turned her back on him in there, he'd decided to re-plant Edith's favourite orchid in the toilet bowl.

But as we walked into the living room, I closed my eyes when I saw the envelope sitting right where I left it.

"Go on then," Jaz said. "Open it." She stepped forward and gave me a nudge, whereupon Stevie quickly wrapped his sticky fingers around my hair. "Oops. Hang on a sec."

She untangled me, and I gingerly picked up the letter of doom. Even now, I wasn't ready to read it, but with Jaz there I had no choice. If I didn't look at it myself, she'd have the list in her hand before I could blink, and even if I locked myself in the bathroom she'd shout it through the door. I had to do it. Holding my breath, I unsealed the flap and slid out the paper nestled inside.

Jaz looked over my shoulder, careful to keep Stevie out of reach as we started to read.

Dearest Ella,

I'd always hoped to be around to see you come out of your shell and blossom into the confident young woman I know is hiding inside you, but as you're reading this, it wasn't to be.

I worry that without someone to give you a nudge in the right direction, you'll let life pass you by, so it has to be me that gives you that push.

That's why I've made you a list of things to do, each one chosen to help you overcome the fears that have been holding you back. You have a year, because I know if I give you forever, that's how long you'll take.

I'm positive you've got it in you to do this, and I look forward to seeing your progress from wherever I've ended up. It will be a sweet moment for both of us when you finish. You'll be ready to take on the world. You only have one life—grab it with both hands, dance with it, treasure it, love it.

Here are your challenges:

1. Get a makeover. You need to stop hiding behind long hair and baggy clothes.

2. Pass your driving test and take a Ferrari out for a spin.

3. Learn to ride a horse and compete in a dressage competition.

4. Go abseiling.

5. Sing on stage in front of an audience.

6. Get up close and personal with an elephant.

7. Try skiing.

8. Take a gamble in a casino.

9. Enjoy some music live by going to a concert.

10. Go speed-dating.

11. Ride on a motorbike.

12. Explore underwater by going scuba diving.

13. Travel overseas.

14. Be an extra in a film.

15. Throw a party. If you've completed everything else, you'll have a reason to celebrate.

Albert will keep an eye on you—don't forget to provide him with the evidence that you've completed each task. Who knows? You might even meet a nice young man on your journey. I'll be keeping my fingers crossed.

Thank you for bringing joy into an old lady's life. I hope I can do the same for you.

Love, Edith

I gulped in a huge mouthful of air as I finished, having forgotten to inhale while I was reading. My fingers shook as I skimmed the letter again, hoping I'd misread it somehow. I hadn't. If anything, it was worse the second time around.

I knew in my heart Edith was right—I didn't so much let life pass me by, it steamrollered me, and I lay down in the road and let it.

"But I can't do all that," I said. "I mean, abseiling? Edith knew I'm terrified of heights."

"I think that's the whole point."

I sat down heavily on the sofa. "And horses? I haven't been near one of those four-legged spawns of Satan since I fell off one when I was seven."

Yes, I remembered it well. My parents had still been alive then, and Mum had decided to capitalise on my obsession with My Little Pony by putting me on a real one. The teacher told me to give it a little kick, so I did, and it shot off, leaving me behind on the ground.

Jaz plopped down beside me and put an arm around my shoulders. "You have to do your best. I mean, at the end of it you'll get this place, and that's a pretty big incentive. I'll help you, I promise."

A tear rolled down my cheek. "I know I've got to have a go. It's just with Edith gone, and now this... It's a lot to take."

"She's right, though. You *have* been hiding away. Especially since Terry."

"I didn't feel like facing people after that. He was cavorting with Demi for ages."

"At least she did the sensible thing and dumped him properly."

I stifled a giggle. She had indeed. It turned out Miss Demeanor commanded quite a following on social media, and she'd used it in her favour. Now half of Reading knew Terry had a dick the size of a peanut and thought a 69 was a kind of ice cream. We'd even become friends after Edith invited her round for dinner as a thank you for the pole dancing lesson. Every so often, we'd meet up for lunch to commiserate over our choice in men.

"She did us both proud, but I'm still not sure I'm ready to meet someone else. And speed dating? I wasn't even good at normal dating." I'd be lucky if I managed to get my name and one half-coherent sentence out before it was time to move on to the next person.

"You'll get better. Some of the things Edith's picked look like a lot of fun."

"You can do them, then."

She smiled and shook her head. "You need to provide evidence you've completed everything. That means photos. I don't think anyone's going to confuse the two of us, seeing as I'm five foot zero and Indian, and you're five foot seven and pale as a ghost."

I sighed. This was a nightmare come to life. I needed a cup of...wine. I needed wine.

As I got up to go to the kitchen, I glanced at Jaz on the sofa and realised there was something wrong with the picture.

"Er, where's Stevie?"

"Oh crap!" She turned pink. "He was just here a second ago."

A crash echoed through the house, and we ran for the dining room. Stevie crouched on top of the table, pushing plates off one by one.

"Shit, I'm sorry!" Jaz rushed past and scooped him up, and he burst into tears.

"It's okay. They were only cheap ones." It was the previous dinner service that cost a fortune, and he'd broken that a couple of months before.

"I don't know what to do with him. The doctor said he'd grow out of it."

How about a straitjacket? "I'm sure it's just a phase."

She carried the struggling toddler through to the kitchen, and I uncorked a bottle of wine. If nothing else, I'd meet new people at the Alcoholics Anonymous meetings I was bound to end up at.

"Do you want a biscuit?" I asked Jaz.

She shook her head and Stevie stuck his hand out. He might have trouble comprehending the word "no," but he understood the names of all his favourite foods.

"I've started Weight Watchers again," she said. "I already ate two cupcakes I wasn't supposed to yesterday, and I've got a weigh-in on Monday after work."

Since I'd known her, Jaz had tried just about every

fad diet going. I was surprised the calories didn't melt off with all the running around she had to do after Stevie, but she resorted to chocolate every time he did something bad. She most likely had KitKats on bulk order.

"I don't know what I'm doing on Monday. I mean, now I'm jobless," I said.

"That's easy. You're starting your list. Actually, no. Why wait? You can start it tomorrow. No time like the present."

"Maybe I should have a bit of a think about it first. You know, work out the best order to do things in."

"You're not getting out of it that easily. Just start at the top and work down. That means tomorrow's makeover day. You can get your hair done, and I'll meet you for shopping after I escape from Barry. The mall's open until eight."

"I don't know where to begin with a makeover."

"Just google some celebrities and find one you want to look like. Then tell the stylist, and they'll do the rest."

"It's that easy?"

"Absolutely. It couldn't be simpler. You should try that new salon next to John Lewis. I know someone who went there last week, and her hair looks awesome."

She made it sound so straightforward. Was it possible I'd made too big a deal out of this?

Maybe.

I desperately tried to see the positive side, and after Jaz and the tiny tyrant departed, I started on phase one of operations—finding my perfect hairstyle.

CHAPTER 4

THE BUTTERFLIES IN my stomach worked overtime as I walked from the bus stop to the hair salon on Friday morning. They probably had Barry in there, yelling at them to flap harder.

Twice I'd nearly turned around and gone back home. Only the fact that Jaz would drag me right back again kept me walking along to my doom. Why postpone the inevitable?

Turning Heads was the kind of place I'd never have dared to set foot into on a normal day. Its glass, chrome, and artfully arranged flowers were far more fashionable than I could ever hope to be. When I nervously peeped around the door, I cringed and waited for someone to scream "imposter" then march me right out again.

That didn't happen, though. The blonde receptionist looked up at me, eyes peering out from under her purple-streaked asymmetric bob. A flash of surprise was soon masked by her professionalism as she asked, "Can I help?"

"I'm Ella Goodman. I have an appointment?"

I half expected her to say they'd never heard of me, but I had no such luck.

"You're right on time. Carly's just finishing up with her previous client. Would you like a drink?"

I presumed she didn't mean a stiff whisky although that was what I needed. "A cup of coffee would be lovely."

I flipped through the stack of magazines as I waited, but they were all celebrity gossip, and I hardly recognised any of them. Apart from my search for a hairstyle I liked this morning, I tended to shy away from such things. I had no desire to know which Hollywood star got pictured falling out of a club drunk last week, or what the latest must-have eating disorder was.

Thankfully, it wasn't long before Carly bounced over. She was one of those endlessly perky people who seem like they've been drip-fed caffeine.

"So, what are we having today?" She picked up some of my split ends between her fingers and tutted.

"I was—" It came out as a croak and I cleared my throat. "I was wondering... Could you do my hair like Jessica Alba?"

"Jessica Alba..." She thought for a few seconds then smiled. "Of course. I reckon that'll really suit you. You'll look like a different person."

That was the idea, according to Edith, but despite her encouragement, the idea of change terrified me. Jessica's hairstyle seemed like a safe option. My hair colour wasn't that different—I just needed some long layers and a few highlights. All I'd have to do was make sure I got photos at the end.

Snip, snip, snip went the scissors, and I closed my eyes as chunks of my hair fell to the floor. *Only a few inches. It'll make it easier to manage.* Once Carly finished cutting, she painted gunk all over my hair and stuck a shower cap thing on my head.

"We need to wait half an hour or so. Can I offer you another drink?"

Okay, maybe it wasn't all bad. This part was kind of like being in a coffee shop. Sipping a latte and munching on a biscuit was far better than being moaned at by Barry all afternoon. I felt a bit guilty that Jaz was stuck at Payright, listening to morons, and decided I'd treat her to dinner after we'd gone shopping. It was the least I could do to thank her for the moral support she'd given me.

I was halfway through an article about the best kind of jeans to buy and feeling a little more positive when Carly skipped back. "Moment of truth. I just need to rinse everything out."

I followed her over to the sink and tipped my head back as the warm water trickled over my scalp.

"Does it look okay?" I'd never had my hair highlighted before, and after Sue's daughter had a bleach disaster that made half her hair fall out, the fear of going bald was very real.

"It looks amazing. You'll love it!"

I almost didn't dare look in the mirror when she led me back to my seat, but in the end, I cracked a lid open.

And stifled a scream.

My jaw dropped, but no words came out. Carly mistook my horror for joy and grinned.

"It looks great, doesn't it?"

"I'm blonde!" And I was. Platinum blonde. Nothing subtle about it—this was straight up Barbie doll.

"Well of course you are, honey. That's what you asked for."

"I said Jessica Alba." I'd done a lot of searching, and her hair was definitely light brown.

"I know, and that's what I've given you. She looked great in *Dukes of Hazzard*."

The stylist at the next station piped up. "That was Jessica Simpson."

"It was?"

"Jessica Alba was the one in *Spy Kids*."

"Oh, yeah." Her cheeks went pink. "Oops."

Half an hour later, I walked out with a thousand apologies, a free haircut, and a voucher to have the colour fixed in a few weeks when my hair had recovered from the bleaching.

I also had tears in my eyes and people kept staring, including Jaz when she caught sight of me. Her eyes went as big as dinner plates. "I thought you said you weren't going to do anything drastic."

"I wasn't. There was a mix up." She was in stitches as I explained the whole Simpson/Alba mess.

"I should give that hairdresser a medal," she said.

"People keep staring at me."

"That's because you look hot!"

"No, I look like a freak. My hair's practically white."

She shook her head. "Oh, Ella, you've got no idea."

It would seem not, because all I wanted to do was put a bag over my head. Did anywhere in Reading sell wigs?

I had no time to search, because when we got to the mall, I found Jaz had enlisted the help of her friend Candy, who worked as a personal shopper in one of the big department stores.

Candy was perfectly put together in a way I'd never be. Everything matched, from her eyeshadow to her impossibly tall heels. I felt like a gawky child as I trailed behind her and Jaz, watching them select items they thought would suit me.

"I can't wear that," I said, pointing at a particularly risqué dress.

"Why not?" Jaz asked.

"It's far too short."

"You've got great legs," said Candy. "At least try it on."

I sighed. Two against one wasn't fair, especially when one of them knew all about my total lack of backbone. The sooner this was over, the better.

An hour later, Jaz and I struggled out of the store, weighed down by bags. I hadn't wanted to buy most of the stuff, but I didn't stand a chance with her involved, and my cunning plan to sneak back to the shop tomorrow for a refund got scuppered when we reached the till and the girl there winked at me.

"Candy's letting you use her staff discount, but it means you can't return anything. That okay?"

I hesitated, and Jaz elbowed me in the side. "Yes, that's wonderful."

Home was too far to walk with all my purchases, so we piled everything into the back of a taxi for the journey back to Edith's. I still struggled to think of it as anything but her house. To me, it always would be.

Once we'd stacked the evidence of the evening's madness up in the hallway, I plopped down on the sofa.

"Takeaway?" I suggested.

Jaz looked at me, incredulity spreading across her face. "We've just spent two hours shopping, you've had your hair and your make-up done, and you want to stay at home and eat a pizza?"

"What's wrong with that?"

"It's Friday night and Amir's babysitting, that's

what."

Okay, maybe I'd been a little optimistic. "I suppose one quick drink wouldn't hurt."

She grinned at me. "That's more like it."

While we waited for a taxi to arrive, Jaz took a few snaps for my challenge album, as I'd taken to calling it.

"It'll be like a diary," she said. "Something that shows how much you change over the next year."

That word again. Change. Every time I heard it, I wanted to crawl back under the duvet and sleep until the year was over, but if I did that I wouldn't have a bed any more. No, the only option was to get everything over with and cause myself the minimum amount of pain possible. I'd accomplished one task, and so far that hadn't gone according to plan. What joy would task two bring?

Jaz supervised while I changed into one of my new outfits, and I wasn't surprised to find out she'd secreted a sparkly top in her cavernous handbag. She tugged it on while I stood in front of the mirror and agonised over my face.

Before we left the store, Candy had got the girl on the make-up counter to "show me a few tricks." That translated into me looking like a clown.

At least, that was my opinion. Jaz said I looked amazing. Apparently, the black gunk around my eyes made them pop. I didn't want them to pop, sparkle, shine, or anything else. I was quite happy with them just the way they were.

"You're not taking it off," Jaz said as I reached for the make-up remover. "No way."

"But..."

She grabbed my wrist and pulled me towards the

front door. "No buts."

This promised to be a long evening.

The music pounded from hidden speakers while we queued up for drinks in the Purple Turtle wine bar. Warm bodies pressed against me as I got jostled from side to side, trying to keep within shouting distance of Jaz. My throat was dry, and I despaired of ever getting a glass of anything when a man behind me tapped me on the shoulder and shouted, "What can I get you ladies?"

Jaz's eyes lit up. "Two white wines, please," she yelled back. Even then, I could hardly hear her above the din. Honestly, it was so loud my head hurt.

Being a few inches taller and, I had to admit, easy on the eye, the stranger soon caught the bargirl's attention. It wasn't long before I had a glass in my hand, and Jaz and I followed the man away from the bar as he cleared a path through the crowd.

"He seems nice, and look at that butt," Jaz shouted in my ear. "He definitely works out. And he's definitely interested in you."

I looked up to see if he'd overheard, but he didn't seem to have. Thank goodness. I put a finger to my lips and she shrugged.

Still, I couldn't resist dropping my gaze downwards. What do you know? She was right.

Our saviour led us over to a table in the corner and waited while a girl in an apron cleared the dirty glasses away. There were only two stools, so he motioned for each of us to take one while he stood. Hmm... Not only cute, but a gentleman as well.

Conversation wasn't easy in the din, but we managed to get the basics out of the way. The owner of the ass was Mike, a student in the final year of his master's degree at Reading university.

Words might have been difficult, but he communicated a lot with his eyes. They barely left me for the rest of the evening. When he left to get us more drinks, Jaz held up her hand for a high-five. "He really likes you. And he's hot! Girl, your luck is changing."

I hardly dared to believe it, but by the time the bartender called out last orders, I had his number and he had mine, and we'd agreed to meet again the next evening. Somewhere quieter where we could actually have a conversation.

"Told you we'd have a good evening," Jaz slurred next to me in the backseat of the cab.

My feet hurt, I felt a little tipsy, and my eyes kept closing, but still I wore a tiny smile. "Yeah, it was okay."

"It's the hair, that's what it is. Men dig the hair."

Maybe the old saying was true? Maybe blondes really did have more fun?

And how much more fun lay in store for me tomorrow?

First thing on Saturday morning, my phone buzzed with a text.

Mike: Lovely to meet you last night. Do you like Chinese?

I loved Chinese! Kung po chicken was my absolute favourite. Things were off to a good start. By lunchtime, we'd decided to meet at Silk Route, a lovely restaurant on the edge of town. I'd been there once with Terry, and while the prices made my eyes water, the food was delicious. What's more, Mike said it was his treat, which made a pleasant change from me always picking up the bill.

As I shimmied into another of my new dresses, I was secretly pleased that Jaz and Candy pushed me into getting them. What would I have worn otherwise? The only other dress I owned was a hideous taffeta affair I'd worn to my school prom, and I doubted I'd even fit into that any more.

The make-up? Well, that was a different story. All the tubes and pots were still languishing in their posh paper carrier bag. One step at a time, eh?

I met Mike just outside the restaurant, and a frisson of excitement ran through me as he bent down and touched his lips to my cheek.

"Lovely to see you again," he shouted.

Why was he shouting? Ah, it must be his idea of a little joke after all the noise in the bar last night.

I got into the spirit of things. "It's good to see you, too," I yelled back, matching his volume.

He gave me an odd look, and that was my first clue as to why he was single.

It turned out the shouting wasn't his idea of a joke. He really did talk like that all the time. Over the starter, he told me and every other patron in the restaurant about the erotic musical he was writing, starring a family of raccoons and a pig named Hamlet. Clue number two.

During the main course, he picked every single beansprout out of his chow mein and lined them up on the side of his plate—clue three—while explaining the plot of Shakespeare's *Othello* with the aid of a bottle of soy sauce and a chopstick holder. The girl at the next table, obviously on a date herself, kept giving me Grade A looks of sympathy.

I couldn't get a word in. Not one. He just kept talking and talking and talking, and with a glass of wine inside him, he got even louder. The man was in desperate need of a volume knob. No, scratch that. He needed an off button.

While I chewed poached lychees and pineapple fritters as fast as humanly possible, we all learned about JavaScript and the many, many, many complications of designing a website. Thank goodness the waiter was quick with the bill.

True to his word, Mike paid, and the waiter was on hand right away with my coat. As he held it up for me to put my arms in, he begged me with his eyes never to bring Mike back. He needn't have worried. There was no danger of that.

"So, your place or mine?" Mike asked as we waited outside for a cab.

Pardon? "Well, uh, I'll go to my place and you can go to yours."

His face clouded over. "Didn't you have a good time at dinner?"

"Yes, it was lovely, but…"

"Then what's your problem?"

My problem? *My* problem? "I don't make a habit of going home with men on a first date." Especially when they'd not only bored me to death but almost deafened me too. Heck, if I took him home, the neighbours would most likely call the police, despite the fact the nearest house was forty yards away.

"Second date."

He was counting yesterday's meeting at the wine bar? "Last night wasn't a date. I was out with my friend."

"But I bought you drinks."

"And that was very kind of you, but we barely talked."

He nodded knowingly. "Oh, you're one of those."

"One of what?"

"A bitch who likes to lead men on. You get yourself tarted up in your short dresses and hooker hair, then go out to see what you can get."

I wanted to sink into the ground. That was how he saw me? At that moment I hated my new look, and Jaz and Edith for forcing it on me. "I'm sorry. I didn't mean to lead you on."

"You need to think about what you've done."

The cab pulled up and Mike jumped in it without so much as a goodbye, leaving me on my own as I sank to the kerb with tears streaming down my face.

CHAPTER 5

IT HAD BARELY turned seven the next morning when my phone rang.

"So, how did it go?" asked Jaz, excitement bubbling in her voice.

Now that I'd slept on it, I realised I couldn't blame her for Mike being an asshole of the highest order. "Do you want to hear the bit where he told the entire restaurant a raccoon love story, or the part at the end where he left me crying at the side of the road?"

There was a long pause. "Tell me you're kidding?"

"Honestly, you couldn't make it up."

"I want to hear everything."

The tale sounded even worse the second time around. So bad that I thought for a minute I might have dreamed the entire thing, but then I looked at the table in the hallway and spotted the bag of fortune cookies the staff at the restaurant had given me as a sympathy gift. When the manager found me sitting on the ground, he'd handed me a glass of whisky, then had one of the delivery drivers drop me home.

"Hang on, he's going to have raccoons spanking each other on stage? Like in *Fifty Shades of Grey*?"

"Apparently so."

"You had a lucky escape there, girl. If you'd gone home with him, you'd probably have woken up shackled to the bed."

A shudder ran through me. That would be worse than sitting through the raccoon show. "I don't want to think about it."

"Then you'll have to take your mind off things with another challenge. What's next?"

I'd had a think about that when I woke up in a cold sweat this morning, in between contemplating the merits of hibernation versus jumping off a bridge.

"I'm going to try the driving." At least if I had wheels, it would make escaping from disasters like the one at Silk Route last night so much easier.

"About time. I don't know what I'd do without my car. I'd have to take Stevie on the bus."

Heaven help the other passengers if she did that. The eight-twenty service would become the portal to hell.

"I need to find an instructor. Who taught you?"

"A friend of my mother's used to give lessons, but he retired last year. Maybe you could look on the internet? Read some reviews?"

That wasn't a bad idea. As soon as I'd had breakfast, I fired up my creaking laptop and clicked the search box. A couple of possibles came up, but one stuck out from the rest with a string of five star ratings. The Wilson School of Motoring.

- *Grant Wilson is the best instructor ever.*

- *Recommended to any lady looking for lessons.*

- *Grant was amazingly patient through my course —I'd definitely give him full marks.*

All of his reviews were like that, so I crossed my fingers and fired off a quick email, hoping he had some slots available.

It wasn't long before my phone pinged, informing me of an incoming text message. Maybe it was Grant? I'd included my number when I contacted him.

It wasn't.

What on earth did Mike want? Surely he'd said everything there was to say last night?

Mike: I've decided you're worth another chance. How about dinner on Tuesday? I can pick you up.

I threw the phone down in disgust. What planet was he on? How could he think I'd want to be in the same room as him again after the way he treated me? The message wasn't even worth a reply.

When my phone rang a little while later I almost threw it across the room, but I was glad I didn't, because this time it was Grant calling.

"Ella Goodman?"

"That's me."

"You were looking for driving lessons?"

His voice was rich and smooth, like a decadent chocolate sauce sliding down my throat. If ever Grant needed a new career, he could make a fortune as a chatline operator. "Yes, that was me," I squeaked.

"I'm usually booked solid, but a girl just cancelled a course because she broke her arm. Would you be interested in Monday at two?"

"In the afternoon?" I stupidly asked, then gave myself a mental slap.

Grant chuckled on the other end of the line. "Yes, Ella, in the afternoon."

I loved the way he said my name. I'd never thought of it as sexy before, but when the Ls rolled off his tongue, I felt it between my thighs.

"Yes, absolutely, I can do two in the afternoon."

I gave him my details, and by the time I hung up, I was fanning myself. I didn't know how long it normally took to pass a driving test, but I hoped for somewhere close to the full year Edith had set for me.

On Sunday afternoon, I laid all my new purchases out on the bed in one of the spare rooms. For a couple of hours, I tried on various combinations, trying to work out what went with what. I couldn't wear a dress for a driving lesson, could I? No, trousers would be better.

What did Grant look like? Would he have the face that went with the voice? Probably not, because that would be unfair to all other men. Knowing my luck, he'd have a nose the size of Mount Kilimanjaro and teeth like a horse. Or maybe he was short.

That didn't stop me from getting out my new make-up and having a go, though. How did the woman in the shop do it? I tried for sultry, but ended up with "panda on crack."

On Sunday night, hot men with no shirts on paraded through my mind, complete with tan chests and rippling muscles. When the alarm clock intruded on my slumber, I almost threw the damned thing across the room. Apart from my dreams, the closest I would ever get a man like that was to buy a calendar or possibly, just possibly, sitting on the other side of a gear shift.

In the end, I went for the simple look for my driving lesson. A pair of dark jeans and a polo neck with a padded gilet over the top. Even though we'd had a few days of sun, the February temperatures were lower than average, and I didn't want to get cold in the biting wind. After one aborted attempt, I passed up on the idea of eyeshadow and went with mascara and a swipe of lip gloss. Even I couldn't mess that up.

Grant was due to arrive at two, and by half past one, I was pacing the floral carpet in the hallway. Only part of my nervousness was due to the driving itself. What really left me trembling was the thought of controlling my libido while he spoke to me in *that* voice for two hours. I'd just made what seemed like my hundredth circuit when my phone beeped. Was he running late?

No. No, he wasn't.

Mike: I haven't had a reply to my previous message. That's a little rude, but I'll overlook it this time. I'll pick you up at 7 tomorrow evening.

My knees gave way, and I sank onto the little sofa by the front door, staring at the screen. Could the man not take the hint? I needed to think of a pithy message to make sure he understood that if he was the last man on earth, I wouldn't go out to dinner with him again, but as I tried to compose something in my head, wheels crunched on the gravel outside, swiftly followed up by a couple of quick toots of a horn. Grant had arrived.

My palms were sweating as I picked up my bag and locked the front door behind me, and I willed my heart to slow down. *It's just a driving lesson. Nothing special.* I did my best to shove Mike into the recesses of my mind—the last thing I needed was to be distracted by that idiot as I tried to concentrate.

Grant drove a cute royal blue Mini, and it was parked neatly at the end of the driveway waiting for me. As I got halfway to it, the driver's door cracked open and a denim-clad leg emerged, followed by the body of a Greek god with the face of an angel. I gave up on the idea of breathing as I drank in the gorgeousness before me.

He smiled—a message from heaven, surely—and stuck out his hand. "Ella?"

What was my name again? Oh, yeah, that was me. I gingerly reached out, and fireworks engulfed me at his touch. No wonder he got so many five star reviews. I'd give him six stars without even getting in the car.

"Y-y-yes. It's good to meet you."

"Nervous?"

"Just a l-l-little."

"It's nothing to worry about. We'll take it slow."

Oh heck, why did he have to say that? Once he helped me into the car, I squeezed my thighs together as he leaned over and adjusted the driver's seat, his face mere inches from mine. Up close, the smell of his aftershave tickled my nostrils, something with a hint of cinnamon. Oh my gosh, he was edible.

Hang on, was I smelling him? I'd lost the plot, big time. I leaned back in the seat and groaned.

"Belt too tight?"

I quickly shook my head. "No, it's fine."

He got in the passenger side, and I did my best to listen as he explained about the clutch and gears and brakes and steering. All I could hear, though, was the deep timbre of his voice, and the sexy pause at the end of each sentence.

Which was probably why I stalled the car as soon as I got out of the driveway.

But Grant had endless patience, and half an hour later, I'd done several circuits of the nearby housing development and mastered going and stopping. Luckily, traffic was quiet in the middle of the day. I hadn't quite got to grips with gears yet, but Grant was doing those for me from his side of the car.

After I'd managed to change up into third for the second time, Grant gave me my next challenge.

"When you get to the end of this road, turn left."

"Isn't that the main road?"

"Yes, but you're ready for it. Just have a bit of confidence in yourself."

I let out a whoop when I managed to get out without crashing. I was driving! For the first time in my life, I was really driving! Maybe Edith's goal of getting behind the wheel of a Ferrari wasn't quite as unattainable as I thought?

By the time we headed back, I'd driven in four different gears and felt a lot more comfortable with challenge number three. At least until we headed for a crossroads.

"There are traffic lights there," I hissed.

"You'll be fine. Don't panic."

They got closer and closer, and a car came towards me. Then my phone pinged, and a vision of Mike popped into my head, wearing a scowl and looking distinctly unhappy.

"I can't!" I squeaked.

"Just pull over then, and take a break."

The car in front got bigger, and I panicked and jerked the wheel to the side. There was an almighty bump, and suddenly I wasn't sitting next to Grant any more. I was suspended above him, the seatbelt cutting into my waist as the car came to rest in a ditch.

For a second, I had no words. If I'd been offered a

one-way trip to Dante's Inferno at that moment, I'd have taken it, and gladly paid extra for express boarding.

Without a hotline to the devil, I tried closing my eyes, but that didn't help. I was still hanging in mid-air.

Finally, Grant spoke. "Next time, don't turn the wheel quite so quickly."

A flood of apologies washed out of me. "Oh my gosh, I'm so, so sorry. I just heard my phone go, and it distracted me, and all I can do is apologise, and if there's anything I can do to make it right, I will..."

He touched my arm. "Ella, don't worry about it. I've got insurance and these things happen. It's not the first time and it won't be the last."

"Really?"

"I once had a pupil accelerate into her own mother's car as we pulled out of her driveway."

I didn't know whether to laugh or cry. In the end, I settled for a gulping sob that sounded like an animal in pain.

"Come on, let's get out of here and sort the mess out."

He reached up and released my seatbelt, and I landed on him in a heap. Under any other circumstances, I'd have been quite pleased with that development, but right now, I barely noticed his muscular thighs or the six-pack pressed up against me. I just wanted to get out of the damn vehicle.

Grant gave me a boost up, and I managed to scramble out of the door above me. As I willed my shaking legs to stay upright, he climbed out himself and put his arm around my waist, steadying me.

"Are you okay? That's the important thing."

"Y-y-yes, I think so. Are you?"

"I'll live," he said dryly.

He eased me down to the ground, and I sat on the damp grass while he called for help. After a few minutes, he knelt next to me and tucked his jacket around my shoulders.

"You need to keep warm. I don't want you going into shock."

I was grateful for the extra warmth, but what about him? "Won't you get cold?"

"I'm a big boy."

Wasn't he just? Once again, I was aware of our closeness, and the heat coming from his body made mine flood south. *Ella, try to act normal.* "So what happens now?"

"There's a tow truck on its way for the car, and my boyfriend's coming to pick us up."

Hang on a second. His *boyfriend*? This perfect specimen of maleness was gay? A tinkling crash sounded in my ears as my already fragile heart shattered, and I slumped forward, drained. My soul wept with the unfairness of it all. Grant, who was sweet and kind as well as hot, went for men. I ended up with assholes like Terry and Mike. Tears prickled behind my eyes as I bit my bottom lip.

Grant tucked me closer to him and stroked my cheek. "It's okay, Ella. It's only a car."

"It's not just that." Everything came pouring out. Terry, Edith, my awful evening with Mike. By the time I'd finished, I was a wreck.

At some point, Grant picked me up and put me in the back of a vehicle then climbed in beside me. I was vaguely aware of him putting on my seatbelt and wrapping an arm around me before we took off for a destination unknown.

Chapter 6

THE VEHICLE EASED to a halt in a car park, and when I looked out the window, I didn't recognise a thing.

"Where are we?" I asked Grant.

"Our flat. You've gone all white. I didn't want to drop you home and leave you like that."

Oh. How thoughtful of him. The door next to me opened, and a small man wearing a fluffy pink jumper and a frown looked in at me.

"I'm Todd, Grant's better half. You're still alive, then?"

I managed to nod. While I hadn't exactly got around to picturing who Grant might be dating, if I had, Todd most certainly would not have been it.

"Oh good. Are you staying for dinner? I've made enough for three. It's lasagne."

I'd rather bury myself under six feet of concrete, but I didn't want to be rude. "Uh, okay."

Todd sashayed on ahead, leaving Grant to help me out of the car.

"Why are you being so nice to me? I mean, after everything?" I asked quietly.

He squeezed my shoulders. "You look like you could use a friend. Plus, I have a feeling you're going to become one of my best customers."

"Am I that bad?"

"You're that nervous."

He shepherded me into the building, and we took the lift up to the second floor. The flat he shared with Todd was as modern as Edith's home was old-fashioned, with a sofa shaped like a buffalo and a chandelier made from little glass toadstools. Grant saw me looking at them and grimaced.

"Todd did the decorating. It made him happy, so I let him get on with it."

The buffalo was surprisingly comfortable, and Todd handed me a glass of wine while he finished off cooking. I offered to help, but he waved me away.

"All under control, sweetie. Relax."

Grant sat down next to me with a beer. "Feeling better?"

Yes, although I hadn't expected to. Now I knew Grant was gay, I didn't feel quite so tongue-tied around him, and when I nodded the smile I gave him was genuine.

"Thank you. Firstly, for being so understanding, and also for...this."

He chuckled. "You can thank me by putting your phone on silent in your next lesson. That way you won't get distracted."

I froze. Oh heck, the phone. I still hadn't checked it.

"What is it?"

"I think it might be a message from Mike. Despite what happened, he still seems to think I'll go out with him again."

Sure enough, his arrogance leapt off the screen.

Mike: I assume you're having a problem with your phone. I'll see you tomorrow at 7. Wear something sexy.

"He knows where you live?" Grant asked.

My cheeks heated. "I might have told him the night we were in the wine bar. I'd had a little bit too much to drink, and I wasn't thinking straight."

Grant patted my knee and sighed. "I'll be there tomorrow at six thirty."

"Really?"

"I'm not going to abandon you to some freak. If he sees me there hopefully he'll get the message."

Relief flowed through me. What would I have done if I'd picked the second driving instructor on the list? Maybe not crashed, but I'd be home alone, googling how to emigrate to Thailand on short notice.

Todd poked his head out of the kitchen. "Dinner's ready."

Not only had he made lasagne, he'd baked focaccia and prepared a tasty green salad. Wow. It was almost worth crashing the car over. No wonder Grant chose to date him.

"So, what made you cry?" Todd asked. "Just the accident, or something more?"

How did he know I'd been crying? I looked at Grant. Did he say something? He gave a small shake of his head.

I turned back to Todd, and he made a circling motion around one eye. "You have a few streaks."

Oh no, my mascara! Despite me trying not to go for the demented panda look, I'd ended up with it anyway.

"Can I just...?" I looked around for a bathroom.

"Sure, but you might as well wait until after dinner. I mean, we've both seen it now."

You know what? He was right. After the car

incident, a few black circles paled into insignificance. I dug my fork in and carried on eating.

"So what else is on this list you have to complete?" asked Grant. I'd told him the gist of it, but not the details.

"What list?" Todd wanted to know.

I started again from scratch, and this time I went through each challenge I had to complete. "So I've got a year," I finished. "But if everything goes as well as the driving, there's no way I'll get through it all."

"Well, the abseiling's easy," Todd said. "Grant can take you. He's into hanging around on ropes and that sort of shizzle. And I might be able to help with the horse riding. There's this guy I went to uni with, his sister runs a horsey place. The party won't be a problem, either." He clapped his hands in glee. "I love parties."

"It's really kind of you to offer, but I couldn't possibly put you to any more trouble. I've caused quite enough already."

Grant totally ignored what I said. "Let's go climbing tomorrow, and once you get to the top, you can abseil down. I'll have to cancel all my lessons anyway until the insurance company sends a replacement car."

I put my head in my hands. "I'll pay for the lessons you can't do."

"Don't worry—I've got insurance for that as well. To be honest, it'll be nice to have a couple of days off. I've been flat out for months. Work, work, work, no time for hobbies, and I've barely seen Todd." He grinned. "This way I get paid to take a holiday."

And that was how, at nine the next morning, I found myself sitting next to Grant in Todd's car on my way to Reading Climbing Centre.

When we arrived in the huge building, with its orange and white walls stretching high above our heads, I nearly turned around and went home again.

"I can't go up there. Do you have any idea how high that is?"

"Fourteen metres. And we'll start small, don't worry."

Don't worry? How could he say that? This made the trip to the salon look easy. I dragged my feet as I followed him to the kiosk to hire the kit I needed, hoping to prolong the inevitable embarrassment.

"Step in the leg-holes."

I hung onto the counter and did so, noting the sharp intake of breath from three nearby women as Grant cinched the harness around my waist.

"Women always stare at you, have you noticed?"

He chuckled. "Yeah. Ironic, isn't it?"

Tragic, more like. And not only were they gazing at him, I got daggers too. Grant just shrugged it off as he rented me some special shoes and a little bag that clipped to my waist to put chalk in.

Properly equipped, I followed him out into the main hall. To my right, a girl lost her grip as her attention wandered from the handholds on the wall to Grant's butt, clad in a snug-fitting pair of tracksuit bottoms. Even as she bobbed around at the end of her safety rope, she couldn't take her eyes off it.

Secretly, I felt a little pleased. As people didn't know he was gay, it certainly upped my street cred to be seen with him.

My smile soon faded when Grant stopped in front of a sheer wall filled with little coloured lumps, and I bumped into the back of him.

"What now?"

He grinned and pointed upwards. Oh dear.

A few seconds later, he introduced another man who came over to join us. "This is Tony. As you're a beginner, we need to have a qualified instructor with us."

"We keep trying to convince him to take the course and work here," Tony said, beaming at Grant. Another member of his fan club? "Let's start with a demonstration."

Tony held the safety rope while Grant climbed up to the top of the wall in two and a half seconds. When he got back to solid ground, he wasn't even breathing hard.

"Think you can do that?" Tony meant to be encouraging, but his words didn't reconcile with what he wanted me to do.

"No way."

Both men laughed. "Don't worry, we'll start slowly and build up."

"I'm not very keen on heights."

"Just don't look down."

First, they had me climb sideways along the wall, a foot or so off the ground. As I wasn't very high up, that gave me a bit of confidence, so when Tony finally told me to try going upwards, I wasn't so scared.

At least until a small child scampered past me, and I lost my concentration and my grip.

"Aaaaaaahhhh." I peeled away from the wall in slow motion, first my right hand then my left, followed by my feet. I closed my eyes and waited for the ground to come up and meet me, but Grant kept hold of my safety rope, so I just swung around like a spider in the breeze as I tried to block out the kid's laughter.

"Reach out and grab the wall, Ella," Grant called. How did he sound so calm?

I forced my eyes open and found the nearest handhold a foot away. Okay, that wasn't so bad. I could do this.

By the end of the afternoon, a miracle had happened and I made it to the top of the wall. I wanted to punch the air, but as I was clinging on for dear life, that probably wasn't a good idea. Instead, I let out an uncharacteristic whoop, which was met with hoots from below.

Great! I'd done it! Now, how did I get down?

"Ready for the abseiling part?" Grant called out. "I want you to lower your bottom until it's below your feet, then let go with your hands, lean back and keep your legs straight, like you're sitting on the ground."

"What if I fall?"

"You won't. I've got hold of you."

"What if the rope breaks?"

"They're designed to hold people much heavier than you. It won't snap, I promise."

Heart pounding, I did as he said, and somehow managed to get myself into the right position.

"Now walk down the wall with your feet. Just make sure you keep your bum lower than them."

Slowly, slowly, I started to descend. By the time I got halfway down, I realised it wasn't quite as bad as I thought, and I actually began to enjoy myself. I was so good at keeping myself in the seated position that my butt hit the ground before my feet did, and I looked up at a grinning Grant and Tony.

Tony waved a phone at me. "I've got photos."

I'd done it! I'd completed a task off the list without cocking it up!

I leapt up and hugged both of them before I realised what I was doing. Tony looked a bit surprised, but Grant squeezed me back. "I knew you could do it."

Well, that made one of us. I had a feeling some of the other challenges wouldn't be quite so easy. "Thanks for helping."

"Pleasure." He helped me out of my gear then held up the car keys. "Time for your non-date."

With all the adrenalin flowing through my system, I'd managed to put Mike out of my mind. Now I'd come back down to earth with a bump. Literally.

"I can't wait."

All too soon, we arrived home, and I looked at my watch. Just after six. Less than an hour to go until the idiot arrived.

"Maybe he'll have changed his mind?" I said hopefully.

"He sounded delusional in those texts. My guess is that we'll see him, but don't worry, we'll be ready."

While we waited, I put the kettle on. "I've only got digestive biscuits, I'm afraid. I need to go shopping. They're not even the ones with chocolate on."

"I'm sure I'll cope."

The clock ticked on, the second hand steady while my heartbeat remained anything but.

It was two minutes to seven when the doorbell rang, the tinny sound of Für Elise echoing through the house. Edith had always loved Beethoven.

"Right, show time," Grant said. Before I registered what he was doing, he reached over, mussed up my hair and pulled my shirt out of my trousers.

"What are—?"

He whipped his own shirt over his head, and my jaw dropped. Did the man have a gym hidden away in his flat? He had muscles on muscles. I was still gaping when he grabbed my hand and pulled me towards the hallway.

Mike had just rung the bell again when Grant yanked the front door open, keeping me half-hidden behind him.

"Yes?" he asked, sounding peeved.

Mike took in the little scene and his features blackened. Without a word, he turned around and stomped off up the driveway, hopping into an ancient Ford Fiesta before accelerating off in a cloud of dubious-looking smoke.

Grant closed the door and held up his hand for a high five. I grinned and smacked his palm.

"That was awesome!"

At least, that's what I thought until the next text message arrived minutes later.

Mike: Why did you sell yourself out like a cheap whore, Ella? I can see you have a lot to learn. Luckily I'm a good teacher.

"What planet is that asshole on?" growled Grant from over my shoulder.

"I don't know, but I'm worried he wants me on it with him."

Chapter 7

TODD'S JAW DROPPED when we told him what happened with Mike.

"I'll make up the bed in the spare room. You can't go home with that madman out there."

"That's sweet of you, but I can't just move out forever."

"He's right," Grant put in. "Mike was pissed when he left. Stay here tonight, and we'll file a police report in the morning. They might be able to give him a warning or something. That last message sounded like a threat to me."

The thought of being alone at Edith's tonight did scare me a little, I had to admit. And then there was Todd's cooking.

"Maybe I could stay for one night. I'll go home tomorrow."

Dinner was herb-crusted sea bass with baby vegetables and a zingy sauce. Maybe I should piss Mike off a bit more often if this was the result.

"What do you do for a living?" I asked Todd. "If you're not a chef, you should be one."

He laughed. "Actually, I'm the executive chef at a contract catering company in London. Not quite as glamorous as Gordon Ramsay's restaurants, but the hours are more civilised. Cooking was all I ever wanted to do. Some people hate to bring their work home with them, but I love experimenting."

Well, Grant had certainly lucked out, hadn't he? Women's magazines had got it all wrong. The days of aspiring to date footballers and male models were over —we should be going for men who knew their way around the kitchen.

After chocolate mousse decorated with sugar flowers, of which I'm ashamed to say I ate two portions, Grant found me a T-shirt to sleep in, and I tried to get some rest. It didn't come easy. Mike was yet another burden on my already troubled mind.

I'd left my phone in the lounge overnight, and when I retrieved it before breakfast, he'd been busy again. I didn't want to look, but I had to. I had to know.

Mike: One more chance, Ella. I'll be round tomorrow at eight. We can eat in.

"Eight in the evening?" Grant asked when I told him, trying to lighten the mood by reminding me of my faux pas in our first conversation.

"Oh, very funny." I bit my lip. "I hope so. What if he's decided to invite himself for breakfast?"

"That would be crazy."

I stared at him.

"I like my toast with marmalade," he said.

By the time Grant turned up the next morning, I'd been shopping and got him two kinds of bread, three kinds of marmalade, and a bottle of freshly-squeezed orange juice.

"You have no idea how much I appreciate this," I said as I let him in.

"What kind of gentleman would I be if I left a damsel in distress?"

He made it sound like nothing, but it was everything.

I felt even guiltier when eight o'clock came and went with no sign of Mike.

"I've got to go out and sort out a new car today, but I'll be back this evening."

"I could cook," I blurted out. "Not as well as Todd, obviously, but it's the least I can do."

"Will there be enough for Todd? He gets grumpy if I abandon him to watch *Downton Abbey* on his own."

"Of course."

"In that case, thank you. Todd insists on cooking every evening, mainly because I burn everything, but he needs the occasional day off."

"That's settled then." At least I could repay a small fraction of his kindness.

The first thing I did after he went was call the police. I begged them to have a word with Mike, but the officer said as he hadn't actually tried to murder me, it wasn't a priority. Not in so many words, obviously, but that was the sentiment. This came from the same force that had sent out a car and two constables when Jaz accidentally parked her car two inches too close to her asshole neighbour's driveway. It was good to see my tax money was hard at work.

I spent the rest of the day experimenting, and by the time the doorbell rang I had a passable imitation of a lamb tagine warming in the oven. Ducking low around the door jamb, I peeked down the hallway and saw two shadows lurking behind the security glass. Thank goodness—it wasn't Mike deciding to arrive early.

"Something smells delicious," said Todd, following his nose towards the kitchen. "We brought a bottle of red."

Was it possible for a straight woman to fall in love with a pair of gay guys? Because I was getting perilously close.

He'd only just put the wine down on the island when the doorbell rang again. We all looked at each other.

"How do you want to play it this time?" Grant whispered.

"I don't know. Maybe...hide?"

I repeated my earlier trick and saw Mike's shadow hovering on the doorstep. The crunch of gravel followed as he moved off towards the dining room. A pause. Then more crunching.

"Shit, he's coming round the back!"

We dropped to our knees and crawled around the kitchen island as he stopped outside one window, then the next.

"Ella, I know you're in there," he called. "A good girl like you wouldn't go out more than one night a week."

Backwards and forwards he went. I imagined his face pressed against the window, his beady eyes violating my personal space.

"Dinner's going to be ruined," Todd groaned. "And these jeans are Versace. They weren't designed for contact with the floor."

"I'm sorry."

"Oh, ignore him," Grant said. "He likes to be a

diva."

Over twenty minutes passed before we heard the ragged engine of Mike's old banger rattle to life. There was a collective sigh of relief. Mine because Mike had gone, Grant's because the floor was cold and Todd's because he could finally start cooking the couscous.

"I can't go on like this," I said, as I picked at my dinner. Todd forked his in enthusiastically and told me it was delicious, but to me it tasted of old socks. "Why does he keep doing it? Is it a challenge to him? A game?"

"He'll probably get bored soon," said Grant. "We can wait it out."

"What if he doesn't?"

"I've got a better idea," piped up Todd. "I spoke to my friend today, and the stables his sister runs offers residential courses. You could have a nice little holiday and knock something off your list at the same time."

"I don't know. What if I got there and hated it?" If I was as good at riding horses as I was at driving, after one lesson I'd never want to set foot near one again.

Grant must have read my mind. "A horse would see the ditch coming and steer round it, so you're all right there. Plus, you've got to complete these challenges, sooner or later. You might as well push yourself and get this one done sooner."

I couldn't deny that the thought of being far from Mike appealed. "Where is the place?"

"In the Cotswolds somewhere."

"That's about an hour from here, right?"

"Yep. And it's got sweet little cottages and good pubs, or so I'm told," Todd said, as if that would offset the horrors of the four-legged fiends.

"I suppose I might as well take the details."

Todd wrote down the website address and his friend's sister Jenny's phone number. Linden Hollow, the place was called. It did seem kind of cute. Mind you, so did gremlins and look at what happened to them when you let your guard down.

I'd cheated with dessert and bought a trifle, but the guys didn't seem to mind. Todd had talked Grant into driving, so we split the bottle of wine, and by midnight I couldn't stop giggling as his impromptu make-up lesson came to a sticky end when he got the lipstick confused with the eyeshadow.

"Time for bed," Grant said.

"Aww, spoilsport."

The stairs gave me a problem, so Grant carried me up them and tucked me in, where I passed out rather than fell asleep while he and Todd let themselves out.

It was the best night's rest I'd had in ages.

Apart from a pounding headache, I felt better the next morning. Mike had been blessedly quiet, and once I'd swallowed a paracetamol, I was ready to face the day.

That feeling lasted until I got downstairs.

In keeping with the style of the house, Edith's front door was one of those old-fashioned ones where the mottled glass panels went all the way down to the floor. And this morning, the outline of a body sat slumped against it. Oh hell, was that Mike? Had he taken his stalking to the next level?

No.

When I crouched and squinted, I made out a mop of blonde hair and Mike's was brown.

I marched up and yanked the door open, not feeling

at all sorry when Terry tumbled backwards and landed on the prickly doormat with a bump. A bunch of sorry-looking flowers and a box of Turkish delight fell from his arms. Clearly he'd forgotten I hated the stuff.

He scrambled to his feet and held out his offerings. I made no effort to take them, and when he realised things weren't going to be as easy as he thought, he sheepishly lowered his hands to his sides.

"What do you want, Terry? It's seven thirty in the morning."

"I need to talk to you before you go to work."

"You haven't spoken to me for three months."

"I know, and with every passing day, the pain in my chest becomes more intense." He paused and took a deep breath. "I made a mistake. I've missed you more than I thought possible, and I want you back."

I could tell my peal of laughter wasn't the reaction he'd been expecting. Who the hell did he think he was? He'd cheated on me, slunk off with barely a word, and now he thought I'd fall back into his arms? Well, he had two chances: None and even less than that.

"I know it can't have been easy, living without me for all this time, but I'll do everything I can to make it up to you."

Yup, definitely delusional.

"You can start by getting out of my doorway." I prodded him with my foot, and he reluctantly shuffled backwards.

Once again, I wished Edith was still with me. The last time he'd darkened the doorstep, she'd threatened to whack him in the unmentionables with a frying pan, and he'd made tracks pretty sharpish after that. I sighed. Why couldn't I have her courage?

"I'm not leaving, Ella. I'm going to stay until you see how much I love you."

Love? Yeah right.

I pushed the door with all my might until it clicked shut then got on the phone to Demi. We kept each other up to date with Terry-related gossip as well as going on our lunch dates.

"You'll never guess who's sitting on my doorstep."

"Terry?"

That was slightly disappointing. "How did you know?"

"I heard at the club last night that he'd split up with his latest girlfriend. You know, the one who works in the clothes shop next to Tesco? They were living together, but she found he'd borrowed her credit card to watch porn on the internet and booted him out. I thought I'd take round a box of donuts later so she could celebrate properly."

"He's homeless?"

"I guess so. I was going to call and warn you after breakfast."

"Sorry, I woke you up, didn't I?"

"It doesn't matter. I'll go back to bed after I've watched Jeremy Kyle. That program always makes me feel so much better about my own life. I mean, I may be single and strip for a living, but at least my significant other isn't shagging my sister's cat."

"I suppose there is that. Do you fancy getting lunch? If Terry's hanging around, I'd rather be out of the house."

"I'd love to. How about the café next to the church?"

By the time I left the house at twelve, the idiot was

nowhere in sight. Obviously his sense of commitment hadn't improved any since we split. Over a tasty slice of quiche, I caught Demi up on the disasters in my life, including Edith's challenges and mad Mike.

"We sure can pick 'em, can't we?" She rolled her eyes. "I'll go speed-dating with you if you like. I've tried everything else."

"Really? I'm nervous about that one. I'm usually tongue-tied for at least an hour when I meet a man, so I probably won't get more than a sentence out."

She giggled. "We can practise what to say beforehand. Once you get a few glasses of wine in you, you'll be fine." Her face turned serious. "At least when you talk, guys listen to you. They never even look at my face."

Demi had been blessed, or cursed as she thought of it, with the kind of chest that men found distracting. When you put that together with her slim figure and pretty face, half of all men were intimidated by her. Most of the rest couldn't see past her exterior, and the few that did got hung up on her job. After a while, I'd realised how lonely she was.

"Maybe we could go to a bar where the lighting isn't very good?"

She gave me a little smile. "You're on. So what's next on your list, apart from the speed-dating?"

"Not driving, obviously. I've put that one to the very bottom. I'm thinking of trying the horse riding. Todd told me about a residential centre that runs intensive courses."

I'd taken a look at the website for Linden Hollow that morning. The accommodation certainly looked pleasant, and it boasted a selection of horses for all levels of ability and a high staff-to-student ratio. I fished out my phone to show Demi, only to find another text from Mike flashing at me.

"What now?" I groaned.

Mike: It was very rude of you not to answer the door last night. I can only imagine you were upstairs behaving like a slut with your visitor. Honestly, Ella, it's not good enough. Your education is going to take longer than I thought.

"What's up? You've lost all your colour."

I slid the phone over to her.

"Wow. The guy's whacked."

"Tell me about it. The police won't help until it gets worse. What do they want? For me to end up as another statistic?"

"You know what I'd do? Go to that horse riding place. A couple of weeks away'll do you good, plus you'll complete something on your list."

"That idea's getting more and more appealing."

When I got home and found Terry lying in the porch again, complete with a sleeping bag and a camping stove, my mind stopped wavering between mad Mike and the evil equines. Decision made.

Linden Hollow, here I come.

CHAPTER 8

MY NERVES JANGLED as I waited for Jenny to answer the phone. Would she teach a complete beginner? And if she agreed to give me lessons, how long before I could go?

I needn't have worried. "You're exactly the type of rider we specialise in," she said. "We've got some lovely quiet horses, and our instructors have experience with all levels."

"Do you have vacancies at the moment?"

"We've got a course starting the day after tomorrow, as it happens. There are two other girls coming. They've ridden a bit before, but we'll assign you a groom of your own to teach you stable management. I firmly believe that learning how to care for the horse is as important as the riding. You build up a much better bond that way."

So I'd be scooping poop? Wonderful. But at least I could go soon. "Do you have any accommodation free? Or should I try to find something nearby?"

"Both the cottages are booked, but we've got a free en-suite room in the barn."

"The barn?" I pictured a cow-stall, complete with straw and a manger for my dinner.

Jenny laughed. "Don't worry—it's been converted into living quarters. You'd just have to share a kitchen and lounge with the others."

"I don't mind doing that." Some company would be nice. I was already feeling a bit lonely now I'd finished at Payright, at least, as lonely as I could feel with a freak stalking me and my ex camping in the porch.

"I'll email you all the details, and we'll see you on Saturday then."

As soon as I told Todd the news, he squealed down the phone line, "That's fabulous news! Have you got the right outfits?"

Outfits? I hadn't even thought about that. What did one wear to go horse riding? I glanced up at one of Edith's paintings, an old hunting scene that took pride of place above the fireplace in the dining room. The riders all wore red jackets and puffy trousers. Surely not?

I needn't have feared because Todd had done the research for me. Two hours later, I snuck out of the back gate into the service road that ran behind the house, wanting to avoid another conversation with Terry, who was still sitting on the doorstep.

"We're going to a tack shop," Todd announced. "I found it on the internet."

Forty minutes later, we pulled into a farm, and Todd led me into a huge warehouse filled with weird and wonderful things, half of which looked like torture implements.

"What do you reckon this is for?" I asked him, picking up a metal thing with a hook at the end.

He turned it over in his hands. "Hanging things on?"

"It's a hoof pick," came a voice from behind us. "You use it for getting the stones out of horses' hooves."

Ick, no way was I getting that close. The four-legged monster would probably kick me.

Todd and the salesgirl laughed. Oops, did I say that out loud?

"Do you need any help?" she asked.

"In every way possible," Todd said.

Thanks, Todd. I poked him in the side. "I'm going on a riding holiday, and I need to buy things for that."

"Do you ride often?"

"I fell off a pony once."

I sorely regretted telling Edith that story as I very much suspected it was why she'd set horse riding as one of my challenges. Many times over the years she'd said, "If you fall off the horse, you need to get straight back on again." Just as many times, I hadn't managed to do it. Now was my chance to prove I could.

The girl's eyes widened. "That's it?"

I nodded, a sigh escaping at the same time.

"So you need everything for a beginner, then?"

"That's right."

I soon found out why horse riding had a reputation as a rich man's sport. A pair of boots, a crash helmet, two pairs of jodhpurs, gloves, and a waterproof jacket set me back almost five hundred pounds.

"You look cute, though. Very *Country Life* magazine," Todd said.

That was all right then. As long as I looked the part. The phrase "all the gear and no idea" sprung to mind. I might get away with the charade for a few hours, but the moment I went near a horse I'd get laughed out of the stable. Could horses laugh?

I'd planned to get the train to Linden Hollow, but Grant insisted on driving me.

"You've packed your own body weight in those two suitcases. I don't know what you've got in there, but I can't see you dragging them round a train station without needing medical attention."

I glanced down at my luggage. Well, Edith's luggage. She used to go on holiday twice a year without fail. Once to Ibiza for the clubs, yes really, and a two-week cruise around the Med. I'd learned my packing skills from her.

"Thanks," I muttered.

He squeezed my shoulder. "Just cheer up. Look on the bright side, your squatter might be gone by the time you get back." Terry had been sprawled out and snoring when Grant arrived, so he'd come in through the back. "I could get some of the guys from the gym to give me a hand removing him if you like?"

Terry was an idiot, but he was harmless. "I'm hoping his presence will deter Mike."

"There is that."

The drive to the Cotswolds took longer than we'd hoped, mainly due to a surfboard falling off someone's roof rack in the fast lane and causing a traffic jam on the M4. Quite why anybody would want to venture into the sea at that time of year was beyond me. The temperatures may have been above average for February, but the water certainly wouldn't be balmy. By the time we reached Linden Hollow, I'd got fidgety and desperate for the loo.

When Grant pulled into the driveway, I saw how the place got its name. The farmhouse, stables and the other buildings nestled into the dip at the bottom of two hills, a picture postcard of perfection. Rolling fields spread out on either side, and even the car park was decorated with tubs of colourful winter pansies.

We'd only just parked when a girl came bustling up to the car. "Hi, are you Ella?"

Panic hit. "No, uh, we're just lost."

Grant rolled his eyes. "Yes, she's Ella." He leaned a little closer. "You've bought all the stuff now. You have to stay."

The girl's puzzled look turned into a welcoming grin. "I'm Jenny. It's great to have you here."

Her age surprised me. I'd imagined her as a tough-looking lady in her late forties or early fifties, but she didn't look much older than I was.

"Er, do you have a ladies' room I could borrow?"

She laughed, a hearty sound that spoke of her confidence. "Sure, I'll show you."

I left Grant to haul my suitcases out of the car while I followed Jenny. Twenty stables formed a U-shape around a central courtyard, and a few curious faces peeped over the half-doors at our approach. She led me over to the far corner, into a room filled with saddles, bridles, and a well-rounded ginger cat. The rich smell of leather permeating the air reminded me of the old sofa in Edith's den. As a little girl, I'd loved curling up there for hours, reading. It sure beat going home.

She pointed to a door at the end. "The loo's in there."

Glamorous it was not. Bits of straw dotted the floor,

and a decade's worth of smudges covered a once white wall. My face stared back at me from a cracked mirror above the tiny basin Why did I go to the effort of blow-drying my hair this morning? I thanked my lucky stars that at least there was a toilet roll, then movement caught my eye and I glanced up.

Jenny and Grant both came running at my scream.

"What is it?" Jenny asked, forehead creased in worry.

I pointed with a shaking finger. "There's a spider." And not just any spider. A steroid-enhanced mutant spider that could most likely take out the cat if he put his mind to it.

Jenny laughed. "That's just Gordon. He's been there for months."

She'd named a spider? Was she mad? The only thing I did with spiders was suck them up the vacuum cleaner. Actually, that was the one thing I missed about having Terry around. He used to deal with them for me.

"Uh, do you have another bathroom?" I may have been crossing my legs, but there was no way I'd set foot back in that one.

She chuckled again. "I'll show you to the one in the barn."

Grant followed along with my cases as Jenny led the way to a wood-framed building with an old red-tiled roof and pots of flowers either side of the door. After seeing the tack room, I'd been expecting the worst, but the barn was actually kind of cute. Once I'd done my business, Jenny showed me my room, and I was pleasantly surprised by that too. Not five-star, but definitely a solid three.

When we went back out to the living area, two other

girls had come in. I may have been feeling overdressed earlier, but beside them I was the poor relation. Both wore country chic and had that snooty air about them that tended to be inherited rather than acquired.

I followed a little reluctantly as Jenny veered in their direction.

"Ella, meet Annabel and Felicity. They'll both be with you on the course this week. They've done some riding before, but you'll be assigned individual buddies to tailor your training."

Annabel looked down her nose at me. "Good. I don't want to be held back."

Wow, that was friendly.

"Do you have your own horses?" asked Felicity.

I shook my head. "I haven't really ridden before."

She and Annabel gave each other a look. *What on earth is she doing here?*

Jenny seemed oblivious. "I need to get back out to the horses. Zoltan needs lunging. You two can finish showing Ella around, can't you?"

They looked as if there was nothing they'd like less, but Felicity grudgingly agreed. The second Jenny stepped out, Annabel ignored me and turned her attention on Grant, tongue hanging out.

"I'm Annabel," she cooed.

"Yeah, I got that," he said. "I'm Grant."

"And you're dating Ella?"

"Uh...we're friends."

That earned him a smile that was almost genuine. "Would you like a tour as well?"

He must have caught the pleading look in my eyes because he sighed nodded. "Okay, I'll come."

With Annabel on one side and Felicity the other,

Grant got shown the paddocks, the indoor and outdoor arenas, and the break room. Annabel pressed up against him as they leaned over each stable door, giving him a personal introduction to all the horses. Poor Grant. I shuffled along behind, feeling like a spare part.

Every so often, Grant would try to involve me in the conversation, but the tag team shut me down pretty quickly.

"Ella, what do you think of this horse?" he asked.

"She looks sweet."

"Yes, but she's old," Annabel interrupted, taking his arm. "Let's go and look at the stallion over here."

Finally, when they'd shown him everything but their bedrooms, we found ourselves back in the lounge. From the way they kept eyeing him up, I suspected they'd both have willingly tested out their mattress springs with him.

"Do you want to stay and have dinner with us, Grant?" Annabel asked. "June comes in from the village to make our meals, and she's a splendid cook."

"Sorry, I can't. I'm going out to G-A-Y with my boyfriend this evening, and I don't want to be late."

Both their mouths dropped open as he bent to give me a kiss on the cheek. "Good luck with that pair," he whispered.

I was going to need it.

"Thanks for bringing me."

"No problem. Just give me a shout when you want picking up."

What had I done to deserve meeting such a kind man? I did share Annabel and Felicity's opinions on one thing at least—it was a crying shame he was gay.

"Enjoy club night," I said brightly, so the other two

could hear.

He put on his campest voice. "Oh I will, dahling, I will."

CHAPTER 9

"WE ALL TEND to eat together," Jenny said as I helped her to set the dining table that evening. "I'm a big believer in teamwork. We'll be working together and riding together, so it makes sense to share a table as well."

I looked around for the Ugly Sisters, conspicuous only by their absence. I'd christened them with that moniker because while they may have looked perfect on the outside, their souls weren't pretty. I doubted they'd bought into Jenny's togetherness concept either.

As I set out napkins, I counted up the place settings. Seven plates, seven sets of cutlery. With the Uglies, Jenny, and I, that made four. "Who else is coming for dinner?"

"Marion and Lenny for sure—they're two of the trainers who'll be doing the one-on-one lessons. Connor's the third, but I'm not sure whether he'll be back tonight. He had to pop into London for a couple of days, and he wasn't sure what time he'd finish there."

Ah well, if he didn't turn up, maybe I could get an extra portion—the tantalising aromas drifting in from the kitchen were making my tummy rumble.

"Do you know what's for dinner?" I asked.

"No, but June hasn't cooked a bad meal yet. Don't forget to save room for dessert."

Marion and Lenny turned up a few minutes before seven and introduced themselves before they sat down. Marion fitted the picture I'd had in my mind for Jenny —older, with a vaguely stern expression and her hair scraped back in a bun. Lenny couldn't have been more than twenty, and his ginger hair flopped over his eyes as he greeted me with an easy smile.

We were well into the main course and chattering away when the two Uglies turned up. A sideways glance saw Lenny turn to Marion and roll his eyes. Annabel and Felicity were like a dam across a river. Free-flowing conversation slowed to an awkward trickle, interspersed with the clink of cutlery on plates.

"Is there any low-sodium salt?" asked Annabel, picking at her chicken.

"Sorry, just normal salt," Jenny said.

Annabel huffed and pushed her dinner around with her fork, occasionally taking a bite, before she gave up and shoved the sorry remains away. Felicity fared a little better but left all her potatoes, citing the evilness of carbs in general and roasted ones in particular.

When Annabel laid down her cutlery, I struggled to hold in my smile

"Want to catch a movie on Netflix?" she asked Felicity.

"That new rom-com's out now."

The pair of them walked off, leaving their dirty plates on the table, and Jenny gave the sigh of a condemned woman.

"It's going to be a long two weeks."

At least with the pair of them out of the way, there was extra trifle for the four of us. I ate two helpings. Okay, two and a half. At this rate, I'd either need to take up jogging or buy bigger clothes.

"That was amazing, June," I said, as I helped stack plates into the dishwasher. I covered my mouth to burp discreetly then turned to find her beaming at me.

"It's good to see a young girl with an appetite. We had one here a couple of weeks ago who would only eat orange food. There's only so many things you can do with carrots and sweet potato."

Wow, that must be boring. "The only thing I'm not keen on is mushrooms. I don't know who thought it would be a good idea to start eating those."

"I'll remember that. No mushrooms." She dried her hands on a tea towel and hung it on one of the cupboard doors. "I'm done for the day, so I'll see you tomorrow for lunch. Breakfast is fend-for-yourself, I'm afraid."

"I'm sure I can do myself a slice of toast."

It really wasn't that difficult, but from the Uglies' reaction, you'd think they'd been asked to harvest their muesli rather than just pouring it out of the box.

"I wouldn't do this at home, so I don't see why I should have to do it here," Annabel said.

"And there's no soy milk for my tea," grumbled Felicity. "I'm lactose intolerant."

"Would you like me to make you a slice of toast?" I asked. Anything to stop them from moaning.

They both stared at me, and Annabel shook her head. "I only eat organic bread, and that isn't."

"And I don't eat carbs before twelve," Felicity said.

Why did I bother offering when all they did was complain? I spread a thick layer of jam onto my own slice and took a bite. It may have been inorganic but it tasted pretty good.

According to Jenny, our course would start today at nine. She'd explained last night we'd ride twice a day, and the rest of the time would be spent learning to care for the horses and doing chores on the yard. The Uglies had looked most unimpressed at the "chores" part.

"What made you come here?" I'd asked them. Surely they could have found somewhere more suitable, a place where the butler brought fancy drinks while somebody rode the horses for them.

"Because everybody knows that if you want to ride the horses movie stars ride, you come to Jenny," Annabel said.

Everybody except me, it seemed. I didn't want to ask for more information in case I sounded stupid. I mean, I already knew I sounded stupid, but I didn't want to sound even thicker.

At nine o'clock, the butterflies started as I walked to the tack room with the enthusiasm of an inmate on death row. I kept my fingers crossed I'd get paired up with Lenny. He'd been cheerful and talkative last night, whereas I found Marion a bit intimidating.

Except when I got to the tack room, the only person there was a stranger leaning against the windowsill. His back was to me as he looked towards a couple of horses in the paddock, running around as the first rays of sun peeped through a gap in the cloud. I cleared my throat and he turned slowly, reluctant to tear his eyes from the scene outside. And that was when I stopped breathing.

From the back, he didn't look like much in his tatty jeans and checked shirt, but from the front... A whole different story. The black beanie hat shoved low over his forehead and a day's worth of stubble suggested a lack of care about his looks, but they did nothing to hide his strong jaw and chiselled cheekbones. But those weren't what got to me. No, it was his eyes. The moment they met mine, they sucked out my soul and replaced it with party poppers.

He stalked towards me with the confident manner of a man who knew women would fall at his feet. I nearly did as well. My knees started to buckle, and I stepped backwards until I hit the wall, thankful for its support.

A couple of feet out, he stopped and gave me the kind of look people reserved for their shoe after they'd trodden in something squidgy. Disgust mixed with mild curiosity.

"I'm Connor."

My mouth opened but no sound came out, so I closed it again. What should I say? My name. I should tell him my name.

I sucked in air and prepared to speak, but Annabel saved me the trouble. She strutted through the door with Felicity in tow and headed straight for Connor like a homing pigeon. A homing pigeon in designer breeches, spotless leather boots, and a white—yes, white—jacket.

He saw her coming and took a step back from me. She didn't hesitate and got straight in there, pulling him towards her to kiss him on both cheeks, European style.

"I'm Annabel," she said, still holding onto his upper arms. "It's lovely to meet you." Her saccharine voice made me long for a pair of earplugs. If it got any higher, passing dogs would stop in to see what was going on.

Felicity gave a little wave from behind her. "I'm Felicity."

"Connor," he said, grinning at the pair of them. His beaming smile would have lit up a small town. If scientists harnessed its power, it would go a long way towards solving the energy crisis.

Jenny arrived at just the right moment. "Right everyone, I'll pair you up, and we can get started." She eyed up the connection between Annabel and Connor. "Connor, could you come this way, please?"

He extricated himself and took his place beside Lenny. My heart was thundering by then, a combination of nerves about horse riding and Connor's mere presence.

"Annabel, I think we'll put you with Marion."

"I want to go with Connor."

Jenny smiled through gritted teeth. "When you signed up, you said you wanted to improve your dressage. Marion's a world-class trainer. She used to work with the Olympic team."

"But..." She tailed off, but we all knew what she wanted to say. Marion didn't have eyes that smouldered or butt cheeks that could crack walnuts.

"I think you'll make a great pairing," Jenny said firmly, then turned to the second of the Uglies. "And Felicity, you said you wanted to work on your jumping technique, so Lenny's the guy for you. He's been competing since the age of ten."

I gulped, only my mouth had turned into a desert and my tongue suddenly felt too big for it so I ended up having a coughing fit.

Lenny leapt forward and walloped me on the back. "You okay?"

Jenny handed me a bottle of water from the mini-fridge next to the sink, and I sipped gratefully. "I'm fine, just a dry throat."

"Good, good," Jenny said. "Anyway, Ella, that leaves you with Connor."

Yes, I'd worked that part out, and it terrified me.

It didn't take a genius to see that Connor was dangerous. He was the type of guy who could take a girl's heart, put it through a mincer, then chargrill the sorry remains. The only saving grace was that he kept making eyes at Annabel and not me.

I perched on the edge of a trunk while a pissed-looking Annabel and a resigned Felicity filtered out with Marion and Lenny, and Jenny gave my shoulder a squeeze.

"You're a bit nervous, aren't you?"

I managed a strangled laugh. "How did you guess?"

"Don't worry, I've picked out a lovely horse for you to start with. She's really kind to beginners."

It wasn't the horse I was worried about. "Thanks."

She walked out, leaving me in the bear pit. Connor gave me an arrogant smile as he walked over and stopped in front of me once again.

"So," he said.

I didn't respond. It was either stay quiet or open my mouth and say something really, really stupid.

"You ready to get started?" His American accent sounded West Coast to my untrained ears. I wished he'd go back there, because then he wouldn't be squeezing my chest in a vice and slowly, slowly turning the handle.

But I could hardly say that. Instead, I nodded to him, dreading the first task.

"We'll start with the fun part—mucking out."

Hurrah.

He demonstrated first, and that was something I could have watched all day. Each time he leaned forward to fork up another pile of the unmentionable, his jeans tightened across his buttocks and the view had me licking my lips before I gave myself a mental slap.

Then it was my turn. Connor left me to it as I started clearing "my" stable.

How people did this every day, I had no idea. My back ached and my thighs were burning by the time I'd finished. Not to mention the fact I smelled disgusting. The only consolation was the two Uglies had to do this as well. No butler, no slave.

When Connor came back, I'd turned into a sweaty mess, with bits of straw stuck all over me and dirt on my hands. I wished I could teleport myself to the shower and, following that, back to Edith's. But no such luck.

He looked over what I'd done with a critical eye. Emphasis on the critical. "You need to add more straw to Folly's bed."

A groan escaped my lips. I'd thought I was finished. With Connor watching, I tried to ignore the pain in my wrists as I picked up the wheelbarrow and headed to the barn again. I'd just finished shaking out the fresh straw when Jenny came back, right on time to witness the coughing fit as dust got up my nose.

"Are you ready for your first lesson?" she asked brightly.

No, I was ready for a massage, a brightly coloured cocktail, and an afternoon on the sofa with a good book, but I saw by the saddle Jenny was carrying I wasn't going to get that.

"This is Folly," she said, without waiting for my answer. Connor had tied the horse outside earlier, and she was still standing patiently as I did my best to ignore her. "She's an old girl now, but she's safe as houses."

I hoped she was safer than my house. Had Terry given up and found himself a new place to sleep yet? Had Mike been round again?

"Are you sure? I mean, she's got four legs and a will of her own."

"She's a sweetheart, honestly. Connor'll show you how to tack up, then I'll start teaching you the basics."

Great. I could hardly wait.

Connor looked as enthusiastic as I felt as he fiddled with his phone. In terms of priorities, it appeared I came somewhere between Candy Crush and mucking out. Welcome to my life.

Eventually, he looked up. "You need to groom her first, then I'll show you how to put her saddle and bridle on."

He handed me a brush and our fingertips touched. A flash of heat ran through me, while Connor seemed unaffected. Blooming heck. If I didn't build up an immunity to his presence sooner rather than later I'd be a shivering mess by the time I left here.

At least brushing Folly was therapeutic. Something about the repetitive motion calmed my nerves, and when Connor disturbed my trance I almost told him to go away.

He held up the saddle. "Time for this. You need to lower it gently onto her back," he said as he demonstrated. "Then smooth out any wrinkles in the saddle pad. The strap that goes under her belly is called the girth, and you need to do it up tightly enough that you can get four fingers under it, no more."

He worked too fast for me to take in the details, but at least he seemed competent.

"Next time, you try. Now for the bridle. You need to hold it like this." He grabbed hold of a random leather strap. "Then when the bit's under the horse's lips, you put your thumb in their mouth to get them to open it."

"Hang on. You put your thumb *in* its mouth? What if it bites it off?"

He laughed then showed me how to do it. "Horses have a gap in their teeth at the top of their lips. It's where the bit sits, and they can't hurt you if you put your finger there."

Folly opened her mouth wide, and what he said was true. Who knew? He put the top part of the bridle, the headpiece he called it, over Folly's ears then buckled up the noseband and throatlash to keep the thing on.

Before I knew it, it was time for my first lesson.

CHAPTER 10

I SETTLED MY crash helmet onto my head as Connor led Folly beside me on the way to the arena.

She seemed placid enough, but I couldn't help being worried by her size. What if she decided she didn't want me on her back? When Connor halted the horse at the entrance, a big part of me wanted to carry on walking, right out the gate and down the road. A gentle stroll, a quiet country pub, maybe a light lunch while I waited for Grant to come and pick me up.

My nerves weren't helped by the sight of Annabel on a beautiful champagne-coloured horse, cantering tidily around the arena. She must have mucked out as well, but she'd certainly come through the ordeal better than I had. Marion yelled instructions at her—turn here, speed up, hands together, heels down—and she followed them all perfectly. I didn't even know how to get on the bloody nag.

"Your turn," Jenny called.

I forced myself to unclench my hands and pasted a smile on my face that I absolutely didn't feel. My legs wobbled as I plodded beside Folly onto the sandy surface.

On her way out, Annabel gave me a condescending look before turning her charms onto Connor.

"Will you be in for lunch?" she asked with a

simpering smile.

"Sure will."

She took off her helmet and fluffed up her hair. Nope, she'd barely broken a sweat, despite all the complicated moves she'd been doing. "I'll save you a seat."

I caught Connor staring after her as she walked away, her spotless white breeches moulded to her like a second skin with no sign of a VPL.

"Connor, can you give Ella a leg up?" Jenny asked, making both of us snap our attention back to her.

"A what?"

"It's to get on the horse," he explained. "Face the horse on its near side then bend your left leg at the knee."

I did that, and he put one hand under my knee and the other on my ankle.

"What are you doing?"

"When I count to three, jump."

I had no time to think. As he lifted, all I could do was spring up as hard as possible and try not to shriek too loudly as the momentum almost took me over the other side of the horse. Somehow, I managed to keep my bottom in the saddle, and as I whispered thanks to someone up there for the break, I leaned forward, flung my arms around Folly's neck, and clung on like a shopaholic guarding my bargains from the sale rail.

Hoots of laughter came from the side of the arena. Annabel and Felicity were hanging over the fence, tears streaming down their cheeks at my expense. Connor chuckled as well, and even Jenny was trying not to smile. I closed my eyes and tried to block them out.

Why had I thought I could succeed? I might as well

admit defeat on Edith's list right now. First the driving disaster, now this...this...nightmare. I could go to Payright and beg Barry for my old job back. If I bought him a couple of dozen donuts, he might find it in himself to forgive me.

"Honey, you need to sit up," Jenny said.

"I can't. I'll fall off," I mumbled into Folly's fur.

"You won't, I promise. Connor's got hold of Folly, and I'm right here to catch you if you wobble. Do you think you could try?"

Oh, what the hell? If I was going to land on my arse, I might as well get it over with. I forced an eyelid open. At least the sand was soft. Maybe I wouldn't break any bones when I hit the deck?

I shifted my grip to Folly's mane, tangling my fingers in her wiry hair, then pushed myself skywards.

Connor looked up at me, the top of his head level with my waist. "You okay?"

Well, I thought I might be until I made the mistake of looking down. I closed my eyes again. Who wanted to see their end coming?

Connor's fingers closed around my thigh, and I jumped like I'd been burned.

"Ella?" The amused look he'd worn before had been replaced by worry.

"I'm scared," I admitted.

His expression softened. "You won't fall."

"You don't know that."

"Well, if you do, I'll catch you. How about that?"

In that case, sliding off didn't seem like such a bad option.

"What now?" I asked in a small voice.

"We'll get Folly to walk. I'll keep hold of her—all

you need to do is sit there. Can you manage that?"

"I think so."

Jenny clicked her tongue and the saddle lurched underneath me as Folly ambled off. As promised, Connor stayed at my side, and when we'd gone twice round the arena, I began to relax slightly. By relax, I mean I loosened my grip enough for some feeling to return to my fingers.

"Are you ready to try holding the reins now?" Jenny asked.

No. Not in a million years, but I wasn't about to say that in front of Connor. I'd come across as incompetent enough already.

"Okay."

Let go of the mane, Ella. I tried, but no...no... Connor had to reach up and un-peel my fingers before positioning them on the leather.

"Now, the reins are attached to Folly's mouth," he said. "So don't pull on them too hard, or you'll hurt her."

I was careful to keep a very light contact as we moved off again. Poor Folly. She was an angel for putting up with me, and I didn't want to make it worse.

After we'd done two more laps, Jenny told me to give a gentle pull.

"She stopped!"

"That's what's supposed to happen. Now squeeze with your legs."

I did, and she started up again. "Did I do that?"

"You did. Let's practise a few more times."

By the time we stopped for lunch, I'd become quite proficient at starting and stopping, and nobody was more surprised by that than me. Maybe I *could* do this after all?

"How do I get down?" I asked Connor. After my exertions this morning, I'd developed quite an appetite, and surely Folly wanted some food as well?

"Lean forwards, swing your right leg over the back of the saddle, then slide down, but..."

Eager to prove I was a good student, I did as he said. Too late, I realised I'd left my feet in the stirrups and tumbled, landing right on top of him. Jenny leapt forwards and grabbed Folly as Connor twisted so he landed underneath me. An "oof" escaped his lips as I squashed the air out of his lungs.

"I'm so sorry!"

I tried to scramble off him, but he had his arms wrapped around me. A few long, long seconds passed before they loosened enough for me to roll away.

"I was going to say 'don't forget to take your feet out of the stirrups.'"

He got to his feet first and as an afterthought, offered me his hand. I took it, and any sparks I might have felt were doused by the wave of embarrassment that rolled over me.

Stupid, clumsy Ella.

I took the seat furthest from Connor and Annabel at lunch. She monopolised him while the others chatted away in...well, it bore a passing resemblance to English but all the terms—martingale, oxer, numnah, pommel —passed right over my head. Rather than admit I didn't have a clue, I concentrated on eating June's sausage and mash. I'm sure it was delicious, but it turned to sawdust as I chewed.

"My hands hurt from Chardonnay's reins," Annabel said to him after an enthusiastic discussion on the merits of Devoucoux saddles versus Hermès. "Could you help me find some different ones?"

"It'd be my pleasure."

They walked close to each other as they left the room, with Connor opening the door to let Annabel go through first. I know that shouldn't have hurt, but it did. All my life I'd craved the ability to fit in like Annabel, but once again, I'd found myself stuck in the corner as life passed me by. How could I change that? The rare occasions Jaz had convinced me to try resulted in disasters like Mike. Perhaps being one of the in-crowd simply wasn't my destiny, no matter how much I might wish for it?

After lunch, we had a break of a couple of hours, and I escaped to my room, finding comfort in solitude and a book. There was nothing like trying to solve a good mystery before the heroine did to keep my mind occupied. I could have a bit of excitement, even if it was all in my head.

The afternoon session came around all too soon. At least this time I managed to get on board and sit up almost straight away. Connor plodded round with Folly while Jenny drilled me over starting and stopping, then turning left and right by squeezing on the reins. By the end of the session, I'd done a rather wobbly circle, and I was quite proud that I'd kept my eyes open the entire time.

"Do I need to get a crash mat?" Connor asked as I prepared to dismount.

I checked my feet were clear of the stirrups. "No, it should be okay this time."

I slithered down and, by some miracle, ended up on my feet. Compared to Felicity and Annabel, I didn't feel as if I'd done much, but every muscle ached and my eyes kept trying to close of their own accord. All I wanted was dinner and sleep.

"We need to bed the horses down for the night now," Connor said once I'd taken the tack off Folly.

A groan escaped at the thought of more work, especially the stinky kind. I was about to pick up the wheelbarrow when my phone pinged. Saved by the bell.

Or maybe not. It was a message from Terry.

Terry: You could have warned me you had a new boyfriend. He woke me up and threatened to chop my nuts off before I managed to resolve things.

For a second I felt bad, but when I realised Terry was still crashing in Edith's porch my sympathy evaporated. More so when Mike followed up with another text seconds later.

Mike: Ella, I can't believe you haven't given your brother a key to your house. It's inhumane to make him sleep in the shed. I'm disappointed in you.

Those...those...those...assholes! Terry was sleeping in Edith's summerhouse? That was my little sanctuary in the warm months. I'd set it up with a couple of comfortable loungers and a bookshelf, and Edith and I would sit out there to catch the last of the evening sun. Now Terry had violated that. I wanted to rip his scrawny bits off myself.

And as for passing himself off as my brother, well, that made me want to skewer his testicles and barbecue them.

Not only that, the fact Mike had found him there meant he'd been prowling around the back of my house again, and that alone gave me the creeps.

But what could I do? I was miles away.

"Problems?" asked Connor.

I jumped at the sound of his voice. I hadn't heard him creep up behind me. What was I supposed to say? He already thought I was an idiot, so I figured one more thing couldn't make it any worse. I might as well tell the truth.

"My stalker texted to say my ex is living in my shed."

There was a silence-filled pause before Connor burst out laughing. "You had me going for a second."

"It's true."

He stopped laughing. "You're not serious?"

I nodded miserably. "It's a long story."

"I'm all ears."

"Uh, it's really not that interesting." I didn't particularly want to rehash my failed love life for a man whose pheromones probably caused girls several counties over to suffer restless nights.

He opened his mouth, maybe to try and convince me, but the sound that hit my eardrums was Annabel's whine.

"Connor, there's no more coarse mix in the bin in the feed room and Chardonnay's hungry. Would you help me?"

"Sure thing, sweetheart."

As the pair sauntered off, I took the opportunity to put Folly to bed and escape, happy I'd survived at least the first day in equine hell.

CHAPTER 11

ON SUNDAY MORNING, the Uglies skipped breakfast, which was a blessed relief. I'd had quite enough of them at dinner the night before. I didn't care if Annabel's family owned a mansion in Surrey and a villa in Spain, or that Felicity's father was head partner at a law firm, but I found out anyway, at full volume and in excruciating detail.

I'd been tempted to skip dessert just to get away from them, but June's treacle tart won out and I'd stayed for a small slice. Okay, slices. Maybe I should take up aerobics?

I glanced down at my stomach. Was it my imagination, or had it grown in the last few days? No, it must be the cut of my breeches—skin tight lycra didn't flatter anyone. I sucked it in as Connor sauntered through the kitchen door, rubbing his eyes.

"Late night?" I asked, trying to keep the sarcasm out of my voice. He'd been engrossed in conversation with Annabel when I'd retired to my room, their heads bent together as he laughed at her witty repartee.

"Yeah, I had things to do."

Things? Or Annabel? I sighed. What was the point in dwelling on it? People who looked like Connor dated the Annabels of this world, not girls like me who couldn't even get off a horse without ballsing it up completely.

The kettle boiled, and I spooned instant coffee into a mug. Usually I was more of a tea drinker, but I hadn't slept well the night before and I needed the caffeine. Visions of Terry and Mike slugging it out in a boxing ring had filled my dreams, blood dripping and teeth flying. The shame of it was I wanted both of them to lose.

"Do you fancy coffee?" I asked Connor. He looked as rough as I felt.

"Yeah. Please."

"What's the plan today?"

"Chores first, then I'll give you a lesson."

"Not Jenny?" At least with her there, I had a buffer between Connor and my hormones.

"She's out today, filming."

"Filming?"

"You didn't know? Jenny doesn't just run riding holidays; she trains horses for film and television work. She's taken two of them out to work on an episode of a new TV drama."

Suddenly Annabel's comment about coming here to ride movie star horses made sense. "Does she spend much time doing that?"

"Her husband helps with that side of the business, but he's away in Scotland with a team of horses for a couple of months working on a Hollywood blockbuster."

"Wow! That sounds amazing! It must be hard for Jenny though, being on her own."

"Yeah, she's stretched quite thin at the moment, but the deal was too good for them to pass up."

She must be exhausted, and sad too. Being away

from the man you loved for weeks at a time had to be difficult.

Being away from Mike and Terry, on the other hand, was a good thing.

I got through the mucking out a little faster that morning and managed to brush Folly by myself before Connor came back.

"You have a go at tacking up today," he told me.

"I'm really not sure..."

"Have some confidence in yourself and try."

It was all right for him to say. He had it in spades. If ever a budding entrepreneur started selling bottles of confidence, they'd use Connor's face on the label.

Hesitantly, I lifted the saddle. It weighed a ton, and my arms felt the strain as I lifted it onto Folly's back. Remembering what Connor had done yesterday. I fastened the girth to one side and ran it under her belly, then tightened it up on the other.

"Is that right?"

"Yeah, it is." He sounded surprised, but his words still made me glow inside.

The bridle presented my next challenge. It just looked like a tangle of leather straps, and I couldn't even work out which way up it was supposed to go. In the end, Connor stepped up behind and helped. The heat from his body radiated against mine as he reached around me to sort out the jumble.

"First, you need to find the headpiece, and if you hold that and give it a shake, most of the time it sorts itself out."

He made it look so easy.

I held my breath as he lifted my hands and helped me to put the bridle on. By the time we did the last buckle up, I'd almost passed out from lack of oxygen.

Luckily, Connor didn't seem to notice as he turned away. "I'm going to get some lunging gear. We'll be doing something different today."

"Something different" turned out to be him standing in the middle and making Folly walk around him in a big circle at the end of a long rope. A lunge line, he called it.

"I'm controlling her, so you only need to worry about your position," he called. "Head up, heels down."

He was wrong. I also needed to worry about tumbling off and Folly walking over the top of me. It took ages before I began to relax. I was almost ready to contemplate letting go of her mane when Connor clicked his tongue and she walked faster.

"Stop!"

"She's fine. Are you ready to try trotting now?"

"Uh, no?" I wasn't sure I'd ever be ready.

"Just have a go."

He clicked again, and she broke into a trot. I clung on to the front of the saddle for dear life as she ran along, praying for it to be over soon.

Why was he smiling? I looked like a total idiot, didn't I?

"Now, the aim is to do rising trot. That means you sit for one beat and stand up for the next, in time to Folly's steps."

I tried it and nearly catapulted off the side. "It doesn't work."

"Sure it does, but it'll take you a few tries to get it."

That might be so for a normal person, but this was me we were talking about. I'd done no better by the time Connor slowed Folly to a walk at the end of the lesson.

"I think I'm a lost cause."

He gave my shoulder a squeeze, making me jump. "You need to practise, that's all."

"Are we doing it again this afternoon?"

"No, I thought we'd go for a hack instead."

"A hack?" Computer hack? Newspaper hack? Life hack? Uma Thurman Kill Bill-style hack?

"It's where we ride out into the countryside. Be one with nature and all that shit."

Oh.

That sounded like a disaster waiting to happen. What if Folly ran off? I had visions of me landing in the mud, or maybe getting impaled by a tree branch if I was really lucky.

"I'm not sure..."

"I am," Connor said, and that was that.

I picked at lunch, too busy worrying about falling off in front of Connor to eat. Luckily, the only person who attempted to speak to me was Lenny, and that was only to complain his team lost at football the night before.

"It's a bloody shambles," he said. "There's nothing worse than watching the other team score a goal in injury time."

Well, clearly he'd never lived my life.

I felt quite pleased when I managed to put Folly's saddle and bridle on by myself that afternoon. At least, I did until Connor pointed out all the bits I'd got wrong and redid it properly.

A few minutes later, I discovered something important—if Connor looked hot off a horse, on one he was incendiary. He sat astride a huge black beast with an easy grace, controlling it effortlessly with one hand.

"This is Captain," he told me. "He's my favourite ride around here."

I almost said, "Even better than Annabel?" but I bit my tongue and followed him up the driveway instead. How ridiculous to be jealous of a horse.

Captain danced around a bit, but Folly plodded along behind. I had to admit the view was very nice, and the English countryside wasn't bad either. After ten minutes, we turned off the lane onto a shady bridleway, and in time that opened up into a grassy meadow. Connor paused to let me walk up alongside him then nudged Captain to go faster.

"Are you ready to trot?"

"Not really." I bit my lip. Obviously I'd have to try it again sooner or later, but I preferred it to be later.

A quick glance at Connor showed his mouth set in a hard line. I don't think he liked my answer.

"You need to keep your hands lower," he said a few seconds later. "A couple of inches above her neck, not under your chin."

I tried that, resisting the urge to hang on to her

mane again.

"Keep your heels down. If you don't, your foot could slip through the stirrup, and if you come off, you'll be dragged along."

What a horrible thought. I immediately shoved them as low as they'd go.

"Head up. You go where you look, and you want to go forwards, not into the ground."

I fixed my eyes forward. At least he hadn't caught me looking at him.

"Sit up straight. Don't slouch... Tuck your elbows in... Your hands have come up again, put them down."

The list went on and on, and I felt like an incompetent toddler as he found fault with everything. Connor may have had good looks, but he also had a bad attitude. I was liking him less and less, which I guess was a good thing.

"I'm trying," I said, hoping I didn't sound too whiny.

"Yeah, very trying," he muttered under his breath.

Now he was simply being rude, and something inside me snapped.

"Look, until yesterday, I'd sat on a pony precisely once, and I didn't get off, I fell off. I can't help being the least co-ordinated person I know, and it would be helpful if you cut me a little slack rather than berating me for everything I say and everything I do."

As soon as I finished speaking, I wished I'd kept my mouth shut. The only excuse I had was perhaps a teeny bit of pre-menstrual tension.

Connor didn't say a word, just looked away. An uncomfortable silence spread between us, heavy on my shoulders, my hands, my heart. I almost preferred his niggling to the suffocating blanket of nothing.

I was tempted to apologise, to cross the void, but the trouble was I'd meant every word. The little bit of pride I still had left wouldn't let me say something I didn't believe.

Then Connor surprised me.

"I'm sorry," he said, so quietly I almost didn't hear him.

"Pardon?"

"I'm sorry. I'm not having a great day, and I took it out on you."

Well, that was a turn up for the books. It obviously hadn't been easy for him to say those words, but still, he'd forced them out. "It's okay. We all have days like those."

"I seem to be having more than most at the moment." He didn't elaborate, just gave a heavy sigh, which was followed by a pause that stretched for a hundred yards of Folly's gentle amble. "Why did you come to Linden Hollow? Usually when people sign up for an intensive two-week course, they're keen on horses. You act scared of them."

"That obvious, huh?"

"When Folly scratched her nose on her leg earlier, you jumped back three feet."

I had to give him that one. "It wasn't my idea to learn to ride. I got challenged to do it. Somehow, I have to ride in a dressage competition, but I don't see how I'll ever manage it."

"Everybody started somewhere."

"How did you start?"

Another silence, as if he was deciding how much to tell me. Finally, he shrugged. "My grandpop was a John

Wayne fan, and every Sunday afternoon, we'd sit down and watch one of his movies together. I grew up wanting to be a cowboy, and after I'd spent years begging for my own quarter horse, he gave in and got a friend of his to let me help out on his ranch in return for lessons."

"A cowboy, huh? Do you know how to rope steers and all that?"

"I'm not bad with a lasso, but Mom banned me from riding in any rodeos. She said she wasn't going to spend her weekends in the emergency room."

"Have you ever been hurt?"

"I broke my leg when I came off barrel racing and the horse fell on top of me. And once I managed to put a pitchfork through my foot."

"Ouch."

"My words were a little more colourful than that."

"I'm sure they were." Why was I so hopeless at having conversations like these? I never knew what to say, and they always fizzled away to nothing. I think that was why I stuck with Terry for so long. He was the silent type.

Connor spoke again, though. "So what, was it like a bet?"

"Was what like a bet?"

"The reason you're here."

"Oh. Yeah." Why did I always turn into a fool in front of him? "Not a bet, exactly. More a series of impossible tasks that I'm supposed to complete within a year." I found myself telling him about Edith and the bucket list.

"She sounds like a hoot."

"Yes, she was."

"So how many things have you ticked off?"

"One. Well, two, if you count the makeover catastrophe."

"What catastrophe? You look good to me, babe."

What? I couldn't believe he just said that. I quickly turned my face away so he wouldn't see the blush creeping across my cheeks.

"The hairdresser accidentally dyed my hair blonde. It's a bit, well...it's not really me."

"Why not?"

"Platinum blondes tend to be outgoing and confident. I'm neither. I want to go back to what suits me."

"Or you could look at it a different way. Why don't you try changing yourself to fit the hair for a few weeks? You might find you like it."

"I can't do that!"

"You need to stop being so negative."

"I can't."

"You just did it again. Try."

"I ca..." I tailed off under the intensity of his gaze.

"Better. Now, what was that other thing you were talking about? Is your ex really living in your shed?"

"It's more of a summerhouse."

"Babe, I don't care about the difference between a shed and a summerhouse. The dude's living in it?"

"I think so. He was sleeping in the porch when I left, but Mike told me he was in the summerhouse now."

"Who's Mike? Your boyfriend?"

"No, he's my, uh, stalker's probably the best word for it."

"Dare I ask?"

Oh, what the hell? Connor already knew enough about me to realise I was a total idiot, so one more tragic tale wouldn't make much difference.

"Babe, you're a walking disaster," he said when I'd finished.

He thought I didn't realise that? And what was with all the "babes?"

"I didn't even tell you about the car crash."

He closed his eyes and groaned. "I'm not sure I want to know."

"That's okay. I'm trying to erase it from my own mind."

"Actually, tell me. I could do with a laugh."

That was all I was good for, wasn't it? Still, I recounted the tale of my first, and so far only, driving lesson. He was snickering by the time I'd finished.

"Remind me never to get in a car with you driving."

Not much danger of that. "I don't want to get in a car with me driving again either."

He laughed louder.

"It's not funny. This is my life."

"Yeah, and it's fucking hilarious. You couldn't make it up. You should have your own reality show."

I shuddered. "No thanks. I can't think of anything worse than being under the spotlight, having every cock-up I make splashed across the tabloids."

When I looked across at him, the humour had gone out of his eyes. He sounded almost weary when he spoke. "Yeah, on second thought, you're right. It's not all it's cracked up to be."

We'd been so busy talking I'd barely noticed how quickly time had gone by, but when we passed a shiny red post box, I realised we'd done a big circle and reached the end of the driveway again.

"We're back!" And I'd survived.

"You didn't do badly once you relaxed," Connor said.

As soon as he said that, I tensed up again. He was right. As soon as I thought about what I was doing, everything went to pot.

"It's gone wrong again."

He pushed Captain closer and leaned down to me. "I'll just have to teach you to relax, then."

By the time his words penetrated, he'd opened up the distance between us. What did he mean by that? Was he into yoga or something? I thought of him doing a downward facing dog wearing only a pair of shorts and let out a little sigh.

Oh gosh, had he heard that?

Thankfully not, as when I looked across, his attention was firmly fixed on Annabel, who was striding across the yard towards us.

"Ooh, Connor, we've been waiting for you to get back. A friend of Felicity's lives near here, and he's having a house party tonight. Do you want to come with us?"

I melted away. I didn't want to be the third wheel in that conversation. There was no chance Annabel would invite me along as well, and I didn't want to suffer the embarrassment of being left out in front of Connor. Instead, I managed to untack Folly by myself and do her bed for the night, then I went back to the barn. June had the evening off, so I took one of the sandwiches she'd left in the fridge and spent the evening in the arms of a fictional boyfriend. At least they were within my reach.

CHAPTER 12

THE HORSES GOT Monday off, but no such luck for the humans. Well, most of the humans. By the time I'd eaten breakfast and gone outside to clean Folly's stable, there was still no sign of the Uglies.

Jenny wasn't amused. "The whole point of staying here is that you learn about the commitment of owning a horse, not just how to ride it. Where are they?"

"I think they mentioned a party last night." Judging by the slamming doors and laughing, they'd got back at two in the morning.

"Party or no party, the horses still need to be done."

Jenny marched off to the barn while I cleaned out Folly's automatic water drinker. She nuzzled me gently from behind, making me jump then giggle. It was funny how a couple of days ago I'd been terrified of her.

"I haven't got any treats, girl, but I'll see if I can pinch you a carrot later, how about that?"

A bleary-eyed Connor shuffled past outside, scratching his head.

"Good morning," I said.

"Not sure about the good part, but yeah, morning."

Annabel and Felicity turned up on the yard almost an hour later, looking furious at having to be there at all.

"This is ridiculous," I overheard Annabel say. "She

said we have to learn about horse ownership, but I already have a horse and a groom to look after it. Why should I have to get up and do manual labour?"

Maybe so you know what it's like to live in the real world?

With no riding on the agenda, I had most of the day to myself. The big, squashy sofa next to the window called my name, but while I was in my room picking out a book to read, the Uglies commandeered the entire lounge to do their own spa day. Soon enough, the place smelled more pungent than a Lush store, and then they added nail varnish to the mix.

Sod it. I slunk back to my room where a text from Mike proved the most exciting thing to happen all day.

Mike: Ella, your brother and I are both worried. Where are you?

He was worried? How touching.

I ignored him.

By Tuesday I'd caught cabin fever, and my jaw hurt from clenching it so much as I listened to the Uglies' screeching. It was almost a relief to get on Folly again.

"We're going to work on rising trot today," Connor said.

"Is that where the horse runs?"

He nodded and laughed. Well, I was glad someone found it funny. He'd put me on the lunge again and paused for a second to fasten a strap around Folly's neck.

"We call it an 'oh shit' strap. If you start to lose your

balance, grab it. Now, when she speeds up, stand up and then sit down in time to her strides."

Having something to hold on to gave me the safety net I needed, and by the end of the lesson, I'd managed a few steps of proper, honest-to-goodness rising trot, and I felt really pleased with myself. I imagine Folly was relieved as well, because having me bopping around on her back all day couldn't be comfortable.

"You look happier today," Connor said as we walked back to the stables.

"Probably because I didn't keep feeling like I was going to tumble off the side."

"You're doing better than you think you are."

"I'm not sure..."

He gave me a sharp look. "Enough. Stop being negative."

"Yes, master."

He chuckled. "That's better. What do you want to do this afternoon? We can ride out again or you can carry on from the lesson you just had."

I was torn. I'd enjoyed the ride out in the countryside. No—I closed my eyes briefly—I'd enjoyed talking to Connor. Not the beginning bit, obviously, but after I snapped at him, he'd thawed out a bit. Under his cocky charm and his rudeness, there was a nice guy lurking, and I'd met him on Sunday.

My heart did a little flip at the thought of getting to know Connor better, and I chided myself. What was the point? After the end of next week, I'd never see him again. I'd come here to ride, to complete my challenge and move onto the next disaster.

"Could I have another lesson?"

He shrugged. "Whatever you want."

I really did manage to tack Folly up by myself for the second session. Connor checked everything and pronounced me good to go.

"You're learning. Two days ago you didn't know where to start."

I was, wasn't I? I couldn't help smiling, and when one side of Connor's lips quirked upwards, a little giddiness crept in.

"You want to try steering by yourself this afternoon?"

"Do you think I'm ready?"

"I wouldn't have suggested it otherwise."

Connor set up a line of cones down the middle of the arena and taught me how to weave in and out of them by squeezing one rein, then the other.

"There's no need to pull hard," he said. "Her mouth's very sensitive. Think how it would feel if someone yanked on a piece of metal sitting on your gums. The key is to be gentle."

I heeded his advice, and half an hour later, I steered around the cones like an old pro even if my circles turned out a little lopsided.

"That's good. Now try it in trot."

Two things at once? That was asking a bit much, but I daren't chicken out. Not with Mr. Hotness tapping his foot in the middle of the arena, waiting for me to speed up.

Oh well, here goes nothing. I pushed Folly into a trot, resisting the urge to reach for the neck strap. I had to do two laps before I felt confident enough to try for the cones, but when I did, I managed to get from one end to the other and couldn't help letting out a small cheer when I reached the far fence.

"We'll stop there," Connor said. "Always end on a good note."

"I did it! I actually did it!"

"It's like riding a bike. Once you get the hang of rising trot, you won't forget. Are you okay to put Folly away on your own?"

"I think so." What did he plan to do? I was curious, but I didn't want to pry.

As it turned out, I didn't have to. Jenny was grooming Captain when I got up to the yard, and I stopped to say hello to both of them.

"Are you going to ride him?" I asked.

"Connor is. Captain had a fall a few months back and lost his confidence jumping. Connor's been helping him get it back again."

"Can I watch?"

"Sure. You might get put to work helping with the fences, though," she warned.

I didn't mind that. It was better than being on my own inside.

When I got back to the arena, Connor was already on Captain, cantering round. He'd set up a pair of brightly coloured jumps halfway down the arena, three feet or so high. It wasn't long before he thundered towards one of them.

My heart went into my mouth as Captain jinked and dived to the side. Connor hung on and circled, then tried the same again. This time, Captain lurched over, an awkward cat jump where he took off with all four legs at the same time.

"You wouldn't think it, but that's a marked improvement on three weeks ago. Then, he spent almost an hour getting him to go over a fence at all."

The same thing happened at the other jump, and Connor patiently cajoled Captain into going over it, patting him when he made it. By the end of the session, Captain was jumping more stylishly, and we'd even put the fences up a couple of notches.

"That was amazing," I said as we walked back to put Captain away. "I don't know how you stuck on for some of that."

He laughed. "If you can stick on a rodeo pony, you can stick on anything."

"I thought your mum wouldn't let you do that?"

"She didn't, but I still did it."

Why was I not surprised?

When we got back to the yard, I helped Connor with Captain's tack. It seemed the least I could do after all his patience with me earlier and earned me another hint of a smile. They were better than currency, and they bought a warm feeling that spread out through my insides like the burn of a good whisky.

But would I end up with a hangover?

That night, I went to bed with a smile on my face for the first time in weeks. Connor's sweetness, June's treacle tart, and the look on Annabel's face when she found out June used real butter in the mashed potatoes all made for a great day. The question was, how long would the happiness last?

The answer? Until the next morning.

"Folly's tail's all tangled," I said to Jenny.

"There's spray conditioner in the storage room next

to the toilet."

After checking the corners of the ceiling carefully for spiders, I stepped inside to look for it. The shelves were filled with boxes and baskets of lotions and potions. What was kaolin paste for? And green oils? I started rummaging, but I couldn't find any hair products. At this rate, it would be quicker to order a taxi, have it take me to the nearest supermarket, buy some L'Oréal because Folly was worth it, and drive back. I was contemplating the feasibility of that when the grating tones of the Uglies pierced the wall.

I recognised the first voice as Felicity's, lower pitched but whinier than Annabel's. "Did you see him in the kitchen this morning? He had his shirt off, and he's got an eight-pack."

"I was doing my hair, but don't worry, I intend on seeing it tonight."

Were they talking about Connor? Topless in the kitchen? How had I missed that? The only other man around was Lenny, and he was more of a one-pack guy. It had to be Connor. I stopped my search and held my breath while they chattered on. Yes, I knew it was rude to eavesdrop, but I couldn't help myself.

"Ooh, I wish I could get a guy like him. My mother's always on at me to find myself a suitable man."

Annabel cackled with laughter. "Good grief, Felicity, I'm not planning to take him to meet my mother."

"You're not?" Felicity's voice belied her confusion.

Before Annabel got a chance to reply, I felt a tickle on my wrist. A quick glance revealed an eight-legged freak the size of a teacup taking a scenic tour of my hand. I opened my mouth to scream then swallowed it down when Annabel spoke again.

"You've got a lot to learn, haven't you?"

Oh heck, I couldn't run out there—they'd know I'd been listening in. I stood, statue-like, as I tried to stop myself from hyperventilating.

Annabel sighed and continued to impart her wisdom. "Look, Felicity, there are two types of men in this world—the ones you take for a wild ride between the sheets, and the ones you introduce to your family. Mother would have a fit if I announced I was dating a stable boy."

"But what if you loved him?"

"I'm not going to fall for someone without a platinum credit card. The Connors of this planet are like paper handkerchiefs—first you use them, then you throw them away. The sooner you learn that, the sooner you'll move up in the world."

What a bitch! Connor might be an arse at times, but he didn't deserve to be treated like dirt, especially by a hoity-toity cow like Annabel.

The spider interrupted my thoughts by climbing further up my arm. When it got halfway to my elbow, I swear it paused to laugh at me.

"Don't you believe in true love, then?" It sounded like Felicity might be a bit of a romantic under her stuffy exterior.

Not so much for Annabel. "Love is something made up by greetings card manufacturers to sell more crap. The secret to a good marriage is a few shared interests and a luxurious lifestyle, that's what Mother taught me."

"Not the sex, then?" Felicity dropped her voice to a whisper and I almost missed it.

There was another trill of laughter from the Wicked Witch of West London. "That's what pool boys and tennis coaches and masseurs are for. And stable boys, of course."

Their footsteps receded, as did their voices, and the second I heard the door click shut behind them I flung my new friend off my arm. I didn't check to see where he landed, but I hoped he got a headache. Instead, I shot out of the closet like I had the fires of hell behind me, and I didn't stop until I hit daylight.

All day, I agonised over whether I should say something to Connor. Did he realise Annabel was using him? That she'd toss him aside without a thought once he'd satisfied her needs? So what if he was "only" a stable boy. He deserved the same respect as anybody else.

But then again, would he care about Annabel's lack of ethics? Wasn't he the type of guy who'd get off on hooking a rich bitch for a few nights of fun every couple of weeks? Surely it was one of the perks of his job? A quick roll in the hay, no strings, no commitments.

At the beginning of the week, I'd have said he was exactly that man, but after another afternoon with him, this one spent talking about the horses he'd ridden as a child and my nightmare working for Barry, I wasn't so sure.

Twice I nearly told him what I'd heard, but both times I held back. I didn't want him to get hurt, but surely he was old enough to make his own choices?

By saying something, I risked making myself sound like a petty, jealous shrew, and I didn't want that. After all, I wasn't jealous, was I? Was I?

I kept telling myself that all evening. That I didn't

have any interest in a man like Connor. That I wanted steady, and I wanted dependable, not a hot-blooded heartbreaker.

I managed to keep the pretence up until the nine o'clock news came on, when Annabel's door opened. Curled up on the sofa with a novel, I got the perfect view of her flimsy silk robe, and her hair and make-up were perfect despite the fact it was bedtime. Or, I quickly realised, because it was bedtime. She paid me no heed as she swept over to Connor's room, on its own in the far corner. She'd forgone slippers in favour of stilettos, and they clicked on the wooden floor as my heart raced ahead of them.

A swift knock, a few whispered words, and she slipped inside. As she disappeared, so did my attempts to convince myself I didn't care what Connor did or who he did it with.

Seeing her with him—it hurt.

CHAPTER 13

I'D GONE STRAIGHT to bed after Annabel got together with Connor the night before. The flimsy doors did little to block out noise, and I had no desire to hear a blow by blow account of them doing the deed.

I put the pillow over my head just in case her moans travelled through two layers of wood, but even then I tossed and turned. In my dreams, I was sitting on Captain, my arms wrapped tightly around Connor's waist as we galloped across lush green pastures and soared over hedges. With Connor, it felt like I could jump the moon.

Then I woke to a cold dose of reality. Another woman was no doubt draped over him at this very moment, and I couldn't even trot properly.

"Hurry up," I muttered at the toaster, gripping the butter knife so tightly it left a dent in my palm. I wanted to get out of the kitchen before anybody else turned up, and by spreading jam like a woman possessed and chewing quickly I managed it.

Folly nuzzled me as I combed through her tail. I still hadn't found the conditioner, but there was no way I'd venture back into the spider's layer.

"Blimey, you're keen," said Jenny when she saw me tying Folly outside under the overhanging roof. It was trying to rain, and I didn't want her to get wet.

"I've decided horses aren't as scary as I thought."

"That's good to hear," she said with a laugh. "Do you fancy giving a hand with a few other things once you've done her?"

"Why not?" Anything to distract my mind, which had spent far too long imagining Connor's abs. Was an eight-pack even possible? I had no idea. And as the only time I'd seen a six-pack in real life was when I picked up Terry's beer at the off-licence, I doubted I'd find out any time soon.

Jenny was showing me how to measure out feed into bowls when my phone rang. Oh, hell. Mike? Terry?

No, Grant. Thank goodness.

"I went round to check on your house. Did you know the dude from your porch is living in your shed?"

I sighed. "I hoped he'd be gone by now."

"He's installed a satellite dish. I don't think he's planning on leaving in the near future."

"Is it still possible to run away and join the circus, do you know?"

"That bad, huh? Do you want us to get rid of him?"

It was a tempting offer, but I still wasn't sure whether Mike had got the message. At least with Terry in the shed, I was unlikely to come home and find Mike had installed himself in my bedroom.

"I'll sort it out when I get back. Terry's annoying, but he's harmless."

"If you change your mind, just say the word. How are the horses?"

I told him about life at Linden Hollow so far, carefully leaving out any mention of Connor. If I mentioned a hot guy, Grant would tell Todd, and Todd would insist on driving up here to rate him out of ten and give me tips on what underwear I should be wearing. Or not wearing, if his imagination had anything to do with it.

"I had to teach a girl like that to drive once," he said, referring to Annabel. "If I wasn't gay already, her attitude would have been enough to turn me that way."

I smothered a bark of laughter. I'd gone outside to take the call, but Jenny looked up out of the gloomy feed room at the noise. "She's the most obnoxious person I've ever met. Well, apart from Mike. Maybe I should introduce them? They'd get on famously."

"One of them would end up getting eaten alive, that's for sure."

A vision of a praying mantis with Annabel's head snacking on my stalker popped into my mind. I hated to say it, but in that instance, I'd be rooting for her. "I can only hope."

Grant promised to pop round to Edith's again in a day or two to check Terry wasn't installing indoor plumbing in the summerhouse, then we bid each other goodbye.

I'd gone back to helping Jenny when Felicity poked her head around the door. "Where's Connor? I can't reach Berry's spare bridle. The hook's too high."

"Connor's not here today. Something urgent came up, and he had to go into town. If you ask Lenny, he'll find you something to stand on."

"Connor's off?" I asked once Felicity disappeared. "He didn't mention it yesterday."

"No, it was a last-minute thing. He should be back tomorrow. Don't worry, you'll still get your lessons—I'll teach you myself."

I couldn't help the pang of disappointment I felt. I

hadn't wanted to admit to myself how much I liked the afternoon session yesterday where we forgot who we were and simply talked. Not about anything of consequence, just easy chat. Connor lost some of his edge then. His attitude receded and his face relaxed. He became the real Connor, I was convinced of that, which made him hotter than ever.

Not only his looks, but his easy smile and the way he laughed from his belly. Whenever our horses closed the distance between each other, my heart beat faster and my skin prickled as his aura encroached on mine.

I was riding into trouble and I knew it, but I wasn't sure I could stop myself.

Or if I even wanted to.

But I couldn't tell Jenny that, of course. When she asked how I was getting on with my lessons, I went with vague. "Okay, I think. Connor's a good teacher."

"Him being able to come at such short notice got me out of a bind, that's for sure."

"What do you mean? I thought he'd been here for ages?"

"I've known him a few years, but he's only here temporarily. My regular trainer ended up in a cast for six weeks, and it wasn't even due to a horse. She spent her life doing riding stunts then broke her leg when she came off her bicycle."

"That's terrible," I murmured. My words should have been aimed at the poor lady who got injured, but instead all I could think about was Connor leaving. "When's she due back?"

"Not for three weeks yet, and she'll need to ease in gently. Connor's been a lifesaver to step in."

"What will he do after that?"

She shrugged. "Probably go home. Or maybe travel a bit. He's been talking about a trip to Europe."

I realised how little I knew about him. Where was home? Somewhere in America, obviously, from his accent, but America was a big place. We'd spent hours talking, and I'd told him about Edith, my list of challenges, Mike, and even how Terry cheated on me, yet I didn't know so much as his last name. I'd learned more from chatting to Jenny for five minutes than I had in five days with Connor.

"You ready for your first lesson?" asked Jenny, cutting into my thoughts.

"As I'll ever be."

I wasn't too bad at the trotting lark now. I could do circles with ease, and even loop back and forth across the arena in a serpentine.

"Connor said you need to ride a dressage test," Jenny said as I brought Folly to a halt at the end of the session.

"That's right. Do you reckon I'll ever be able to?"

"Of course. There's a low-key unaffiliated competition just down the road next week. Why don't you enter it?"

I froze. "That soon? I can't even canter."

"You'll be able to soon enough. Connor can get you started tomorrow morning."

The idea of going that fast brought me out in a cold sweat, even as I untacked Folly. What if she turned into some wild demon at the promise of a bit of speed? That thought stayed with me through the afternoon and evening, meaning I wasn't in the best of moods over dinner.

When Annabel and Felicity shared an animated

discussion about what they were going to watch on television that night, all I could hear was fingernails on a blackboard. I accidentally huffed, and Annabel locked her gaze on me.

"So, how have your pony rides been going?" she asked, her tone condescending.

"Fine," I snapped. "At least I've managed to stick to riding of the horse variety."

I honestly don't know why I said that. Even as the words left my mouth, I clapped a hand over it, horrified with myself.

Annabel's face turned an alarming shade of beetroot, which clashed terribly with her green eyeshadow. "You little cow. You probably don't even know what it's like to get laid."

I deserved that. I opened my mouth to apologise, but before I could do so, she stormed off with Felicity at her heels like a faithful spaniel.

As her bedroom door slammed, Jenny burst out laughing. "I've been dying to say that for days. You've got balls, lady."

I buried my head in my hands. "I don't know what came over me. It just popped out."

"It was only what we've all been thinking. She's been trying to get her claws into Connor from day one."

"She doesn't have claws; she's got talons."

We both hooted with laughter again, and I glanced over to Annabel's door, worried in case she heard us. It remained firmly closed.

But it wouldn't stay that way forever. I sobered up at the thought of spending an uncomfortable evening with the Uglies, watching *Project Runway*. I didn't even like the damn program. I'd suggested watching

Dancing with the Stars the other day, but Annabel rudely informed me she didn't go in for all that celebrity rubbish. Neither did I, but I liked the dancing. "Isn't *Project Runway* a reality show?" I'd asked. She rudely informed me it was "art."

Nope, I didn't want to spend a second longer than I had to with either of them.

"I'd better go back to my room before they come out again," I said. "I know I'll have to deal with it in the morning, but I have a saying—Never do today what you can do tomorrow."

"Oh, you shouldn't have to lock yourself away. Why don't you come back to the house with me? We were planning to watch a movie."

"We?"

"Me and Connor."

Connor was there? "I thought he'd had to go away suddenly?"

She shifted uncomfortably. "Not exactly. There was a bit of an incident last night. You hit a sore spot just then with your comment about only riding horses."

"What do you mean?"

Jenny glanced over at Annabel's door then lowered her voice. "Annabel went to Connor's room last night and told him a story about wanting advice on lateral work. Except when he turned round from closing the door, she'd dropped her robe and was standing there starkers."

I thought he'd have leapt at that opportunity, but Jenny's tone implied otherwise. "What happened?"

"He told her she'd got the wrong idea, and she said she hadn't then tried to kiss him. He ended up manhandling her out, and apparently she was none too happy about it. I figured it was best to give everyone some space by having him take the day off."

Wow! She'd handed it to him on a plate, and he'd knocked her back? That had to sting. And then I'd said what I said and poured salt into her wound.

"So what about tomorrow? Do you think I should keep a low profile as well?"

"Girls like Annabel turn up with plenty of money, no manners, and a disgusting sense of entitlement. I've seen it before. She won't forgive and forget like a normal person. I hate to say it, but avoidance is probably the way to go unless you want to feel her anger."

I gulped. "I'll keep out of the way."

"You're coming to watch a movie, then?"

The alternative was another night in my room. It may have been comfortable enough, but the walls were closing in on me. And though I didn't want to admit it, even to myself, I wanted to see Connor. I couldn't deny that hearing he'd knocked back Annabel lit a little spark of happiness deep inside me.

"Why not?"

At her house, Jenny held the door open for me, and I found myself in a hallway which could best be described as lived-in. A show home it wasn't, but there was something comforting about seeing the coats slung over the bannister and the row of shoes next to the front door.

But that wasn't the part that made my breath hitch. In the living room, Connor lounged barefoot on the sofa in a worn t-shirt and faded jeans, idly flipping through TV channels like he owned the place. Dark hair flopped over his forehead, and he pushed it back as he met my gaze.

Oh, yes. I was in trouble.

CHAPTER 14

CONNOR RAISED A dark eyebrow at Jenny, questioning.

"Another refugee from the gruesome twosome," she said.

A bubble of laughter escaped before I could tamp it down. "Gruesome twosome?"

"Connor's idea, but I thought it was appropriate."

"I've been calling them the Uglies. They're polished on the outside, but not so nice on the inside."

It was Connor's turn to chuckle. "Yeah, you got that right."

"Drink?" Jenny asked.

"I think I need one."

"What's your poison?"

"White wine, if you have any?"

I stood in the lounge, not sure what to do with myself. As well as the squashy leather sofa, there were two armchairs, but one of them had a saddle on it. If I took the other side of the sofa, Connor might suspect I liked him, but if I sat in the chair, would he think I didn't? What should I do?

I'd never been in this situation before. When I met Terry, I wasn't looking for a date—we'd simply got talking. Later, he'd claimed fate pushed us together.

Fate, or perhaps stupidity.

Jenny made my decision for me in the end when she handed Connor a can of cola and me a large glass of wine then flopped back into the vacant chair.

"It's been a long day," she said.

I gingerly perched on the sofa, careful not to spill my drink. Connor popped the top on his, took a slug, and resumed channel surfing.

"Any preferences?" he asked.

"No slushy romance," said Jenny. "And no zombies. They give me nightmares."

"Ella?"

"Uh, I don't mind." I didn't watch many movies, and I always picked rom-coms with happy endings, but I didn't want to cause a fuss.

We watched an action film. Well, Connor and Jenny watched an action film while I snuck glances at Connor out of the corner of my eye, thankful Jenny switched the light off before she sat down so she could see the screen better.

When the closing credits rolled, Connor yawned and stretched, his T-shirt rising up to give me a glimpse of the muscles that Felicity had so admired. I tried to count, but I'd only got to four when he lowered his arms again.

"What was that?" Connor asked.

"What was what?"

"It sounded like you sighed?"

"Oh, er, I'm just tired." Oops.

"Connor, will you walk Ella back to the barn?" Jenny said.

"I'll be okay on my own."

It was nice of her to offer his services, but if I spent any more time near him I'd end up having a hot flush.

What was wrong with me? He wasn't my type at all, but he still did funny things to my insides that I couldn't control.

"No, it's dark out, and you've had three glasses of wine," she said.

Connor heaved himself to his feet. "I'll do it." His tone left no room for argument.

"Alrighty then." Did I just say that? Way to go, Ella. How to make yourself sound like an idiot in two easy words. I could have accepted graciously, but instead I chose to imitate Ace Ventura.

Connor stuck his feet into a pair of boots in the hallway then opened the front door for me. I shivered as I stepped outside. The sky was clear, and the temperature had dropped a few degrees since I arrived.

A couple of seconds later, a jacket settled over my shoulders.

"You look cold," Connor said, shrugging. He hadn't even put a sweater on, and I could tell he was chilly by his pointy, er, I really shouldn't be looking there. My gaze dropped downwards. Not there, either. Ella! Behave!

I forced my eyes up to his face. "Thank you."

Silence stretched between us as we covered the short distance back to the barn. Thankfully it was dark and quiet when we arrived, with no sign of the Uglies. I guess they got bored after *Project Runway*.

Connor held the door open once more, and I brushed against him as I walked through, the flimsy contact stroking fire over my skin. A shiver ran through me again, and this time it wasn't from the cold.

"Keep the jacket," Connor said. "I'll pick it up tomorrow."

Keep it? I ended up sleeping in it, with Connor's sweet musk wrapped around me like a blanket.

It was the wine, I told myself when the alarm woke me up at seven the next morning. That was why I'd behaved like a lovesick schoolgirl the night before. There was simply no other explanation for it.

I went to roll out of bed, but my head had other ideas. The instant I moved a fireworks display started, lights flashing behind my eyes while a headache pounded along in time.

The groan that left my lips didn't even sound human. How big had those glasses of wine been? Maybe a few more minutes of sleep would help? Yes, that was the answer. I rolled over and closed my eyes.

A few minutes later the pounding started again. I shook my head, trying to clear it, but it carried on, and white-hot needles of pain spread through my temples.

"Ella, what are you doing in there?" came Connor's muffled voice. "It's nine thirty."

Wha-wha-what? I looked at my watch. Holy hell, I'd overslept by two and a half hours!

Energy I didn't know I had made me leap out of bed, and before I'd had time to think, I yanked the door open.

"I'm sorry, I overslept."

He of course looked as if he'd just stepped out of a photoshoot for an equestrian clothing catalogue. "I got that. Are you using my jacket as pyjamas?"

My blush started at my toes and rose up my body

faster than I could blink. I looked down, trying to make out that it was as much of a surprise to me as it was to him. "Uh, yes?"

His only answer was, "Babe," then he walked away, chuckling.

What did that mean?

I dragged myself into the shower and turned it on cold in an attempt to both wake myself up and cool my overheating libido. It worked on one of those counts.

Connor was sitting at the kitchen table when I made it out of my room, and he slid a cup of coffee over.

"My hero," I said, trying to sound perkier than I felt.

He glanced up at me. "You've got your sweater on inside out."

Was it possible to have one day, just one day, where I didn't make a fool of myself in front of this man?

At least riding went a bit better. I was getting reasonably proficient at walking and trotting now, at least if you didn't put me side by side with somebody who could actually ride.

I thought we were finished when Connor gave a grin I didn't like very much. "You ready for a canter?"

"Is 'no' an acceptable answer?"

He gave me a sharp look. Guess not.

"When you get to the next corner, go into sitting trot, press your inside leg on the girth and slide your outside leg back. You might want to hold onto the saddle with one hand."

Might? I gripped it so hard I was amazed it didn't crumble, and when I did as he said, there was a lurch as Folly leapt forward. My free arm flapped as I bounced around, and while Connor laughed I somehow pulled Folly to a stop.

"What's so funny?"

"You looked like you were doing the funky chicken."

I put my hands on my hips. "And you didn't the first time you tried cantering? I thought I was going to be catapulted right over the fence."

"You look cute when you get all indignant. Now have another go."

I didn't know whether to melt at him calling me cute or panic at the idea of having to do it all over again. What I needed was Velcro, to stick my ass to the saddle, my elbows to my sides, and my stupid thoughts at the back of my churning mind.

Without it, I concentrated hard on pinning my arms down as Folly popped into canter again, and managed to keep them reasonably still. The only problem was, my legs started jumping around like a demented marionette instead. Honestly, this was impossible.

"Try again," was all Connor said.

If he hadn't been there, I'd have given up, but he was so I didn't, and by the end of the afternoon I'd managed to do a lap of the arena without holding on.

"Did you see that?"

"Couldn't miss it, babe. You were squealing the whole way round."

"I was?" I hadn't even noticed. Were my ears faulty?

He chuckled to himself as he walked off. "Yeah, cute," I was sure I heard him say.

Dinner was a tedious affair. Jenny and I made small talk while Annabel and Felicity yacked away at the tops of their voices about their ambitions to ride in Horse of the Year Show. When we'd finished, I was ready to make a dash for my room when Jenny grabbed hold of my wrist.

"We're popping out for a quick drink, if you want to join us?"

The sensible option would have been to shake my head, mumble an excuse, and go back to my novel. A headache, tiredness, feeling a little bit queasy—anything, in fact. But when Jenny said "we" I assumed she meant Connor, and so the dumb part of me overruled.

Stupid, stupid me.

Chapter 15

I SWEPT A pile of straw off the seat and climbed into the back of Jenny's Land Rover while Connor took the front. Jenny drove, and that in itself was enough to make me regret coming. I hit my head twice as we bounced over the potholes.

"Where are we going?"

"The Port and Pickle," Jenny answered.

"The what?"

"The local pub. The landlord wanted something memorable."

"I'll say," I muttered as she slowed for the car park, and I looked up at the sign. From that angle, the pickle was doing something to the port no child should see.

"He also tends to do a lot of his own product testing."

That seemed quite likely. As we approached the front door, the beat of loud music floated out, and when we got closer, I heard a wailing over the top, akin to an animal in pain. The three of us exchanged glances. What on earth...?

Connor pushed the door open, and we were greeted by the sight of a woman on a raised stage that someone had knocked up out of plywood. Gaudy disco lights flashed red and blue, illuminating the crime against music being committed in front of us.

It wasn't the terrible singing that made our jaws drop, nor the fact that she must have been at least seventy. No, what was remarkable was her outfit. She'd gone for the Madonna look—straw-coloured wig, fishnet tights, and a leotard complete with conical bra over the top.

And she was working it.

We stepped through the doorway as if drawn in by an invisible tractor beam. The performance was so terrible I couldn't bear to watch, but at the same time I felt compelled to. The rest of the patrons appeared to feel the same way as they crowded in front of the stage, clapping along while she wailed "Like a Virgin."

Beside me, Connor rubbed his eyes and blinked a few times. "Is that really happening?"

"Either that, or we're stuck in the same nightmare," I told him.

"I need a drink."

Jenny looked at him sharply. "You said you'd drive back, which means you're on the soft drinks."

He murmured something that sounded suspiciously like "Heaven help me" as Jenny ordered us both large glasses of wine, with a Pepsi for Connor.

"What's with the, er...?" She jerked her thumb at the lady, who was still shaking her hip replacements in time to the beat.

The landlord grinned. "One of those business advisors came out from the bank, said I should try diversifying. Figured I'd try a karaoke night. Place is packed, so I reckon he knew what he was talking about."

There was a good reason people were reaching for the alcohol, I thought, as a toupee-wearing Elvis impersonator replaced Madonna. Nobody would get the full benefit of this sober.

We snagged a table at the side and laughed until we cried through a playlist that included Celine Dion, Bruce Springsteen, and Bon Jovi. After a young girl got up and did a version of Adele's "Someone Like You" that was actually quite good, the landlord announced a short break before the second "act."

My sides ached as I reached for my drink. We'd given up on ordering by the glass and got a bottle of white between us. "This is hideous," I said. "It's better than the outtakes for the *X Factor*."

"It's like watching a car crash," said Connor. "Are we coming back next week?"

"It's not on next week," Jenny said. "The landlord's taking the diversification thing very seriously. Next Friday's drag queen night."

Hmmm, maybe I could invite Grant and Todd to that? I had a feeling Todd would be the star of the show.

"That only gives you tonight then, Ella," Connor said.

"Sorry, what?"

"Wasn't one of your challenges to get up and sing on stage?"

I didn't like his sly grin, and my alcohol-addled brain whirred away and saw where he was going with this. "No way."

"Wait, what challenges?" Jenny asked.

Connor filled her in, and she clapped her hands in glee. "Oh, this is perfect. You have to get up there!"

"But I can't sing. I was planning to take some lessons before I even attempted it."

"Look around, babe. Nobody else here can sing, either. There's a stage, there's a microphone. What more do you need?"

Courage. I needed courage.

"You don't need courage. You just need wine," Jenny said, topping up my glass.

Did I say that out loud? Clearly the answer was yes.

"I'm not getting up on that stage by myself and singing. Everyone'll be staring at me."

Connor's evil smile came back. "Then I'll get up there with you. Jenny can take the photos."

"No, no, no, no, no."

I protested until the moment Connor picked me up and deposited me in front of the crowd, right in the centre. I tried to run away, but he had hold of my hand and he wasn't letting go. Someone thrust a microphone at me, and I blinked in the glare of the spotlight aimed into my eyes.

"What are we even singing?" I hissed, furious that he'd done this.

He grinned down at me. "No idea. I told them to surprise us."

If I hadn't had the microphone in one hand, and he hadn't been holding the other in a death grip, I'd have walloped him. As it was, the only thing thumping was my heart, which threatened to explode. Actually, it mightn't have been a bad thing if it did. In hospital, I could have escaped singing in front of a bloody audience.

There was the screech of microphone feedback then the speakers crackled with the opening bars of Pink's "Just Give Me a Reason."

There had to be a hundred expectant faces staring

up at me, and I realised that the only thing worse than me butchering a song I loved would be not to sing at all. At least I knew the words, that was a saving grace.

Cringing, I launched into a slightly slurred attempt at the first verse. So far, so mediocre. It was when the second verse started I got my next shock of the night.

Connor could sing. I mean, really sing.

Until that point, there had been background chatter and the clink of glasses, but the rest of the pub fell silent as everybody stopped to listen. Me included. I completely forgot to start my next bit until he nudged me and muttered, "Sing!"

I garbled my way through it, thinking only of hearing him again. He hit every note perfectly, his voice like molten chocolate, and standing there while he sang to me, I believed every word.

When the music died down, it was replaced by a couple of voices chanting.

"More! More! More!"

Others joined them, and soon the whole pub was shouting for Connor to sing again.

For the first time ever, he seemed a little embarrassed. "Perhaps we should sit down now."

No way was he getting away with that. He'd dragged me up there, so he could damn well stick around and do another song. "Don't you bloody dare. You're staying here if I have to tie you up."

He waggled his eyebrows at me. "You promise?"

"Oh, just sing, will you?"

Someone cued up the music, and I realised he was still holding on to me. I had no choice but to stand next to him like a spare part as he got the crowd to its feet with "Died in your arms tonight."

They cheered for him to sing again at the end, but he wasn't having any more of it. "Done now," he said as he led the way back to our table.

The landlord came over with more drinks. "Think you deserve this, lad. The ladies loved you," he said, placing a couple more glasses of wine and a pint of beer on the table. "On the house."

"I got that," Connor said, placing a scrunched up pair of knickers on the table. "Someone threw these at me."

"Eeew!" squealed Jenny. "Who knows where they've been."

He held them aloft. They had to be at least a size twenty. Smirking, he scanned the room and winked at a larger lady on the far side who was staring at him with her tongue hanging out. She started fanning herself.

"For crying out loud," Jenny said. "I can't take you anywhere."

"Did you get the photos?" I asked. That was all I cared about. If I had photos, I could prove to Albert I'd got up on stage and sung. Well, squawked. I'd been there, and that was what mattered.

"Loads of them. Facebook here we come."

"No! Please don't," I begged. I didn't want my moment of shame broadcast to anyone who might recognise me.

"But you were great," she protested.

Connor caught her eye and gave his head a little shake. "Jen, no."

She looked contrite. "Oh, yeah. I forgot."

I was about to ask what she'd forgotten when a gaggle of girls surrounded us, ignoring Jenny and me while they fawned over Connor.

"You're amazing, you should be on telly."

"Have you taken singing lessons?"

"Are you going to be here every week?"

"Our friend's having a party. Do you want to come with us?"

"I'm sure I've seen you somewhere before—are you in a band?"

"Can I get your autograph?"

Four girls became eight, and eight became sixteen. Someone jostled the table, and the pint of beer fell over and drenched me. I tried to blot it up with napkins while Connor disappeared under a sea of females, all chattering away excitedly. More were coming our way when Connor's hand appeared like a drowning man's reaching for a lifeline.

I grabbed it and pulled, then Jenny grabbed my waist and tugged as well. The crowd surged and Connor popped free, landing on top of us as we all fell onto the sticky floor. He got to his feet first and hauled us both up, and we ran, or in my case stumbled, for the door.

"Bloody hell," Jenny said once we were in her Land Rover with the doors firmly locked. "What happened?"

"Eighteen-year-olds and alcohol," I muttered. "They wanted Connor's blood." I turned to him. "You should have warned me you could sing like that." I thought back to something one of the girls said about recognising him. "Have you been in a band somewhere?"

"Not unless you count messing around in the garage with a few friends when I was twelve, no."

"So how did you learn to sing?"

He shrugged. "Just one of my many talents."

"Is modesty another of them?"

He turned and grinned as he started the engine. "That one passed me by."

CHAPTER **16**

YESTERDAY, I THOUGHT I had a headache. Now I knew the truth. That wasn't a headache; it was a mere ripple on a millpond compared to the tsunami raging between my ears this morning. Whose idea had it been to drink all that wine? If I remembered I'd be having a few choice words with them.

I had two priorities. Coffee and painkillers. And was that bacon I smelled? I lurched out of bed and stumbled towards the kitchen. Annabel was coming the other way, her face like thunder.

"Oh, look what the cat dragged in."

I'm sure I looked a fright, but there was no need for her to be so blunt about it. "Good morning to you, too."

"Had a good night last night, did you? Trying to punch above your weight's never a good idea."

"Sorry?" What was she talking about?

"With Connor. He may only be a stable lad, but even he would never stoop down to the gutter."

My face must have betrayed my confusion, because she just laughed at me, a drop of spit landing on my cheek.

"Bloody hell, you really are as stupid as you look. You can embarrass yourself by getting drunk with Connor, you can follow Connor around like a lovesick puppy, and he might even take pity on you and fuck you, but you'll never *have* Connor. You might as well stop living in your fantasy world and get over yourself."

I was left open-mouthed as she stomped off.

Was I being that obvious? I hadn't thought about it, hell, I hadn't thought about anything last night. My synapses stopped firing after my first pint of grape juice, but did my subconscious? Had it gone on a hormone-fuelled rampage? I sagged back against the wall, shaking. Did I like Connor? Yes, I had to admit that despite his faults, of which I could compile a double-sided list, I did. Something about him drew me in and fired me up, made me clench my thighs together to relieve the ache between them whenever he was near.

But Annabel was right, wasn't she? Connor was the sun and I was a moth. I'd burn up before I got anywhere near him.

Suddenly, I didn't want paracetamol any more, or coffee. I wanted to cry. I made it back to my room before the first tear fell then crawled back into bed and soaked my pillow.

Soft knocking disturbed me a few minutes later. "I'm..." sniff, "busy."

"Too busy for a bacon sandwich?" Connor's muffled voice came from the other side of the door.

Oh heck, I couldn't let him see me like this. My nose was running, and I hadn't combed my hair. I always looked as if I'd stuck a finger in the mains in the mornings, and with my hangover, the effect had to be worse than usual.

But I really, really liked bacon.

"Could you leave it outside?"

"Sure. I'll just set it down on the floor."

I waited until I heard his footsteps walking away, then shuffled over and opened the door.

"You bastard. You snuck back."

He held the plate just out of my reach, looking better than should be legal at that time of the day.

"I heard what she said," he said softly.

I couldn't meet his eyes. All I wanted to do was slam the door, but he blocked it with his foot. Sodding bacon sandwich. My appetite had fled, and I didn't even want it any more.

Connor took a step, forcing me backwards. And another, and another, until the back of my knees hit the bed and I fell onto it. There was a clatter as he dropped the plate onto the nightstand.

"Look at me."

I couldn't. They say eyes are the window to the soul, and I didn't want him to see mine.

"Look at me, Ella." He reached down and tilted my chin so I had no choice. He saw me in all my tear-streaked glory.

"Annabel's a bitch and she's a bully, and she believes the world should fall at her feet. When I didn't, she took it out on you. She talks shit, and you need to ignore her."

"I don't know why she's so upset. It's not like she wanted to take you home to meet the family." I paused. "Sorry, I shouldn't have said that, but it's true."

"She told you that?"

"I overheard her talking to Felicity."

His laughter wasn't what I expected. "Babe, no girl wants me to meet their mother. Well, one girl did, only her mother was divorced and as soon as her daughter went out the room, she grabbed my junk and told me I should pick vintage over Beaujoulais Nouveau."

I tried to laugh and ended up choking as my throat had gone dry. After my coughing fit subsided, I wiped my eyes. "She never said that?"

"Swear it's the truth."

"What did you do?"

He stared at the wall and let out a thin breath. "Tried the vintage."

My jaw dropped. "Are you serious?"

"As a coronary." His tortured sigh tugged at my heart. "Ella, I'm not one of the good guys. My life's a train wreck, and I've hurt more people than I can count." He ended on a whisper. "I don't want to hurt you."

My voice came out as a croak, which was fitting as I was the frog nobody would ever kiss. "There is good in you. I've seen it."

He took a deep breath and closed his eyes. "Eat your breakfast, Ella. I'll see you outside when you're ready."

Eating the bacon sandwich was like chewing leather wrapped in cotton wool. Nothing to do with Connor's cooking, more my state of mind. If it hadn't been him who made it, I'd have dropped it straight in the bin.

As it was, I abandoned it halfway favour of crawling into bed again, but the second I pulled the duvet over my head my phone beeped with a message.

Terry: Mike came round again. He thinks you're avoiding him. I'm supposed to be meeting him for a beer tonight—what should I say?

Great—I'd managed to block Mike and Terry from my mind for a couple of days, but now they lined up front and centre again. Why couldn't they both just leave me alone? I started a new list to go alongside Edith's for when I got back, and evicting Terry came at the top of it. Yes, Grant had offered to help, but he'd already dealt with enough of my mess.

Mike, well, I had no idea how to get rid of him, but I kept my fingers crossed something would come to me over the next seven days.

And while I was thinking about home, I needed to call Jaz. We usually went out every week, and I'd missed her. That and I wanted to check Stevie hadn't burnt the house down.

"Hang on a sec," she said as soon as she picked the phone up.

In the background I heard her chiding Stevie, then she came back. "He's worked out how to unstrap himself from his buggy. Every time I turn my back he's escaped again." I pictured her tearing at her hair. "Do you think they make straitjackets in an extra small?"

"Social Services might get upset about that." Although they hadn't cared when one of my foster brothers set fire to my hair, or when my foster mother locked me in my room and forgot me for two days.

"I know, you're right. Sometimes I just don't know what to do with him."

"I'm sure it won't last forever." Was being possessed something a child grew out of?

"I hope not. I'm getting to the end of my tether. Amir and I tried to go out for dinner yesterday, but Stevie bawled so loudly we got asked to leave before the main course came out."

"I'll babysit for a night when I get back." I'd regret it, like I did every other time, but Jaz was always there for me so I braved Stevie at least twice a month.

"You would? That's fantastic. I'll have something to look forward to."

And I'd have something to dread. Last time I'd spent an evening with Stevie, the little devil chewed one of my new ballet pumps. "Of course I will."

"So how are the horses?" Jaz asked, sounding a bit brighter.

"I've been riding a mare called Folly. She's a sweetheart." I filled Jaz in on everything except Connor then rang off with a promise to get together for a catch up as soon as I got back.

Okay, I'd successfully wasted half an hour. Connor had been waiting for ages, but I couldn't face him. What did one say after a revelation like his? He made out he was the devil, but I'd felt the flutter of his wings.

Instead of venturing outside, I picked up my phone again and fired off a message to Grant and Todd, just a quick text to let them know everything was fine. I even included a photo Connor had snapped of me on Folly yesterday, just to prove I really had been on a horse.

Then I did the same with Demi. She'd be asleep after working the late shift, but at least I wasn't ignoring her.

Foot tapping, I scrolled through the menus on my phone, but it was no good. I'd run out of friends and excuses.

Mouth furry and skin greasy, I stumbled through to the bathroom, then stifled a scream when I caught sight of myself in the mirror. Not only did I look like I'd been standing in a wind tunnel, my face reminded me of a coal miner after a twelve-hour shift. Whoever said that brand of mascara was waterproof should have been done for false advertising.

And what was more, Connor saw me like that.

I shook my head, tangled blonde rat-tails flapping around my face. What did it matter? I wasn't a fine wine, anyway. I was more... Ribena.

When I swallowed the last of my pride and ventured outside, Connor was cinching up Folly's girth. I tried to smile at him, but I don't think I pulled it off.

"Are you ready to ride?" His voice held a tightness that hadn't been there yesterday.

"I guess."

I got on by myself using the mounting block then Connor drilled me through more exercises. Turn this way, go that way, speed up, slow down. It might have been repetitive, but each time I did it, it got a little bit easier.

Apart from cantering, that was. I still bounced like a sack of potatoes every time I tried it.

"How do you get your bum to stay in the saddle?" I asked Connor.

"Practice, that's all. We'll go out for a hack later, and you can try a longer canter in a straight line. That way you won't have to think about anything but your position."

And not falling off, of course.

"How's it going?" Jenny asked over lunch. We'd staggered ours so the Uglies ate first and we didn't have to talk to them.

"Good, apart from cantering. That's a disaster."

"You know the secret, don't you?"

I shook my head. "What secret?" If there was one, I'd have sold a kidney to find it out.

"A damn good shag the night before. Really opens your hips up."

I spluttered apple juice onto my plate. Luckily Connor had stepped outside to make a phone call so he didn't hear that little suggestion. "You're kidding?"

"Not at all. I've always scored higher marks in dressage if we've gone for at least two rounds the night before."

I glanced out of the window, where Connor was still pacing up and down with his mobile clasped to his ear. "Even if it did work, there's a small flaw in that plan."

She followed my gaze and smiled ruefully. "I wouldn't suggest trying anything with Connor. He's...well, he's complicated. But there are plenty of nice guys in the village. How do you fancy a girls' night out?"

I got her point about Connor, but was the alternative any better? "Last time I did that, I acquired Mike."

"I know most of these guys. I'll steer you clear of any weirdos."

"You promise?"

"Cross my heart."

CHAPTER 17

IT WAS ALMOST midnight when Jenny and I stumbled through the door, holding each other up. Connor stood in the kitchen, watching us, and his smile gave way to concern when Jenny walked into the doorframe.

She made it through on the third attempt, hobbled over, and patted him on the cheek. "See, we made it back. I told you we would. We can look after ourselves."

He caught her as she tripped over her own feet and lowered her onto one of the wooden chairs that sat around the old oak table. Head lolling, she kicked off her shoes.

"Bloody heels. Whoever invented those should be shot," she slurred.

I collapsed onto the seat next to her. "You said no weirdos, Jenny. You lied."

"Trevor's not so bad."

"He collects tractors."

"This is the country. Most men around here love their farm machinery."

"His bed's shaped like a tractor, and he uses a tractor wheel as a coffee table." He'd told me all about it, with every painful detail. "He recycled a plough and made it into a coat stand. Oh, and the best bit, he wants to go to his wedding on a tractor. He asked if I was okay with that?"

Jenny let out an unladylike snort and Connor covered his mouth.

"Okay, I'll give you that one. He was a bit odd," she said, then dropped her head onto the table and closed her eyes. Seconds later, a gentle snore came from her lips.

I looked up at Connor. "Probably I should go to bed."

"Probably you're right."

I went to get up, only it didn't work out so well, and I ended up sprawled at his feet. Jenny was definitely right about the stilettos. I never should have borrowed them.

"You okay, babe?" Connor pulled me to my feet. Wow, look at those muscles!

"Yeah, I'm good." I clutched onto the counter for support.

He shook his head at me, and before I knew it, I was cradled in his arms as he strode out the door.

I clung around his neck, inhaling his musky scent. He was all man. And he was carrying me! It was like that scene in *The Bodyguard* where Kevin Costner carried Whitney Houston. I might have sighed.

Connor walked across the car park, the silver moonlight tracing the angles of his face. His warmth flooded into me, and the contours of his abs rippled against my side. As he walked, the gentle rocking motion made me feel...queasy.

A lump rose in my throat as I struggled to get down, and I just made it to the nearest bush before losing most of a bottle of wine and several neon-coloured cocktails. Probably the surrounding plants would die from that little lot. I certainly felt like I was about to.

Movement behind brought me back to reality. Oh heck, Connor hadn't run at the first heave and not only that, he was holding my hair back. Death couldn't come soon enough. I looked around for a high bridge or passing freight train, but of course there wasn't one.

"You okay, babe?" he whispered, his lips grazing my ear.

"No." No point in lying. I'd just thrown up in front of the hottest guy I'd ever met, or indeed was ever likely to meet, and now he'd made me feel worse by being so damned nice about it.

I shuddered as he slung an arm around my shoulders and gave me a squeeze. "We need to get you into bed."

"That's the best idea I've heard all evening." A vision of Connor with fewer clothes on flitted through my mind, and I gave myself a mental slap. No, I was not going there. He'd meant it in a kind way, not an I-want-to-strip-you-naked-and-do-bad-things way.

Once more, I found myself in his arms, and this time we made it back to my bedroom. Well, bathroom. Connor propped me up in front of the sink and stared at my reflection in the mirror. I closed my eyes. If I did that, the blonde eyesore I'd become would disappear, right?

"Brush your teeth," he said.

"Huh?"

"Your mouth'll taste like shit, and it'll make you feel better."

As I tried to put toothpaste onto the brush with shaking fingers, I swayed a bit and grabbed for the basin. Connor's arms snaked round my waist and held me up until I spat and rinsed, branding me with his touch.

My efforts earned me a half-smile. "Well done. Now, bed."

He made no attempt to undress me as he tucked me under the duvet, just drew it up to my chin and turned off the main light, leaving me only the glow of the lamp on the nightstand. My eyelids grew heavy, and I could keep them open no longer. There was a pause before Connor's footsteps crossed the room and then the door clicked shut.

But before that, before he walked away, had I imagined his warm breath on my cheek and the brush of his lips against my temple?

I didn't know how to face Connor the next morning. What must he think of me? Hmm... How about if I just packed and snuck out? I could call a taxi, and it would be here in fifteen minutes. Okay, thirty, because I'd need a shower first, and...

My door opened.

"It lives," said Connor as he walked in with two steaming mugs of coffee. The aroma tickled my nose and I inhaled deeply. Delicious.

Hang on a sec. He hadn't even knocked!

"You can't walk in here like that!"

"Just did."

"What if I'd been naked?"

"A guy can live in hope." He dropped onto the edge of the bed and looked down at me. I expected to see annoyance, but what I saw was worry. "How are you feeling?"

"Not great," I admitted, turning my head and burying my face in the pillow. "I threw up in front of you."

"At least you didn't throw up on me."

That made me giggle. "That would have been worse."

"Trust me, it is."

There was something about the way he said it. "Wait, someone's done that to you?"

I thought he wasn't going to answer, he paused for so long. "Other way round."

"You threw up?"

"My date never spoke to me again."

That new piece of information sunk in. Connor puked on a girl? How, when I'd never even seen him drink? "But you're always so sensible."

"I haven't always been that way." He stood up. "I'll see you outside."

His confession made me feel a little bit better, but a couple of nights out had taken their toll, and I was shattered when I got outside. My tiredness showed up in my riding ability, or rather the lack of it.

When we'd ridden out yesterday afternoon, with Folly cantering along nicely beside Captain, I'd finally got the hang of sitting still, but this morning my balance deserted me.

"I can't do it," I said, frustrated.

Connor patted Folly on the neck, no doubt commiserating with her for having an idiot on board. "You can, but you're not in the right frame of mind today. We'll go for a hack this afternoon, the horses have got tomorrow off, and we can start fresh on Tuesday."

Tuesday. We'd be well into week two then. "Jenny said there was a dressage competition on Saturday. There's no way I'll be ready for that."

"You don't have to win; you just have to get round. If you focus for the rest of the week, you'll do it."

"I don't see how I can."

He took a step closer and laid a hand on my knee. "Babe, you need to lay off the wine. It's not helping you."

How did I explain it was the wine that gave me courage? When I was tipsy, I could imagine another, braver girl inhabited my body. One able to look him in the eye without shrinking away.

He squeezed my leg.

"Okay," I blurted.

I was rewarded with a grin, teeth included.

It was when we were walking back to the barn after dinner at Jenny's in the evening that he leaned down to me. "Tomorrow, I'll prove you can have fun without alcohol."

"What?"

"Wear jeans."

Before I could ask what on earth he meant, he'd disappeared into the darkness, leaving me to spend a sleepless night worrying about what he had planned.

The next morning, I got up early to put Folly in the field and muck out then took a shower. Remembering what

Connor said, I pulled on a pair of black skinny jeans and a turtleneck jumper. Hopefully that would meet with his approval.

I smothered a yawn as I sat down for breakfast, and Annabel sneered at me. "Late night?"

"I didn't sleep that well."

"I can tell by the big, black circles under your eyes." Beside her, Felicity giggled. "You should get a decent concealer. What were you doing all night, plotting what you can try next to snag Connor?"

"No, I—"

A roar from outside interrupted me. A blur zipped past the window, and we all ran to look, just in time to see Connor swing his leg over a black motorbike and take off his helmet.

Seconds later, he arrived at the door and grinned at me, then his smile faded as he looked past my shoulder. "Good morning, Annabel, Felicity."

Felicity said, "Good morning," but Annabel merely scowled.

Connor shrugged and looked back at me. "Ready to go, babe?"

I poked my head out the door. "On that thing? You expect me to sit on that? It's a death trap on wheels."

He laughed. "No, it's a Suzuki GSXR."

"You can ride it?"

"No, I flew it here on a magic carpet."

Yet again, I'd managed to sound stupid.

"I'll go for a ride, Connor," Annabel purred from beside me, obviously having a change of heart.

He gave her a scathing look. "I bet you would."

Turning his back on her, he took my hand. "Come on, you can tick off something else from your list."

I'd been so busy freaking out at the thought of having him between my thighs, I'd forgotten all about that. Could I pass up on the chance of completing another challenge? I'd achieved precious little so far, and who knew if another guy would be willing to take me out on a motorbike again?

"Will you go slowly? I like slow."

"I will." He leaned in close so nobody else could hear. "But not on the bike."

Call an ambulance. My heart was going to give out if he kept saying things like that. I fanned myself then stopped when Annabel stared at me.

"Put this helmet on."

Connor helped me to fasten the strap under my chin, and steam hissed out of Annabel's ears as I hopped up behind him onto the tiny pillion seat. I felt around. Where were the handles?

"What do I hold onto?"

He grinned and looked down at himself before pulling his helmet over his head. "Me."

The vibrations from the engine rippled through me when Connor started it up. With the Uglies still watching, I gingerly put my arms around his waist, keeping them loose, trying to ignore the sensations between my legs. I hadn't had time to gather my thoughts when Connor twisted the throttle, and the bike surged forward.

I couldn't help shrieking as I grabbed on for dear life. As he accelerated along the lane, I ended up plastered to his back, the scent of his leather jacket invading my nostrils.

The bike tilted as he went round a corner, and I squealed again. What if it fell over? Didn't he care about gravity? Apparently not, since I could hear his laughter over the throb of the bike as another bend came up.

"Slow down," I yelled.

"Babe, we're only doing forty."

We were? It seemed much faster with the tarmac rushing by so close to my feet. I didn't even know where we were going. All I could do was cling on as Connor sped through the countryside, cottages and fields and hedgerows and streams zipping past in a blur.

It took a while, but when I didn't die I began to enjoy myself. Shivery thrills raced through me as I leaned into the turns with him, and the slow burn between my legs made me fidget. I itched to reach down and relieve it, but that was out of the question. Was it possible to have an orgasm from riding a motorcycle? I didn't know, but I was well on my way to finding out.

The peak of ecstasy was coming close when Connor pulled into the car park of a quiet country inn, and a groan escaped my lips. "Why did you stop?"

He pointed at the blackboard next to the door. It advertised what claimed to be the best full English in the South of England. "I interrupted your breakfast."

As if on cue, my stomach let out a grumble.

"See," he laughed. "It agrees with me."

When we walked in the door, he waved at the guy behind the bar to get his attention. "Two full Englishes and a couple of coffees, please." Then he took my hand and led me over to a table in the corner. My palm sizzled where it touched his, and I had to concentrate to stop myself from panting.

When he let go, I slid into a bench seat on the far side and Connor took the chair opposite. "So, what do you think of the bike?"

I wanted to dissolve into mush but tried to play it cool. Even then, I couldn't keep the grin off my face. "It's all right."

His expression matched mine. "You love it."

"It's all right," I repeated.

"I'll get you to say those three words by the end of the day."

"Nice to see you're up for a challenge."

"I've got my own list, babe."

Why did I feel so flustered when he gave me his secret smile? The one that made me want to peel off his clothes and lick him all over? I shoved that thought away as the guy from the bar brought our drinks to the table and tried to regain my composure as I concentrated on adding cream and sugar.

"So what else do you have planned for today?" I asked.

"Not a lot," he admitted. "This was a spur of the moment thing. I called up an old buddy yesterday evening to borrow the bike. I figured we'd ride around a while, have lunch, maybe dinner?"

A whole day with the perfect excuse to wrap myself around Connor? The chance to spend a couple of hours eating good food and trying to pretend I wasn't drinking him in with my eyes? "Sounds good to me."

It was ten o'clock and pitch black by the time we got back to Linden Hollow, and I peeled myself away from Connor with difficulty. We'd gone west and ridden around half of Wiltshire, broken up only by a shared bag of chips for lunch then a cosy dinner in an out-of-the-way pub.

He put the bike on its stand and helped me off, holding me up as I stumbled sideways.

"You okay?"

"My bum's numb and my legs are stiff."

"Stiffness has been a problem for me today too."

Oh good, at least I wasn't the only one. "It's a shame the bike isn't yours to keep."

"So you love it now?"

"It's all right."

He walked forward, pushing me back against the fairing. "Say it."

I looked away and giggled. "It's all right."

He pinned me in place with his hips, and suddenly his earlier comment about stiffness made sense. I gasped, given no choice but to look at him when he gently grasped my chin and turned my head.

"Say it," he murmured.

His lips hovered inches from mine, and his breath washed over my face, still chocolatey from the dessert we'd shared. My legs started to buckle, and he held me up. Did he know what he did to me?

"I love it," I whispered back, and at that moment I suspected I wasn't only talking about the bike.

Every nerve ending begged him to kiss me, but he stepped back, leaving me a gooey mess. "That's one of *my* challenges ticked off."

CHAPTER 18

I AWOKE ON Tuesday to the sound of rain lashing against my windows.

"Annabel's riding first in the indoor school, then Felicity. We'll take our turn after so we get it to ourselves," Connor said.

That gave me the chance to groom Folly thoroughly and fit in breakfast with Connor afterwards. He munched on a slice of toast, and although he'd made me coffee and pulled out my chair for me, the closeness we shared yesterday seemed to have receded.

Had I imagined it? I didn't think so. If I closed my eyes, the hardness of his cock still pressed into my hip, and there was no way he faked that.

But I could hardly ask him about it, could I? Instead, I kept my confusion to myself as we walked to the arena.

Jenny stayed to watch me ride and gave me a round of applause at the end of my first pretend dressage test. As Connor called out the movements, I gave them my best try, but as I trotted around everything felt kind of wobbly.

"That was great! I can't believe how much progress you've made. I'll call the show secretary and get you entered for Saturday—you'll have no trouble riding one of the prelim tests."

"Really?"

"I wouldn't say it otherwise."

"Can we practise again this afternoon?"

"Sure," Connor said. "I'll ride Captain afterwards to give him a workout."

My second lesson went better than the first, and I began to believe they were right. Maybe I *could* do it? Maybe some of Connor's confidence was rubbing off on me?

With that in mind, I pushed my worries about his distance today to one side and stopped him before he walked back to Jenny's house. "Do you want to have dinner together tonight?"

"Wish I could, babe, but I've got plans I can't cancel."

My spirits plummeted. "That's okay. It was only a thought."

"Tomorrow, yeah?"

I nodded my agreement. At least it wasn't an outright no.

I spent the evening wondering where he'd gone, but when I asked Jenny a few subtle questions over dinner regarding his whereabouts, all she said was that she'd dropped him off at the train station.

As I tried and failed to learn my dressage test from the sheet Jenny had given me, I imagined the worst. What if he had a girlfriend hidden away somewhere? Or he just wanted someone for the night and she wasn't me?

Annabel's imagination was working overtime as well. "Bored of you already, is he? Can't say I blame him."

Next, I attempted to lose myself in a novel, but even

that proved impossible. In my head, the hero looked like Connor, only my version of the story didn't have a happy ending. Another restless night beckoned.

I was brushing Folly the next morning when I heard footsteps behind me and a pair of hands covered my eyes.

"Guess who."

"The Easter Bunny?"

"No, but I did bring you chocolate."

Connor shyly held out a bag to me. He'd bought me a present? I took it from him and peered inside, finding a box of luxury chocolates decorated with a big red bow.

"You dug the dessert the other night. Did you know you moaned while you were eating it?"

"I did not."

"Did too." His voice went high pitched. "Ooh, Connor, this is sooo good. More, I need more."

I shoved him in the chest. "I did not sound like that."

He captured my hand in his and held it against his heart. I felt it beating, hammering almost as fast as mine. "Not far off, babe."

What would it feel like if we didn't have his clothes between us? Unlike Felicity, I hadn't seen him shirtless. Would his skin be silky smooth? Or perhaps have a smattering of dark hair? Surely it wouldn't be gorilla-style?

He cleared his throat, disturbing my reverie. "You

ready to ride?"

"Yup."

"Dressage practice this morning, hack in the afternoon?"

I needed to run through my test as many times as possible. I'd be riding Prelim 14, which included movements in walk, trot and canter. Simple exercises, Connor said, but to me it was as simple as learning to Riverdance with my shoelaces tied together and a couple of glasses of wine inside me. And I still hadn't memorised the instructions. Jenny had promised to lend me her show jacket and stock, and when I tried them on for size after dinner yesterday they'd fitted perfectly, so I couldn't use that as an excuse not to compete either. But even with all that pressure, I still wanted to go for a hack. Nothing beat riding out with Connor in the countryside.

"Yes, I'd like that."

Connor was more critical of me that morning, endlessly correcting my position or the patterns I was riding.

"It's to help you be the best you can on Saturday," he explained. "A judge is going to be looking for all these things."

He worked me hard, and my legs ached by the time I dismounted. I felt sorry for Folly as well. Her sheen of sweat showed how hard she'd been working. We'd both enjoy an easier time in the afternoon.

I helped Connor out on the yard before lunch, which earned me the right to some of the delicious chocolates he'd given me when we got back to the barn. First a caramel, then a praline, a nougat, a truffle, a strawberry crème.

"I feel a bit sick," I said. "But these are good."

He grabbed my hand, which was halfway to my mouth, and steered it in his direction instead. "Don't get sick. Give them to me instead." He popped the chocolate I was holding into his mouth and sucked my finger.

His touch travelled all the way through my core, and a throb started between my thighs. If he planned to repeat that move, he could have the rest. Then I'd go out and buy another box.

Annabel made a gagging noise behind us. "Would you stop it? You're making the rest of us feel sick as well."

Without missing a beat, Connor scooped up the box and grabbed my hand. "Of course, what was I thinking? We'll continue this in private." He dragged me into the bedroom he never used, leaving Annabel open mouthed behind us.

As soon as the door closed, we stared at each other then started laughing.

"Did you see the look on her face?" he asked.

"It was priceless. I'm surprised she didn't have an aneurysm."

We stayed in there long enough to give her something to wonder about, then Connor untucked his shirt while I buttoned my blouse wrongly and messed up my hair.

"Look okay?" I asked.

"Perfect." He gave me a thumbs up and slung an arm around my shoulders as we marched past the Uglies and out to the horses.

"Sometimes it's the little things that are the most satisfying," I said.

He waggled his eyebrows. "Big things can be more satisfying." His tone left me in no doubt as to which "big thing" he was referring to. I wasn't sure whether he was joking or not.

The dirty part of me, the part that wanted to melt the remaining chocolates over him and slowly lick them off, hoped for "not."

We tied the horses next to each other while we tacked them up, and as we did so, I mulled over Connor in my mind. When I first arrived at Linden Hollow, I'd thought he was an arrogant sod, but underneath the rude exterior he'd turned out very different to the persona he projected. The hidden Connor, sweet and sensitive, made my heart ache. Sure, he still blew hot and cold—yesterday's distance was a case in point—but the upshot of it was that I liked him. I mean, really liked him.

And I had only four days left to find out whether he felt the same.

The thing was, if I confessed my feelings and it went wrong, I'd probably lose him as a friend. And above all else, he'd become a friend, someone who made me laugh, someone I could hang out with and talk to.

I tried to put those thoughts to the back of my mind while we rode, but now I'd had them, they were hard to ignore.

"Do you want to canter?" Connor asked when we got to the woods down the road. There was a nice clear path ahead of us, and I'd thoroughly enjoyed whizzing down it the other day.

"Yeah, go on then." Cantering didn't scare me anymore. I'd found out Folly had good brakes, and the speed gave me the same thrill as freewheeling down a steep hill on my bicycle. But fast or not, it didn't come close to riding behind Connor on that Suzuki.

I urged Folly on beside Captain, unable to resist the occasional glance across at Connor, relaxed and smiling as he rode one handed, western-style.

And then it happened.

One second I was cantering happily along, the next, Folly lurched forwards, and I flew through the air as she fell onto her knees.

I heard a scream, and it took a second to realise it came from my lips. A log at the side of the path flew towards me, and as I hit it, I swear I heard the crunch as something broke. An unbearable pain shot through my chest. Silver flashed on the edge of my vision as one of Folly's hooves passed inches from my face, and that was the last thing I saw before everything went black.

CHAPTER 19

THE WORLD MORPHED from black to red as hot pokers invaded my conscious. I tried to roll, to get away from the agony but it came with me, more intense with every movement.

"Stay still, Ella." A man's voice seeped into my brain, echoing from far away.

I stopped moving and a hand held mine. I gripped onto it, as if by squeezing I could make the pain disappear. More words filtered through, little snippets jumbling round in my brain: "Folly fell, and she came off...need an ambulance...think she's coming round."

I tried to open my eyes, but my eyelids were heavy, as if someone had threaded tiny weights onto each eyelash to hold them closed. Damp seeped through my clothes, and with it came a chill. Was this what death felt like?

I tried to fight it, but the shadows got closer, surrounding me and blanketing my thoughts. I gave in and embraced the darkness, for with it came peace. Like a switch had been thrown, the lights went out.

Then the pain came back, needling at my side. Hands reached underneath me, and some bastard tried to drive nails into my ribcage with a hammer. An awful wail left me, then a gasp as I was lifted clear of the ground, floating skywards as if being summoned to heaven.

No, that couldn't be right. After what I did to Grant's car, surely I had a space reserved for me down below? My eyes popped open as I tried to work out where I was.

Connor's face hovered above me, first ashen then blue in the flashing lights. I tried to reach out for him but he stepped back, quickly obscured by the green uniforms and high-vis jackets of the paramedics as they transferred me onto a waiting stretcher. Connor tried to follow me into the ambulance, but the paramedics blocked his way.

"We can only take the patient, sir."

"But—"

I thought he was going to start arguing. "It's okay," I croaked. "I'll be okay."

My words were of little comfort—he still looked terrified as they closed the doors.

The lack of siren on the journey was a little disappointing, but we still arrived at A&E quickly. I hadn't been there for years, not since my foster brother glued my fingers together the day before my ninth birthday and my foster mother spent hours complaining while we waited for a nurse to separate my hands. The furniture didn't seem quite so big now but apart from that, nothing had changed. A doctor shone a torch in my eyes and asked me a lot of questions, most of which were irrelevant. How was the date of my last period relevant to chest pain, and why did he care what my plans were for Saturday night?

My swollen side already looked like Stevie had been at it with his painting set by the time they whisked me off for X-rays. The purple clashed horribly with the remains of my red top, and I had an awful feeling I knew what the outcome was going to be.

"You've fractured three ribs, Miss Goodman," the doctor said, peering at my chart. "The good news is that they're only small breaks, but you won't be up to much physical activity for the next six weeks."

Yup, it was as bad as I thought. Then it got worse.

"You've got a concussion as well. We'll need to keep you in overnight to monitor the head injury. It's lucky you were wearing a crash helmet. It took the brunt of the impact."

Lucky? I didn't feel lucky. I closed my eyes and took a long breath, then gagged with the pain. Okay, he was right. It could have been much, much worse. "Is there anything you can do for my ribs? Do I need a cast?"

"Nowadays we don't tend to strap up that sort of injury. We can give you some anti-inflammatories, but apart from that, you just need to take it easy. Let the pain be your guide—if it hurts, you probably shouldn't be doing it."

It was all very well for him to say. Even breathing was agony, and I couldn't very well stop doing that, could I?

When Connor arrived, he didn't look much better than I felt. It seemed like he'd aged ten years in the space of an afternoon. He dragged the uncomfortable-looking visitor's chair up to the side of my bed, and his fingers closed around mine, carefully avoiding the IV line sticking out the back of my hand. The top of the bed was raised, so at least I could see him properly.

"Babe, I'm so sorry."

"What on earth for?"

"You got hurt when you were with me."

"It was an accident. Just an accident. You couldn't have stopped it." I took another deep breath then immediately regretted it. "How's Folly?"

"The vet came out and scanned her legs. She's got an inflamed tendon so she needs a few weeks off to recover, but she'll be okay."

A weight lifted off my mind. I'd been worrying about her fate since I came round. "And how are you?"

"You're the one in hospital and you're asking how I am?"

"You look terrible."

He managed a chuckle. "You're stealing all my lines."

"You still haven't answered the question."

"I've never been so terrified as when I saw you come flying past me without the horse. Every time I close my eyes I hear you scream."

"Perhaps I was better off being unconscious." I tried to joke, but I soon discovered laughing was out for the foreseeable future as well.

The look on his face told me he didn't find it funny. "You wouldn't wake up. I couldn't make you wake up."

"I'm awake now." I squeezed his hand. "Please don't think of what didn't happen."

"Fuck, if it had been worse, I don't know what I'd have done."

"It wasn't. Now stop it."

He looked away, and I saw a hand come up to swipe at his cheek.

"Connor, I'm okay. Look at me." He didn't, so I gave his hand a little tug. "Look at me."

His eyes glistened when he finally turned, and I knew right then I was seeing the real Connor. All of him, even the parts he tried to hide away under his veneer of cockiness. He might come across as having endless confidence, but underneath it he was scared.

"I'm okay," I repeated, and not knowing what else to do, I brought his hand to my mouth and kissed it. He copied the gesture, and as his lips brushed over my skin, I knew Annabel had been talking rubbish. Connor was mine, and I was his.

The nurses let him stay half an hour past visiting time, but even his charms weren't enough to get him a bed for the night. Four nurses escorted him to the door, and not long after that, the ward sister who'd been drooling over him helped me out with a packet of Co-codamol and told me to get some sleep.

I wasn't sure I could, but in the end, I lay there counting the abs I imagined Connor to have in my head, and that sent me off.

The real Connor woke me as soon as visiting hours started. I'd been asleep for ages, apart from a brief moment in the night when a nurse shook me awake to check my brain was still working.

My eyes widened as I saw what he was carrying. "What did you do, rob a candy store?"

"I thought you liked chocolate?"

"I also like being a size ten, and I won't be one for much longer if I eat that lot."

He looked hopeful. "I could help."

I recalled the finger-sucking incident that almost caused me to orgasm on the spot. "Okay, deal."

A nurse offered me dry toast, and after half a slice I gave up and ate half a dozen pralines instead, each one fed to me by the man-god before me. There were definitely some advantages to being ill.

"When do you get out of here?" Connor asked.

"Later today, I hope. The doctor needs to come and check on me first." At least, that's what the nurse said last night after prodding all my sore bits. "Oh crap, do you know what happened to my phone?"

"It broke when you fell. Here, use mine, and I'll get you a new one later."

"You don't have to do that."

"I'm doing it anyway."

"I'll give you the money."

"No, you won't." He fished his phone out and dropped it into my palm.

"I don't want to take advantage of you."

"Is something not clear? I'm here because I want to spend time with you. A lot of time. And in some of that time, I'm gonna buy shit for you, and no, you're not going to pay me back." He guided my hand into his lap. "And for the record, I'm very much looking forward to you taking advantage of me."

Holy shit! Was it possible to discharge myself? I tried to shuffle further up the bed, but the vice crushing my chest was a harsh reminder that I wouldn't be taking advantage of anything for the foreseeable future.

I groaned, and even that hurt.

"What's up, babe? You need a nurse?"

"No, I need an orgasm, but my ribs aren't sharing the sentiment." I went red as soon as the words left my mouth. I seriously needed to work on my brain-to-mouth filter.

Connor laughed, then sobered up as realisation dawned. "These six weeks are going to be the most frustrating of my life. I'm gonna be ready to explode by the end of it."

"I'm counting on it," I murmured.

The mere anticipation left me hot, bothered and ready to ignite, and all that from a man I hadn't even kissed yet. Oh, hell—what if he thought I was a terrible kisser? I'd only had Terry to practise with, and he wasn't exactly Mr. Charisma. Was that why he'd turned to Demi? Maybe I kissed like a kipper and he just hadn't told me. And, oh my gosh, what about the sex? Terry had never been very adventurous, and I'd bet my bicycle that Connor had tried at least ninety percent of the Kama Sutra.

And speaking of Terry, was he still in my bloody summerhouse? If Connor planned to visit, and I sincerely hoped he did, I needed to get rid of Terry sooner rather than later.

"What are you thinking?" He ran a finger across my brow. "You're giving yourself worry lines. I don't want you to worry."

I didn't dare mention the sex part. Maybe I could get a bluffer's guide on Amazon? Or ring Demi for tips? Flipping heck, this was going to be a disaster. I'd finally got a hot man, and with it came a crisis of confidence of epic proportions.

And he was still looking at me, waiting for an answer. What was the question again? Oh yes, why was I worried?

"Terry's still living in my shed," I blurted.

His mouth hardened into a thin line. "Terry won't be living in your shed as soon as I get there."

My my, hello Mr. Alpha. "You won't hurt him, will you?"

"I'll have a chat and explain the position."

Oh, that was okay, then.

"And if he doesn't leave right away, I'll tie him to the back of my truck and drag him off your property."

I gulped. Hopefully Terry would see sense. "You have a truck?" I didn't remember seeing one.

"Not at the moment, but as it looks like I'm gonna be spending some time in the UK, I'd better buy one, hadn't I?" He gave me a look that would have melted my underwear off if the nurses hadn't taken it all and given me an ugly paper gown instead.

"Uh, how is this going to work?"

"How is what going to work?"

"Us." I whispered the word, hardly daring to believe that there was indeed an "us."

He leaned back in the chair. "Fuck, that's gonna take a bit of sorting out. I guess we'll go back to Jenny's for now, if that suits you? I've still got three more weeks to do there, and I don't want to let her down."

"You think she'll be okay with that? I've been nothing but trouble for both of you."

"I know she will. She feels bad about the accident too."

Which was how, that evening, I found myself in Jenny's Land Rover as Connor drove very slowly back to Linden Hollow. My ribs hurt too much to wear a seatbelt, and every tiny bump caused me to wince.

When we arrived, Jenny fussed around, holding the door open and plumping up the cushions on the sofa.

"I'm so glad it wasn't worse. When Connor called and said you'd come off badly, I'd never been so scared in my life."

"The doctors said I'll make a full recovery. The concussion was only mild, and the ribs will heal in a few weeks."

"They're bloody painful, I bet. I've put extra pillows on the bed. I know when I broke mine, it hurt to lie flat for a few weeks."

"You've broken your ribs?"

"Four of them, and my sternum. Got double barrelled in the chest by a youngster, and I've never felt pain like it."

"How long did it take for them to stop hurting?"

"Six weeks isn't a bad estimate. You can stay here as long as you like, but I've let your room in the barn out from next week, I'm afraid. You'll have to sleep in Connor's bed, and he can take the sofa."

I looked at the sofa, then looked at Connor, who was at least six inches longer than it. "Uh, that's not very fair. I'm shorter, I can take the sofa."

"You're having the bed," Connor said, and that was that.

For the next three weeks, I was stuck inside, surviving on a cocktail of paracetamol and Connor's endless supply of expensive chocolates. He bought me an eReader, and I read novel after novel, devouring complicated plots and romantic heroes as if they were sustenance. Then, in the second week, I did something I never thought I'd have the courage to do. I picked up pen and paper and started writing a book of my own.

Well, more of a journal, really—the story of Edith's challenges and the complete balls up I'd managed to make of every one of them so far.

Connor spent most of his time outside. With an influx of guests, he taught from dawn to dusk, everyone from a nervous mum to a teenager who made Annabel look sweeter than candyfloss.

I got him in the evenings, though. Jenny let him off dinner after the first night, when the aforementioned teenager tried to play footsie with him under the table and ended up ramming her not-so-dainty size six right into his crotch.

"I might never have children," he said as he walked into the house, doubled over.

I stopped myself just in time before I offered to kiss it better. My filter was improving, I was pleased to note.

That evening, I snuggled into him on the sofa which conveniently happened to be the only position that felt comfortable. "How are your...er, you know?"

"Blue."

"I'm sorry." I looked away, unable to meet his eyes, both out of guilt and a fear I might laugh. "This is all my fault."

"It's not." He pressed his lips to my temple. "And you're worth the wait."

But he didn't wait. He leaned over and laid his lips on mine, resting a hand on the back of the seat so he didn't squash me. I gasped as he caught me by surprise then pressed back against him as my lips parted. I longed to hold him, to feel him against me, but I didn't dare. Instead, I slid my tongue into his mouth, relishing the sweetness from the chocolate he'd just eaten as I explored.

I thought the kiss was never going to end, nor did I want it to. His tenderness surprised me, and when he did move his head, it was only to flutter soft kisses along my jawline and murmur in my ear.

"Until you're healed up, this is what you get. After that, all bets are off."

The happy glow spread from my chest and out to my extremities. If someone had turned the lights out, I'm sure I'd have lit up the room.

Connor managed to stick to his promise for six more days. Six days of sweet words and even sweeter kisses. As he helped me up from the sofa late one evening, I noticed he'd started moving with a stiffness absent before, and more than once I'd seen him trying to work out the kinks in his back in the morning.

He turned back the quilt for me and when I'd climbed into bed, he pulled the covers up to my chin and leaned over to kiss me good night. As he had done every day, he whispered, "May your dreams come true."

"Make them. Stay." I took hold of his hand and gave it a little tug.

"Are you sure?"

I wasn't, but I nodded anyway. "Just to sleep."

I didn't need to say it again. He kicked off his shoes and climbed in beside me, lying flat while I propped myself up on a mountain of pillows. He entwined my fingers tightly with his, clasped against his chest. Anyone looking at us might have thought our hands were the only thing connecting us, but I knew better.

We were linked by our hearts as well.

Chapter 20

LATE ONE SUNDAY, Jenny's husband finally returned complete with a huge lorry and four beautiful Spanish horses. I was able to get up and walk by then, as long as I didn't breathe hard or move my arms or touch anything.

Folly snaffled an apple from my palm before I went along to get a better look at the newcomers, now happily ensconced in their stables. I'd seen them from a distance as they were being unloaded but I wanted to say hello properly. Connor was with me, of course. When he wasn't working, he'd barely left my side.

"Look at his mane," I said, as I peered over the first door at a white stallion. "It's got to be two feet long. And his tail's down to the floor."

"Yeah, it looks good now, but you wait until he's been in the field tomorrow morning. You won't recognise him from all the mud."

"Is he friendly?"

"He'll mug you for food, but if you hold out a carrot he'll be gentle."

Once I'd given all the horses a treat, my muscles ached a little. My body was taking its sweet time to recover from the accident. Connor offered me his arm and helped me back to the house. "You ready for the big off tomorrow?" he asked.

I nodded, but in truth I was a nervous wreck. Connor was coming to stay with me in Reading before he flew back home to San Francisco the following Saturday.

He must have seen my glum expression because he slung an arm round my shoulders and kissed my hair. "Wish I didn't have to go, but I need to pay for the truck." He'd been offered a few days' work and said he couldn't afford to turn it down.

"You mean your penis extension?" He'd just bought it, a big, black Mitsubishi Warrior covered in shiny chrome.

"Don't need one of those, babe, you know that," he reminded me.

Oh yes, I did indeed. The morning before last, I saw him getting out the shower, and if it was any longer I'd end up in hospital again. I also knew that Felicity hadn't miscounted when she'd said he had an eight-pack, and his chest bore no resemblance to a gorilla. His well-muscled pecs were smooth and tanned, crying out for a girl to run her fingers over.

All I needed was for my bloody ribs to heal because I couldn't wait to feel skin on skin.

"What do you do for work?" I asked.

I still didn't know an awful lot about him, but whenever I started with any questions, I always got distracted by his sweet lips and clever tongue. Every time he kissed me, I decided his biography could wait.

"I'm in marketing. Just freelance."

"Oh, like a consultant?"

"Something like that."

Not what I'd expected, I had to admit. I'd always assumed he did something outdoors. After all, it was obvious how much he loved the countryside in general and horses in particular.

Still, his trip should only take a week, and then he'd promised to come back and see me.

Meanwhile, I was determined to enjoy my last night with Jenny and her husband, Taff. According to Connor, Taff once played for the Welsh under-19's football team, and he'd certainly kept his athletic physique as well as his accent. I enjoyed listening to the soft lilt of his voice as we chatted over dinner, and before long, I told him all about my list of challenges.

"That's a good old selection. If you're needing to cover off the film extra one, I'm out on set again tomorrow just down the road. I'm sure they'll let you stand around if you like." He turned to Connor. "Unless you'll be sorting that one out with your brother?"

"Brother?" I asked. Connor had barely mentioned his family, and I'm sure I'd have remembered if he said anything about a sibling.

"Yeah."

"And he does something with films?"

I caught a surprised look from Jenny. Maybe he hadn't told her either?

"Yeah, he's done a bit of that kind of thing, but mostly in the States. Taff, if you reckon you could sort it, that'd get one of Ella's tasks done. We can easily stick around for another day or two."

The thought of knocking something else off the list made me extraordinarily pleased. I'd kind of given up on it until my ribs healed, so if I could complete another challenge before then it would be a bonus.

"Ooh yes, that would be amazing."

And so it turned out not to be the last supper after

all.

On Tuesday, I craned my neck out of Connor's truck as we drove onto the set of a BBC period drama half an hour away from Linden Hollow. Taff left before us with Lenny, who'd been tasked with helping him out for a few days. The girl Connor had been standing in for was also back, so Jenny had a full complement of staff again.

I'd never been on a film set before, and it was more laid back than I'd expected. Assistants bustled purposefully around, hugging clipboards as if they held the key to life, while a team of jeans-clad designers artfully arranged props around a mock-Mediaeval village.

We found the horses over in a quiet corner, standing around, eating hay. They were far less interested in everything than I was—clearly they were old pros.

Taff took me over and introduced me to the wardrobe mistress, and she got her assistant to sort me out with a costume. The casting lady gave me a job playing a peasant girl, and all I had to do was stand in the background and look shocked as the bad guys galloped past. Surely I could manage that?

In the meantime, I joined the leagues of people hovering outside the trailers looking bored. Connor found us both polystyrene cups of tea, and I sipped mine gratefully, holding it tight to warm my hands. The chilly fingers of the early morning air nipped at my skin. Thank goodness I wasn't really a peasant girl because I'd have frozen to death if Connor hadn't lent me his coat.

A guy munching on a croissant paused to clap Connor on the back, and the chair-carrying assistant following almost walked into him.

"Connor! Long time no see."

"Yeah, it's been a while."

"How's your brother?"

"Not too bad."

"Give him my best, would you?"

"Sure, I'll be seeing him next week."

The man looked over at me and his eyes dropped, taking in our joined hands. "You've found a good woman to keep you on the straight and narrow then?"

Connor looked down at me and smiled the smile that made my knees go weak. "I have."

"Good to hear, son, good to hear."

He wandered off while Connor leaned down and brushed a kiss on my lips.

"Hey, watch my make-up."

He laughed. "Those aren't words I ever thought I'd hear you say."

I blushed. "I'm not very good at putting it on myself."

"Don't change. One of the things I love about you is that you don't trowel it on. You look perfect without it."

Did he just say the "L" word? My knees, already wobbly, buckled a little. "Is there a chair anywhere?"

He helped me over to the catering truck, and I sat at one of the little tables clustered outside. "You feeling okay?"

"I came over a bit giddy, but I'm fine now."

He looked at me suspiciously.

"It's probably low blood sugar. I think the tea's helped."

"Stay there. I'll find you something to eat."

He came back with a chocolate bar, and I ate a few squares to keep him happy. Okay, I ate the whole thing. Better safe than sorry, eh?

It wasn't too much longer before I needed to do my bit. According to the dog-eared script I'd borrowed from one of my fellow peasants, the assistant chief bad guy was supposed to gallop in, pull the struggling maiden onto the horse in front of him, and speed off. His minions would follow, and me and my co-extras would stare on in horror.

That was the plan, anyway.

"And...action," the director yelled. He turned out to be the same man who'd stopped to greet Connor earlier.

The bad guy, who'd foregone armour in favour of something more ninja-like, cantered in on Smokey, one of Jenny's team of Andalusians. Hang on. Wasn't he supposed to be able to ride? His chicken was even funkier than mine. He bent at the waist to grasp the maiden, and then landed in a heap as Smokey cantered on without him.

"Cut!"

After he'd dropped the maiden once, fallen off twice more, and the director had yelled "cut" twelve times, I came to the conclusion the naughty knight had told a small porkie pie on his résumé.

My teeth were trying to chatter, and the ordeal of watching the man trying to steer was wearing a little thin. Looking round at my co-extras, they shared that sentiment. Expressions of horror had faded to mild distaste on the latest take.

The director dropped his pile of papers on the floor and marched over to the incompetent idiot, looking royally pissed.

"I thought you said you could ride?" The director poked him in the chest with each word.

"I took a couple of lessons a while back. Honestly, I didn't think it was that difficult," the man whined.

"You're managing to make it that way."

"I'm doing my best."

"Not good enough. You're wasting everyone's time." The director looked around in despair until his eyes settled on Connor, who was lounging behind the camera looking as bored as I felt.

"Connor," he boomed. "Would you do me a favour?"

Half an hour later, we were ready to go again, except this time Connor sat astride Smokey. We got through the scene in one take, and when the maiden swooned, no acting was required. Connor looked so sexy up there, I almost forgot to do my horrified look.

"How did the director know you could ride?" I asked Connor as he dismounted.

"I might have mentioned it," Taff said. "Sorry."

"Don't worry about it. I'll get a couple of days pay and a credit out of it," Connor said.

"A couple of days?" I asked.

"He convinced me to come back and do the rest of the dude's part. I know it's dull, but I'll make it up to you."

"I'll hold you to that."

He bent to whisper in my ear. "And I'll hold you to

me."

I shivered, and not from the cold. A few more days on set might not be so bad if I brought a book and a blanket. When I thought about it, it was kind of cool to be able to say I was dating an actor, even if the novelty only lasted for a day or two.

By Thursday, Connor had stomped around looking moody, berated several minions then died rather convincingly, and it really was time to go home. I gave Jenny a very gentle hug and promised to come back as soon as I could.

"I still need to do that dressage test."

"Folly will be waiting."

She was walking better now, her bandages off. Jenny planned to give her a few more weeks of rest in the field before she came back into work. I'd left a big bag of carrots with Folly's name on it in the feed room, and instructions to feed them to her morning, noon and night.

"Well, that was certainly an experience," I said to Connor as we got in the truck.

"Looking forward to going home?"

"Yes and no. I miss my house and my friends, but I could do without Terry and Mike. And grocery shopping. I hate grocery shopping."

Although I hadn't heard from Mike in weeks. When Connor bought me a new phone, I'd expected a slew of messages ranging from creepy to demented, but there was nothing. I kept my fingers crossed he'd finally lost interest.

"I'll help with the shopping, babe. I'll be eating the food too. And don't worry about Terry and Mike."

What did I do to deserve this man?

As we drove eastwards along the M4 motorway, his hand rested on my thigh, mine over the top of it. I couldn't deny I was a little apprehensive about my new life, but with Connor in it, it was bound to be more colourful than the old version.

CHAPTER 21

THE CLOSER WE got to Reading, the more fidgety I became. What if Connor hated my house? The decor still screamed "old lady," and there wasn't much I could do about that unless I managed to complete all my challenges.

And what would happen with Terry? I only hoped he agreed to go quietly.

When we drew up outside the house, the curtains were open and everything lay quiet. The only sign of habitation was the plume of smoke rising from behind the garage.

Wait a second. Smoke? Why the hell was there smoke?

Lost for words, I pointed at it, my hand trembling.

Connor's eyes followed my finger. "I take it that's not supposed to be there?"

I quickly shook my head.

Connor was out of the car in an instant, pausing only to help me down and tow me along with him. Together we marched around the side of the house.

Well, Terry had made himself right at home, hadn't he?

He and four of his no-good mates from uni were slumped in plastic garden chairs, shouting at a flat-screen TV visible through the open summerhouse door.

A fifth waste-of-space flipped charred-looking meat on a family-sized barbecue, the origin of the plumes of smoke.

Connor marched right up to the lot of them and lowered his voice to a growl. "What the fuck?"

Terry turned from his position on a sun lounger—one of Edith's, I noticed. "All right, Ella? You should have said you were coming back. We'd have got extra burgers."

Connor tucked me in behind him. "You've got ten minutes to get off Ella's property before I help you on your way."

Behind Terry, I noticed the rest of his little gang sidling away. Angry Connor was not a sight anyone wanted to be confronted with.

"Keep your hair on, mate. I know Ella. We go way back."

"I know exactly who you are, and I also know she doesn't want you here."

"No need to be so touchy. She's just helping out an old friend."

I couldn't leave Connor to fight this on his own. It wasn't his battle.

"We're not friends, Terry. You cheated on me with Demi."

"But that was just sex. It didn't mean nothing. I needed a bit of time with someone that got what they were doing down there, know what I mean? Demi was a bitch, anyway."

Oh. My. Goodness. Did he just tell Connor I sucked in bed? Or rather, that I didn't suck? It wasn't my fault Terry smelled like old socks and made me want to gag. Or that he made those weird animal noises when he got close to coming that threw a bucket of cold water over my libido.

Did I say any of that? No, I just stood there open mouthed as Terry's face took on a look of smugness.

"What you did was horrible," I finally managed to get out.

"Oh, lighten up." He jerked a thumb at Connor. "You've been quick enough to hop into the sack with someone else."

"You can't stay here." Because if he did, I might be tempted to punch him.

"Look." His tone turned wheedling. "I'll get some grass seed for the burnt bits before I go, and I'll even empty the chemical toilet."

I looked round, taking in the charred patches of lawn that spoke of the disposable barbecues he'd used before getting a proper one. And what toilet? Tell me he hadn't been shitting in the summerhouse?

I didn't get the chance to ask because Connor dove forward and rugby tackled him. There was a bit of a struggle, and seconds later Terry got carried to the front of Edith's property and deposited on the pavement.

Connor pointed down at where the tarmac changed into gravel. "Cross that line and I'll kill you, got it?"

Terry had gone white with a hint of green by that point. He nodded quickly.

Without another word, Connor put his arm around me and steered me back up the driveway.

"That was easier than I thought," he said.

In the garden, Terry's mates were still standing around, unsure what to do with themselves. I noted they hadn't lifted a finger to help.

"You've got five minutes to clear that." Connor pointed at the mess outside the summerhouse. "Before I call the cops and get all of you arrested for criminal damage."

After a few beats, they shuffled to the shed with the enthusiasm of the undead. Connor supervised as they carried everything out to the kerb, including the bloody porta-potti.

"Don't s'pose you can give us a lift, mate?" one of them tried, eying up Connor's truck.

Connor simply stared at him until he backed away, tripping over Edith's potted pelargoniums as he did so.

Soon, all that remained was a sad-looking lawn and a broken deckchair. Connor threw that in the wheelie-bin, and the dead flowers we found in the porch with a card from Mike attached joined it.

Day was turning to dusk when we finally started unloading our own cases. Connor brought less stuff than me, a state of affairs I found a little depressing considering he'd been staying with Jenny for twice as long. He carried everything upstairs and dumped it in the larger of the two guest rooms.

"We can unpack tomorrow," he said.

Not having had a man stay before, I was unsure of the etiquette. Should I offer him a wardrobe for his things? Or would that seem too forward? A wave of tiredness washed over me. Connor was right—we could deal with the issue in the morning. At the moment, I needed food.

"Been a long day," Connor said after we'd grabbed a quick dinner. Nothing exciting, just reheated lasagne from the freezer.

We leaned against the kitchen counters opposite each other, waiting for the kettle to boil. The thought of having to reach into the cupboard for mugs brought on a yawn, and I barely had the energy to reach up and cover my mouth.

"That's the spirit, babe, open wide."

I snapped my jaw shut, and he laughed. Only it wasn't funny. Terry had basically told him I was terrible in bed, and the shame of it was, he was probably right.

Connor took a couple of paces and ended up by my side. "What's wrong? You look worried."

We'd come too far for me to lie to him. "It's what Terry said."

"About jumping into bed with me? I know you're not the kind of girl who hops from one guy to the next without a second thought."

"No, not that."

"What, then?"

"About me not knowing what to do." I cast my eyes down at the floor.

He took half a step back and turned my chin up so I couldn't avoid his gaze. "I taught you to ride a horse, right?"

I nodded.

"That's not the only thing I'm gonna teach you to ride. And in the bedroom, I'm the fucking professor."

Oh my giddy aunt, it was a good thing I was leaning on the cupboard, because I wouldn't have stayed standing otherwise.

He leaned closer and murmured against my lips. "Babe, I'm gonna light you up." His finger lightly stroked between my legs. "Then I'm gonna blow you out."

I clutched at his shirt to hold myself up, and he laughed again.

"I don't care what that punk said. If he reckoned you were shit in bed, it's because he didn't know how to use it. And I..." He leaned his hips forward into me so I felt his hardness. "Know how to use it."

I ground against him. We were both wearing far too many clothes. I reached down between us, and for the first time, I gripped his bulge. His eyes hooded and his arms snaked around me, pulling me forward for a searing kiss.

I gasped as our lips met, but it wasn't from pleasure. "Could you loosen your arms a bit?"

He sprang back. "Fuck, babe, I'm sorry. Did I hurt you?"

"I'll be okay."

He pinched the bridge of his nose. "I should have been more careful." He looked furious with himself.

I leaned forward and captured his lips with mine. "Don't," I whispered against them.

With his hands gently resting on my hips this time, we made out until my lips and chin burned from his stubble. My skin wasn't the only thing on fire, though. If I didn't get some relief from the ache between my legs soon, I was going to self-combust. When we broke for air, I couldn't help sighing.

"What is it?" Connor asked.

"I just... I just want you."

"Feeling's mutual, babe."

"Maybe we could, I don't know... I could prop myself or something." I heard the tinge of desperation in my voice, but I didn't care. Damn these stupid ribs! They still ached like hell when I lay flat.

"The first time I'm inside you, I'm not holding back. We're waiting until you can take it."

And he thought that would cool me down? By the time I could "take it," I'd be nothing more than a puddle on the floor.

"That's not helping."

He leaned forward and kissed me again.

"Still not helping."

He reached for my zipper. "You gotta promise to tell me if you hurt."

Better. "Mmmm."

His fingers stilled, and he looked at me sharply. "Babe, you gotta promise."

"I promise," I breathed.

Slowly, oh so slowly, he slid my jeans down. My limbs were so wobbly that when I tried to kick a foot out of one of the legs I ended up lurching inelegantly to the side. Luckily, Connor caught me before I lost my balance and lifted me up onto the kitchen island in front of him.

Then he dropped to his knees.

It didn't take many swipes of his tongue before I gripped the edge of the counter and screamed, a wild mewl that for a second I didn't even realise came from me.

He prolonged the ecstasy by sucking gently at my most sensitive spot, the sensation so intense it bordered on pain. I saw stars. No, scratch that. I saw supernovas. By the time the feeling subsided, I was shaking like a jelly on a Power Plate.

Holy mother of orgasms!

Connor got to his feet and kissed me again, softly this time, without the desperation that had been there a few minutes ago. I tasted myself on him, something I'd always imagined would make me cringe, but on Connor's tongue it sent a fresh wave of heat flooding through me.

"You scream any louder and I'm gonna have to gag you," he said once he pulled back.

"Mavis next door is deaf, and the kids the other side have always got their music on."

"Fuck, don't tell me things like that."

"Just saying."

"When I get back, and you're healed, I'm gonna bury myself balls deep in you and then I want to hear you scream my name."

"It's a deal," I whispered.

I fell asleep reluctantly that night as I knew it would be my last beside Connor for a week. How I wished we could fast forward to a time when not only was he back, but I could cuddle him properly. Simply holding hands was no longer enough for me.

As he breathed quietly alongside, I mused over the bizarre twist of fate that brought us together. If somebody told me a month ago that I'd have lost my heart to a guy who shovelled poop for a living, I'd have helped them straight back to the nearest asylum. It was hardly the stuff of fantasies, was it? But Connor embodied everything I wanted in a man. Kind, dependable, and trustworthy, with the added bonus of being tasty enough to eat.

And now a new phase beckoned. We hadn't spoken

about the future beyond a few weeks, but I couldn't help imagining it. Until my last day at Payright, "impulsive" wasn't even in my vocabulary.

Connor said he didn't have his own home in America. Most of the time he stayed in his brother's spare room, or occasionally with his parents.

"Doesn't that get awkward?" I'd asked.

"My brother travels a lot for work, and his wife goes with him. I've got the house to myself most of the time, so I've never got around to buying my own place."

If I managed to complete Edith's list and inherited her home, was there any chance he'd want to live in it with me? Would he consider swapping San Francisco for the joys of Berkshire? I closed my eyes and leaned back into the pillow. There was no point in daydreaming until I'd ticked off a few more challenges.

With that in mind, I texted Grant as soon as I woke up.

Me: Any chance you could fit me in for driving lessons next week?

A few minutes later, he replied.

Grant: Monday at three? I'll bring Valium and body armour.

Me: Oh ha ha very funny. See you Monday :)

Maybe I could achieve something before Connor came back? Oh, who was I kidding? If I just managed to not crash it would be a miracle.

As Connor slumbered, I watched the hands of my Mickey Mouse clock sweep closer to the hour of agony. Connor's train to the airport left at one, and even though my chest ached from yesterday's exertions, I insisted on going to the station with him.

"You should stay home and rest," he said as we lay

in bed.

I shook my head, biting my lip as I held back tears. What would Connor think if I broke down? Women probably cried over him all the time, and I didn't want to add to the list.

"At least let me get the groceries?"

"Okay." A sniffle escaped and I turned away.

"You all right?"

"I might be getting a cold."

"You want me to pick up some Nurofen?"

"Yes please." Maybe the pills would dull the ache in my heart.

As Connor's train pulled out, I felt like I should be in one of those old movies where the girl runs along the platform, waving her handkerchief and dabbing at her eyes.

Instead, I managed a sniff that had the businessman reading the paper next to me looking up in disgust, and then smeared my mascara.

As I dodged round a couple of lost-looking tourists wheeling their suitcases, I got one last look at Connor through the window, smiling sadly back at me, a scruffy hat pulled low over his eyes.

I was hollow inside as I sat on the bus back to Edith's. I'd spent over a month with Connor around, and the thought of just a few days without him felt like someone had scooped my heart out and put it in cold storage. What was wrong with me? When Terry went to Benidorm for a week with his mates last year, I'd helped him lift his suitcase into the taxi then gone back to watching *MasterChef*.

Connor hadn't even got to the airport yet, and I was ready to plead on my knees with him to come back. Was this what love felt like? I had little experience in matters of the heart, but if it was, I'd fallen in it.

CHAPTER 22

I COULDN'T BEAR going back to Edith's alone that Saturday night, so I went to see Jaz instead.

Weeks had passed since we spent any time together, and apart from text messages and a few hurried phone calls, we hadn't spoken either. I'd been a terrible friend.

When Connor did the shopping, he'd picked up a gooey chocolate mousse from Tesco and a nice bottle of wine. I resisted the urge to wallow in self-pity and snarf both of them down because when I called Jaz earlier, she'd offered to cook dinner. As long as I didn't mind sharing the table with Amir and Stevie, anyway.

Even Stevie's company was better than my own.

The devil child was sitting in the kitchen when I arrived, strapped into his carry seat. Jaz had put duct tape over the buckle, and Stevie scratched at it with his fingernails, escape the only thing on his mind.

"Keep an eye on him, would you?" she said when I walked in. "He's already got out twice."

"You need to put mittens on him."

Her face lit up. "That's a brilliant idea! I've got a pair in the coat cupboard."

Five minutes later, he glowered at us from the other side of the room as we finished chopping vegetables.

"Where's Amir?" I asked.

"He phoned to say he was running late. He should be back any minute."

Half an hour later, the roast was cooling on the table as Amir dashed in, shedding his coat in the hallway and dropping a bag of shopping next to the fridge.

"Took your time," Jaz said.

"It wasn't my fault. I had to go back to Tesco for milk and bread. I tried to go in the morning but they'd closed the store."

"Closed Tesco? What on earth for?" she asked. I could tell she didn't entirely believe him. "You didn't go to the betting shop again, did you?"

"No! The checkout lady said some famous actor came in this morning. Hollywood's wild child, apparently. Nobody recognised him at first because he'd changed his hair colour and looked more cheerful than usual, but then a couple of girls put two and two together and all hell let loose. He had to escape out the back."

I wondered if Connor saw any of it when he went to pick up dessert. He didn't say anything, so I figured he got there before the chaos, and a good job too. If I'd needed to do the shopping today as well as deal with the pain of him leaving, it would have broken me.

Jaz huffed. "Well, at least you're here now. Can you open the wine?"

Amir fished through the drawer for the corkscrew, then poured us our liquid happiness. I'd barely touched the stuff over the last few weeks because I hadn't needed to with Connor. He'd given me all the happy I wanted. Also, I'd noticed he wasn't a big drinker. Come to think of it, I couldn't remember seeing him touch alcohol at all.

Finally, we settled at the table, and I cut into my chicken. Jaz should have been a chef, the way it melted in my mouth. If I knew how to cook like that I'd never need to visit a restaurant again.

"Have we got a problem with the heating?" Amir asked, looking over at Stevie.

"No, why?" Jaz said.

"Stevie's wearing gloves."

"It's harder for him to open the buckle that way."

"Oh, good plan."

By dessert, Stevie had chewed halfway through one of the straps, and I was seriously considering having my ovaries removed. I nervously fished the packet of contraceptive pills out of my handbag to check I'd taken today's. Yep, I had. I hoped to be getting some soon with Connor, and I wasn't ready to risk a Stevie.

"Catch up next week?" Jaz asked when I was ready to leave. "I want to hear more about your mystery man."

Despite her questions, I'd skimmed over all things Connor. "I'll tell you everything soon, I promise. I just don't want to jinx things, not while he's away. I mean, what if he comes to his senses and stays there?"

"Oh, don't be ridiculous. The man just spent a month nursing you through three broken ribs. I'd say that shows commitment."

I hoped she was right, but I couldn't help the niggling suspicion in my guts that something was going to go pear-shaped.

At least it wasn't the next afternoon's driving lesson in the temporary car Grant's insurance company had provided. I managed to get through a whole two hours without hitting a single obstacle. He only grimaced a little bit when I crunched the gears, and the dual controls worked perfectly when I came up to the back of a truck a teeny bit quickly.

"That wasn't as bad as I thought it would be," I said when we got back to his place.

"Apart from the near thing with the delivery van."

"Who knew he was going to pull over like that?"

"Tomorrow, I think we'll work on stopping distances. Are you staying for dinner? Todd's making chocolate soufflés for dessert."

"Race you inside."

Grant won, because he took the stairs two at a time while I waited for the lift. Damn these aching ribs and my lack of ability to breathe properly.

Todd went to hug me when he opened the door, dressed in a frilly apron and holding a rolling pin. Then he must have seen the fear in my eyes because he dropped his arms.

"Oh, Ella, how are your ribs?"

"A little tender from the seatbelt today, but I couldn't have worn it at all this time last week so they're definitely getting better."

"How about a nice glass of rosé to take your mind off them?"

"I wouldn't say no."

He turned and sashayed back to the kitchen, his dangly earrings swinging as he walked.

One glass became two, and dinner was a long affair as I told them of my adventures over the last six weeks. Like with Jaz, I was light on the details of Connor, even when Todd threatened to withhold dessert.

"I need to get to know him better myself. Even

though we were staying together, he spent most of the time working, and I was zonked out on painkillers in the evenings."

"So do you think he could be The One?" Todd bounced up and down on his chair excitedly.

If the fact that I'd thought of barely anything but him since he'd left meant anything, I'd say it was a definite possibility. Still, I wasn't ready to admit that to anybody but myself. "I like him," was all I said.

Between driving lessons, a dinner out with Jaz and a couple of lunches with Demi, plus studying for my driving theory test, the week passed faster than I thought it would.

I'd only managed a few quick conversations with Connor—between his work and the time difference, it was difficult for us to talk. That made me miss him even more.

Still, it was Saturday morning, and Connor's flight landed in the early afternoon at Heathrow. I'd spent yesterday afternoon at the salon with Demi, getting "ready for bed" as she put it. We'd invited Jaz too, but Barry wouldn't let her have the time off work. Boy, was I glad to be out of that place.

"Are you sticking with blonde?" Demi asked.

"It's grown on me." And Connor seemed to like it. Maybe the saying about blondes having more fun had an element of truth in it?

After the stylist touched up my roots and tidied up my split ends, Demi led me back to the beauty rooms.

Or torture chambers, as I now preferred to think of them.

"Ayeeeeeee!" I screamed when the beautician ripped the first strip of wax away, taking my leg hair and a couple of layers of skin with it. Demi, damn her, glanced up from *Dirty* magazine and smirked. How could she stay so calm?

"It's not funny," I told her.

"You have a low pain threshold. I have this done every fortnight."

Flippin' heck, that didn't bear thinking about. And, it turned out, my legs were only the start.

Once my pins were shiny and smooth, the beautician got a gleam in her eye I didn't like. She beckoned Demi over and the two of them had a consultation.

"What do you reckon?" she asked. "Brazilian? Hollywood? Parisian?"

They were speaking in code. "What are you talking about?"

"This." Demi poked at my bikini line.

"What about it?" Then it dawned on me. "Oh no no no no no. No way."

Demi put her hands on her hips. "You can't leave it like that."

"I wasn't planning to. I have a razor at home."

The beautician sniggered and Demi shook her head. "Honey, a razor's not gonna cut it. You need a lawnmower down there."

I turned quite pink. "Really?" I asked in a small voice.

Connor hadn't said anything when he was, er, down there the other day. But what had he been thinking? I'd be kidding myself if I denied he'd had a bevy of beauties before me. What if he'd been comparing me to them and I'd come up lacking?

"I'll be honest with you because you're my friend. There are definite improvements needed."

I screwed my eyes shut and took a deep breath. "Okay, do the necessary."

At least the broken ribs had gone some way towards preparing me for the pain. Seriously, if the US government ever needed to get information from terrorists again, they should forget the water boarding. A bowl of bubbling wax and a spatula would be enough to get even the most hardened terrorist to confess his sins.

I screwed my eyes shut throughout the ordeal, trying to visualise the good things in life like ice packs, painkillers and soothing aloe vera gel. After an excruciatingly long time, Demi squeezed my hand. "Okay, it's over."

I lifted my head and peered down. Sparkles swam before my eyes and I shook my head, trying to clear my vision. Nope, they were still there. I propped myself up higher.

"Holy hell, what have you done?" I didn't know whether to laugh or cry.

"It's a vajazzle," said the beautician. "They're ever so popular at the moment."

What little hair remained had been trimmed into a heart shape, dyed red and decorated with diamantés. My jaw dropped, and the lady mistook my horror for glee.

"We call that design a 'Heart Attack,'" she told me, smiling.

I could see why. Connor would certainly have one of those when he saw it.

"B-b-but it's red!"

Demi grinned. "He'll love it, trust me."

I glared at her. "Have you ever had one of these?"

"Sure. I got mine done in a rainbow last month. My date ate it up."

"Who were you seeing? Stevie Wonder?"

"Ella, Ella. Relax. I'm the master when it comes to these things."

The beautician poured me a glass of champagne, which helped a little, and I lay back to have my eyebrows done. It was tame in comparison, and as she plucked I wondered how to explain to Connor that we'd have to abstain for the next four or five weeks, which was how long I estimated it would take for the red bits to grow out. I could hardly tell him I'd decided to save myself for marriage, could I? He'd run a mile.

But Ella Lowestein, that sounded all right, didn't it? Ella Goodman-Lowestein. Connor and Ella Goodman-Lowestein.

Ella! Stop it!

When I got home, I tried to pick off the gems, but they were stuck fast. The woman must have used superglue. Short of asking for help at A&E, which would bring its own problems, they were there to stay. I considered shaving the red hair off, but the skin underneath had taken on a pink hue, so I'd be left looking like I had a particularly nasty rash.

Dammit. Why was my life such a disaster?

The first thing I did the next day was check whether the vajazzle had been a particularly nasty nightmare, but when I peered under the duvet the beacon of insanity was still there, twinkling at me. I tried to put it out of my mind and focus on the positive as I boiled a couple of eggs for breakfast.

Connor was on his way back! Only a few hours until I'd feel the sweet touch of his lips on mine. My body ached for him, but in a good way this time. I'd never felt such longing before, and being honest, it scared me a little.

Connor called at eleven to say the flight had landed a few minutes late, but he was on his way. I'd yet to think of a way to explain my latest mishap, but I'd gone beyond caring. I just wanted him.

We were about to sail into uncharted territory, and I hoped we'd be able to weather the storm.

CHAPTER 23

A GRIN BURST onto my face when Connor stepped out of the taxi, and my feet left the ground as I threw myself into his arms and hugged him as tightly as I could without wincing.

"Feeling better, babe?"

I buried my face in his neck. "I am now," I said, my words muffled.

He dropped a soft kiss onto my hair. "Me too," he whispered.

The taxi driver cleared his throat behind us. "That'll be forty-five quid, mate."

Connor had gone back to the States with one small suitcase, but now he unloaded two large ones from the boot of the car. The sight of them made my heart jump.

"That's a lot of stuff."

"I'm planning to stick around for a while."

The instant we got in the front door, the luggage was forgotten as Connor's lips landed on mine. He pushed me back into the wall, and I rubbed myself against him like some brazen hussy. His stubble grazed my cheek as he nipped at my earlobe before trailing kisses along my jaw, and I felt my favourite part of his anatomy growing against me.

It was rubbing right against those fucking diamantés.

Vajazzle or no vajazzle, I couldn't help myself as I wrapped my legs around his waist and ground my centre against him. He kissed me again before he pulled back.

"We can't," he panted.

My face fell. "What? Why? I'm hardly sore at all now."

"It's not that. I have a surprise for you, and I don't want us to be late."

A surprise? How sweet! "What is it?"

He rolled his eyes at me. "Which part of the word 'surprise' do you not understand?"

I unwrapped my legs and dropped to the floor. "Not even a tiny hint?"

"It's indoors."

"That's it? That's all I'm getting?"

"Yep."

"When do we have to leave?"

"The cab's coming back in a half hour."

I squeaked and ran for the stairs. He expected me to get ready to go out in thirty minutes? Before I met him, that would have been easy—drag a brush through my hair and add a quick swipe of lip-gloss. But now I was with *Connor*. I had to look perfect.

His steady footsteps climbed the stairs behind me as I dashed for the bedroom. When he arrived, I was pulling clothes out of the wardrobe onto the bed. Why hadn't I gone shopping this week? I needed to buy more outfits.

"What are you doing?" he asked.

"Panicking—what does it look like?"

"Why?"

"Because you've just told me we're going out, and I

need to find something nice to wear and sort out my hair and do my make-up and—"

He silenced me with a kiss. "You look beautiful."

I glanced down at myself. I was wearing a pair of skinny jeans, cowboy boots and a loose knitted sweater. It was great for lounging around the house in, but for going out? No.

Connor, on the other hand, looked like he'd just stepped out of a Levi's advert.

"I'm not dressed to go anywhere."

He wrapped his arms around my waist and held me still. As his grip tightened, I stopped trying to wriggle away and took the chance to inhale his musky scent. He'd worn cologne today. Something fruity and refreshing, and it reminded me of our rides in the woods.

He smiled down at me. "When I first met you, you were wearing no make-up, a pair of old jeans and a baggy jacket, and I wanted you. My feelings aren't gonna change just because you're wearing something sparkly or a coat of lipstick."

He still hadn't seen the "something sparkly." He might change his mind then.

"Maybe I'll just change my top."

He lay on the bed and propped himself up on his elbows.

"What?" I asked.

"Just waiting for the show."

Four attempts later, I finally found a top I liked—a pretty silver one with a cowl neck at the front.

"Don't lean over in that," Connor said. "I don't want other men looking at what's mine."

His. I shivered when he said it. My heart belonged

to him, as did the rest of me. No doubt about it.

I snuggled up to Connor in the taxi but kept an eye out of the window to try and work out where we were going. I knew we'd gone all the way east along the M4, but once we got into London, I gave up, sat back, and enjoyed the ride.

It was over an hour before we stopped, and I looked up at a white tent-like building that I'd only ever seen on television.

"We're at the O2?"

He grinned, his teeth bright in the car's interior light. "Surprise."

"But why?"

"You have to go to a music concert."

Oh my gosh, he was helping with one of my challenges! I gave him a smacker on the lips. "Connor, I..." I managed to stop myself right before I said, "I love you." Thank goodness. I wasn't ready to say it, and I had no clue whether he was ready to hear it. "I can't thank you enough," I finished.

He helped me out of the door. "You can thank me by enjoying it."

"Who are we going to see?"

"Indigo Rain."

Holy crap! They were the biggest band to come out of LA in years. I adored their energetic vibe, not to mention their insanely hot lead singer. "I thought all their concerts sold out months ago?"

"I bumped into an old friend while I was in LA. He

got me the tickets."

"Don't you live in San Francisco?"

"Yes, but I had to go down to LA for work."

Lucky him. Los Angeles was on the list of places I'd love to visit. I wanted to touch the stars on the Walk of Fame and see the Hollywood sign and cruise along Sunset Boulevard. I'd always been nervous about going, though. Everything was too perfect, not least the people. I'd be the poor relation in a city of glitz and glamour.

Before I could ask Connor more about what he did there, we got swept along in a wave of people, all heading for the entrance. Connor held my hand, keeping me tight against him so we didn't get separated. He seemed a little tense, like he was expecting the worst to happen. Maybe he didn't go to concerts often either?

For a last-minute thing, we sure ended up with a good view. Our seats were to the side of the stage, near the front, level with the performers. I saw every detail of Travis Thorne as he strutted up and down with the microphone, sweat glistening on his face. There was no denying the man was a rock god, but still my thoughts kept straying to Connor, sitting next to me with his arm curled protectively around my shoulders.

Was he enjoying the band or not? Part of the time he seemed to be, but every so often, he'd fidget and look around.

"Are you okay?" I asked.

He gave me a tight smile and nodded. I sighed. He was an angel to bring me, especially if rock wasn't his thing.

Despite his glumness, he did oblige by taking some photos of me with the stage in the background. Between that and the ticket, I'd have proof for Albert that I'd completed the task and more souvenirs for my challenge album, which I'd fallen drastically behind on with all the distractions.

When we finally left in the early hours, my ears were ringing. The band came back for not one encore but two, and the whole crowd leapt to their feet to sing along. Even Connor joined in and hearing his sexy voice in my ears had been the icing on the cake.

Connor turned out to be a full-service kind of guy, and he'd already booked a taxi to take us home again. I needed to insist on chipping in for some of these costs —it wasn't fair for him to keep paying for everything. But that was a conversation for another time, one when tiredness hadn't fuddled my brain. Fatigue caught up with me, and I put my hand over my mouth as I yawned. Today had been wonderful but long.

We were almost at the car park when a blonde girl ran up to us.

"Connor?"

He turned at the sound of his name. "Yeah?"

"I almost didn't recognise you! Are you coming to the party?" She was bright and bubbly, wearing a pair of denim hot pants and a tiny top that seemed impossibly cold for this weather. Her bright red lips and flawless skin put my fledgling beauty routine to shame.

He leaned down and kissed her on the cheek, and

my blood ran hot. "It's been a long time, Lori."

"Too long." She giggled. "So are you coming?"

"I need to take Ella home."

She looked over as if noticing me for the first time. Then she smiled brightly and giggled again. "She can come too."

He shook his head. "I can't."

Her perfect lips formed a pout so effective I figured she must practise in front of the mirror. "Aw, you've changed."

"Maybe another time."

"Awww…" Her eyes lit up, and she waved as she spotted someone else she knew then turned back to Connor. "Fine. I'll see you when you're being less boring."

She turned and strutted off in the direction of her friend, her petite frame quickly swallowed up by the crowd. Connor stared after her, looking troubled.

"Who was that?" I asked.

"Just somebody I used to know."

"From San Francisco?"

"LA."

"Did you spend a lot of time there?"

"A bit," he admitted.

"Did you know her well?" My voice shook. From his evasive answers, and the way he wouldn't meet my eyes, I had a horrible feeling he'd known her intimately.

He still refused to look at me, and his feet appeared to have taken on a new fascination. "If you're asking me what I think you're asking me, I'm not gonna lie to you. The answer's yes."

The bottom dropped out of my world. I knew I wasn't his first, far from it I suspected, but I never dreamed I'd actually meet any of the women who came before me. I could still see her perfect breasts and perky smile in my mind. She looked like she split her time between the gym and the tanning salon. How was I supposed to compete with that?

Connor turned my chin so I was facing him. "Babe, speak to me."

"I don't know what to say."

He pulled me close and laid his forehead against mine. "If I could turn the clock back, I would. But I can't. She's in my past, and you're my future. There's no one I want more than you."

I slipped my arms around his waist and squeezed him tighter against me, blinking back tears. The situation was awkward, but he'd found exactly the right words to soothe my turbulent thoughts. I only hoped that he meant what he said. A broken heart loomed on the horizon if he didn't. No, worse than broken. Shattered.

As he helped me into the taxi and held me by his side, a worry niggled at the back of my mind. How well did I really know Connor? And did he have any more skeletons in his closet?

CHAPTER 24

I AWOKE THE next morning in bed, still wearing my underwear. Connor lay next to me breathing softly, his expression untroubled. I tried to tiptoe to the bathroom, but I'd only got one step when he woke and caught my hand. When I looked back to him, he wore a frown, and his eyes were questioning, pleading almost.

A vision of Lori popped into my head, and I forced her out. Meeting her shook me yesterday, but I refused to let thoughts of her ruin what I had with Connor. I crouched next to him and kissed him on the lips. "I'll be back in a minute. I just need to use the bathroom."

His face relaxed slightly, and he squeezed my hand. "I'm not going anywhere."

A few minutes later, I slipped back under the quilt next to him, and he rolled over to face me. There was a vulnerability about him I hadn't seen before, almost child-like in its appearance.

That was followed by desperation as he kissed me.

I couldn't help but respond, and he pulled me over to straddle him. Between my legs, I felt two things: a throbbing ache and his... Oh, wow. It was huge. And I knew one needed the other.

"Please," I gasped.

"Please what, Ella?" A little of his old cockiness returned.

"I need you," I reached down and stroked his length, and he shuddered. "I need this."

He pulled me forward and kissed me roughly. "Then you'll get it."

Without taking his lips away, he unzipped and released himself, letting me feel all of him for the first time. Boy, it was worth the wait. I spread myself wide and ground my core against his cock until he held my hips still.

"Not so fast, babe. It's your turn first."

Effortlessly, he flipped me onto my back and murmured sweet yet dirty nothings as he sucked, kissed and stroked his way down my body. I drifted off to heaven, floating away on a fluffy white cloud. Was this what it felt like to have an out-of-body experience?

His lips went lower, and his finger grazed my side as he dragged my panties over my hips. Finally... Finally!

Then I heard laughter.

My eyes sprang open, and I looked downwards. Connor was staring wide-eyed at my bits. Oh, shitting hell, with all the distractions I'd managed to put the Heart Attack out of my mind.

"Uh, I can explain..."

His eyes twinkled as he tried, and failed, to stop laughing. He rocked back onto his knees. "Babe, because this is you, I know it's gonna be good."

The spell broken, I blurted out the details of my nightmare visit to the beauty salon. "And they won't come off. I even tried prying them with a nail file."

He bent down and sucked on one. "You're right. Stuck fast." He looked up and grinned. "I know it isn't one of the challenges, but I still feel we should get a photo of this."

Thank goodness Edith hadn't known what a vajazzle was because she surely would have added it to the list. "No! No pictures."

He shrugged. "Never mind. We'll just have to make the best of it."

I had to admit that the sight of his face right below it did make the red furry mess look a lot better. And by the time I screamed out for the first time, it might as well not have existed.

Lunch was a box of chocolates, served up on Connor, just as I'd always dreamed of doing. Once I'd finished licking, we washed off the sticky remains in the shower and stayed in there until the hot water ran out.

By the time we flopped down on the bed again afterwards, I was having trouble standing, and I was pretty sure I'd run Connor dry.

Even so, I looked at him hopefully.

"Don't give me those eyes, babe—there's nothing left in the tank. You'll have to wait a few minutes. We could do with something to eat as well."

I looked over at the remains of the box of chocolates on the nightstand. Two left. I ate one and gave the other to Connor.

He leaned over and licked the last traces of caramel from around my lips. "I was thinking of something more substantial."

Blimey, according to the clock on the nightstand, it was almost five o'clock. "Isn't it a bit early for dinner?"

"We didn't have proper food for lunch, and what we did have, we've sure worked off."

I flopped back on the bed. "I'm not sure I've got the energy to cook. Pizza?"

He turned his head and grinned. "Did I mention I'm keeping you?"

We managed to throw on clothes and get downstairs by the time the delivery guy got there. Connor paid and told him to keep the change.

"You can't keep paying for everything," I said once he'd shut the door.

"Watch me," he said.

I trailed him into the lounge. "Seriously, you can't. You don't work full time. I should contribute."

"You don't work at all."

"No, but Edith left me enough money for a year, and I'll start looking for another job soon."

"Look, if you want to buy shit for yourself, feel free. But if it's stuff for us, I'm buying it."

"You can't do that."

"Yes, I can. Now eat. The pizza's getting cold."

He'd dumped the box on the coffee table, and I flipped back the lid. The delicious aroma of cheese and pepperoni floated out at me. After Connor, it was probably my favourite smell in the world. "Fine, but this discussion isn't over."

"You keep telling yourself that."

How could I both love someone and want to throttle them at the same time? Honestly, sometimes he was beyond impossible. But right now, pizza.

I was full to bursting by the time I sat back on the sofa. Connor and pizza—what more could a girl want?

The man himself took the seat beside me, pulled me

against him and kissed the top of my head. "You and pizza. Best day ever, babe."

Guess I wasn't the only one to think that way. I snuggled into him, feeling happier than I could remember.

"I had an idea for your next challenge," Connor said.

"Does it involve moving?"

"A bit."

"Oh."

"Not right now. Tomorrow. I had a look on the internet, and there's a casino just down the road. How about going there tomorrow to put a few bucks through the slot machines, take some photos, and check off one more thing?"

"That's a great idea! Vegas here we come."

Well, not exactly Vegas, but the Grosvenor Casino on the main road into Reading. Hardly the glitz and glamour of the famous Strip, but not quite the price tag or the jet lag either.

Connor dressed in his usual uniform of jeans, but I decided to put a dress on and do my hair. It wasn't often I got a night out.

"Didn't bring your tuxedo?" I kidded.

"I didn't think I'd need it, so I left it at home," he joked.

At least I thought he was joking. Maybe he wasn't? Did he need a posh suit to go to marketing conferences and the like? There was still so much I didn't know about him but for tonight, I put it out of my mind and gave him a twirl. "What do you think of this dress?"

"You'd look better out of it."

"Put your tongue away. You can take it off me later, but we need to get this casino thing over with first."

Did I just say that? I sounded so...brazen.

And I liked it.

The Grosvenor was the kind of place I'd never have had the guts to go into by myself, whereas Connor merely nodded at the doorman as we swept past.

"Have you ever been to a casino before?" I asked.

"Only in Vegas."

If you planned to go to one, that was the place to do it. "I don't suppose this one'll be a patch on that."

"Sure it will. It's got you in it."

He was the best boyfriend ever. Did I mention that? I pinched myself quickly just to check this was still real then gripped his hand more tightly as he led me into the depths of confusion.

"I don't even know where to start."

"Right here."

He sat me down at a brightly coloured slot machine and showed me what buttons to push to make it eat my money. After ten minutes, I'd won two pounds and lost twenty.

"Smile." Connor pointed his phone camera at me.

I mugged for the lens. "Is there something else we can do? I'm bored of the slot machines now. How do people sit and play on these all day?"

He shrugged. "Beats me."

A casino employee wandered up to us. "Can I interest you in joining the poker tournament that's about to start?"

"How much is it?" I asked.

"The buy in's fifty pounds."

"Why not?" I said. After all, I'd only live once, and playing poker sounded a lot more glamorous than pushing the big yellow button.

"Do you know how to play?" Connor asked as we followed the casino guy.

"No, but I figured I might as well lose at something different for a change. Do you?"

"I've played occasionally. Do you want me to explain?"

I leaned over and kissed his cheek. "Please."

The game was due to start at eight, which gave us twenty minutes to wait. I nabbed a table in the bar while Connor ordered us drinks, and I couldn't help feeling a little guilty as he set his coke down next to my glass of wine.

"We should have got a taxi."

"I don't mind driving."

"But you're stuck on soft drinks."

He took both my hands in his across the table. "I'm drunk on you."

That sounded so cheesy we both burst out laughing. But I couldn't deny I appreciated the sentiment. Having a man as special as Connor be so open about his feelings for me gave me a high like no other. I drank in every plane of his gorgeous face while he gave me a brief rundown on what all the cards meant.

"Okay, I can remember that aces are good and a

pair is quite good, but I've forgotten the rest. Can you go over it again?"

He did, but after the third time, I didn't have the heart to tell him it was getting mixed up with the alcohol and evaporating out of my brain.

"Time to sit down, ladies and gents," the man with the cards announced.

"Better do what the croupier says, babe," Connor said.

Oh well, wish me luck.

I'd hoped to sit next to Connor, but the croupier pointed across the table and along a bit instead. Connor ended up next to a sour-faced woman who looked fifty and dressed thirty. She kept staring at him like he was a prize stallion, and I suppose that wasn't far from the truth. He was definitely hung like one, anyway.

The first two cards were dealt, and try as I might, I barely remembered anything Connor told me. I didn't have a pair. Therefore, I had nothing. I lost the bit of money the croupier charged me at the beginning then folded.

That was kind of how it went on for the next few rounds. If the croupier held out his hand, I gave him chips. If not, I folded and watched Connor. His pile of chips slowly grew, and he certainly seemed to know what he was doing. Plus he looked hot.

That carried on until I was dealt two queens. A pair! That was good, right? I shoved some chips into the middle and then some more.

"Three of a kind," the croupier said and shoved the whole pile back at me.

Three? Where was the third one? Was I missing something? Oh yes, there it was in the middle. I remembered now.

Now I had lots of chips. I spent time stacking them into pretty coloured piles while I motioned to the barman for another glass of wine. This was great. Why didn't I come to the casino more often?

I lost a few chips with a pair of threes and won a handful with a pair of tens. By then, there was only me, Connor, the cougar-lady and a shrewd-looking gentleman left at the table.

I was ever so happy when the woman shoved her chair back angrily and stomped off. At least she wouldn't be staring at my boyfriend now. I watched the cellulite on the back of her thighs, mesmerised as she marched over to the bar and ordered a fancy drink with little umbrellas in it. I wanted one of those. It was such a pretty shade of pink. I waved at the barman again, and he happily obliged. Mine even came with a couple of cherries on a stick.

Connor licked his lips as I sucked one of my cherries. Did I mention he was hot?

"Sir, are you going to call?"

Connor tore his eyes away and glared at the croupier then pushed some of his chips into the middle. I slipped a shoe off and ran my foot up Connor's leg. At least I thought it was his leg until the casino dude leapt back like he'd plugged his fingers in a live socket. Oops.

We each got more cards, and Connor traded stares with the other man left at the table. Me? I only had eyes for one man. Tonight he looked dark and dangerous and... Oh, the casino dude wanted more chips. Here you go.

"Awww." I couldn't help being sad when the mean-looking man took all Connor's chips.

Connor shrugged and left the table, pausing to drop a kiss on my lips as he passed. Heat flooded downwards. I started to get up and follow him, my mind on his delicious, tight bottom, but the croupier gave me a dirty look so I sat back down again. The bastard held his hand out for more chips.

I glanced at my cards. A seven and eight of hearts. Well, Connor certainly had mine, and right now, I wanted to go home and give him other parts of me as well. Oh, what the hell? It was only fifty quid. The sooner I lost, the sooner I'd be on the way to my first orgasm of the night. I shoved my whole pile of chips into the middle and pushed my chair back.

"Straight flush," the croupier said, and gave all the chips back to me. Oh, dammit, did this mean I had to stay?

The furious and slightly fuzzy-looking man opposite me got up and stormed off. Hang on, had I won? I looked at Connor, and he was beaming at me.

"Well done, babe. I though you said you hadn't played before?"

I swayed alarmingly as I tried to walk towards both of him then fell into his arms. Swooned. Swooned sounded much better.

"Did you have a bit too much to drink?"

I can't remember what my response was, but I think there was a hiccup in there.

The last thing I recalled about that night was Connor carrying me up to bed and laying me gently down on the mattress. He climbed in beside me, just in time for my victory speech.

"Ha, now I can buy the pizza."

CHAPTER 25

TUESDAY WAS HANGOVER day.

"I need a fry up," I mumbled to Connor.

"No you don't. That's just a rumour. You need painkillers, a smoothie, and a lot of water."

"That all sounds far too healthy. And could you stop shouting?"

He laughed, and the sound ricocheted around my skull like a bowling ball. "I'm not shouting. And trust me, it's the only thing that helps. I've tried everything."

"But you don't even drink."

"Not any more. I used to." He leaned forward and stroked my hair off my forehead then planted a kiss on it. "Stay there, and I'll go get you some juice."

I groaned and rolled over. I felt like I'd gone ten rounds with Muhammad Ali in my sleep, and now a troupe of break-dancers was practising in my head. The constant throbbing made me screw my eyes shut, and at least that blocked out the daylight.

My hero came back soon enough with a packet of paracetamol and a jug of water. But what was in that other glass? It looked vile, and when I took a mouthful it tasted even worse.

"Ugh, what is it?"

"Orange juice, banana, kiwi, kale and avocado."

"It's disgusting."

"It's good for you."

"I'd rather be bad."

He grinned. "I thought you'd never ask."

I tried to raise my head, but it didn't want to play the game. "Urgh."

Connor dropped onto the bed next to me. "On second thoughts, I'm not into necrophilia. Why don't you get some more rest, and I'll wake you up for lunch?"

Perfect. Connor was perfect. That was my last thought before I dropped off again.

Lunch was salad. A big bowl of green stuff accompanied by grilled chicken breasts and more water.

"It's to help get rid of the toxins. It's got antioxidants in it," Connor said as he took a seat opposite me.

"Are you secretly a nutritionist?"

"No, I just like to know what I'm eating." He poured me another glass of juice. "While you were lazing around this morning, I sorted out your next challenge." He looked ever so pleased with himself.

"Are you going to tell me what we're doing this time?"

With the things I'd ticked off so far, there weren't that many tasks left. It would be nice if we were travelling to another country, but that seemed unlikely if he'd only come up with it this morning.

"We're going to the zoo."

"The zoo?"

"You need to see the elephants." He slid over a piece of paper he'd printed out.

I'd given him the password to my computer the other day so he could check his email. For a minute, I'd struggled to remember it but then it came to me. Legolas. I'd set it up when I was going through my Lord of the Rings phase. Apart from using the laptop to slowly and painfully type up my coursework when I was at uni, I barely turned the thing on.

The gift certificate informed me he'd booked us a day out at Colchester Zoo, which included a VIP tour of the elephant house and a chance to feed them. That had to count as Edith's "up close and personal," right?

"Thank you," I said softly. He really had gone out of his way to make me feel special.

"Anything for you, babe."

I got up early the next morning to pack us snacks and drinks for the trip. Lunch was included, according to the blurb, but as it would take a couple of hours to get there, I thought we might get peckish. Normally I hated long journeys, but as I'd be shut in a car with Connor it wouldn't exactly be a hardship.

"I've made sandwiches, and I've got crisps, biscuits, and bottles of water," I told him when he came downstairs, his hair still damp from the shower.

"Sounds good."

I ran the back of my hand along his cheek. "Forgot to shave today?"

"Thought I'd go with the natural look for a change."

"It's hot." Different but hot. I nuzzled him with my cheek. "But it might chafe, especially on my thighs."

I went pink as I realised what I'd said, but Connor only laughed as he pulled me in for a gentle kiss.

"I'll shave for you later."

Connor wasn't big on talking while he was driving, but we put the radio on and sang along to a couple of tracks, which made the journey go faster. Well, I started off attempting to sing, but I soon left the words to Connor. His velvety voice almost had me begging him to pull over into the nearest Travelodge.

I was a little nervous as we drew into the car park at the zoo, but not shaking like when I had arrived at Linden Hollow. Now I'd been around the horses I wasn't quite so scared of animals in general, not to mention the fact that Connor was with me, really with me, for moral support.

Johnny, the keeper who would be showing us round, met us at the visitor centre and from there it was a short walk to the Elephant Kingdom.

"We've got five elephants," Johnny told us. "One bull, three adult females, and our latest addition, a baby girl."

He showed us around the spacious indoor quarters then took us out to the paddocks, pointing out the waterfall and pool area.

"Why is that one all on its own?" I asked, pointing.

"That's the male. In the wild, the bulls are solitary creatures, so it's not unusual for him to be alone. He's got his own enclosure."

"Aw, look, there's the baby." She was peeping out from behind another elephant.

"Yes, we're part of the European Endangered Species Breeding Programme. We hope to have great success with it."

"I can't believe she's so tiny. She's like a proper elephant that got shrunk in the wash."

Johnny laughed. "Yes, she is that. Do you want to feed her? She hasn't been getting enough milk from mum, so she gets bottles as well."

"I'd love to." That would definitely be something Edith would smile about if she could see me now.

He led us back to the elephant house, and the baby followed with mum ambling along behind. Once inside, Johnny herded us into a roped-off area while he went to get a couple of bottles.

"They're kinda cool, aren't they?" Connor said, looking up at the mother. "Even bigger than I thought. Wouldn't it be fun to see them in the wild someday?"

"You mean go on a safari?"

"Yeah, why not?"

"With you?"

"You got any other men you're seeing?" He raised an eyebrow.

"Well, no, it's just... I guess that seems like a big step."

"Babe, I spent most of last night buried inside you, and you think taking a trip together is a big step?"

"Well, when you put it like that..." I broke into a grin. "I'd love to go on holiday with you."

Johnny came back with the bottles. "If you stand over here by the gate, she'll come and take the milk."

I did as he said, and the baby soon started feeding. Connor stood back and took plenty of photos of me grinning away. The baby finished the first bottle and pushed at me to get the second.

"Aw, she nudged me. Did you see that? She—" She shoved me again, and I lost my balance. "Oh shit."

And it was, literally. It went squelch as I sat in it, and judging by the warmth that seeped through my trousers, it was fresh, too.

My cheeks burned as I looked over at Connor. The bastard was doubled over laughing. Johnny pushed the elephants out of the way, and I noticed he couldn't keep the mirth off his face either.

"Oopsy daisy," he said. "I don't think that's ever happened before."

Oh, that made me feel much better. It was great to know I was the first person to totally embarrass myself by landing in a steaming pile of elephant poop.

I tried to smile rather than cry. "It's always good to be a trailblazer."

"I'll see if I can find something for you to change into."

Connor was wiping his eyes by then.

"It's not funny," I snapped.

"Yeah it is. I got it on film, too." He held up his phone.

I made a grab for it, but he held it out of reach. "That better not go anywhere near YouTube, or...or..."

"Or what, babe?"

I put my hands on my hips. "No more blowjobs."

I heard a snicker from behind me and slowly turned. Johnny stood there, holding out a pair of green trousers, surgical scrubs like doctors wear.

"You heard that last bit, didn't you?"

"Hard to miss." He tried to look more serious but didn't quite manage. "One of the vets said you can have these. They've got a drawstring so they should fit."

"Thanks," I said, taking them. "Where can I change?"

He pointed me towards the ladies' room, and I slunk off, wondering whether it would be practical to simply keep walking and never come back.

It was a long way home. In the end, I changed into the ugly new trousers and bundled my jeans up into the plastic bag the scrubs came in. It was a good thing Connor found it all so amusing. He'd need his sense of humour when he smelled the inside of his truck tomorrow.

Desperate to look like I wasn't mortally humiliated, I finished the rest of the tour with Connor. I got a few funny looks from other visitors for my attire, but thankfully most of the female guests were too taken with Connor to notice what I was wearing. I could have been in a tutu, and they'd still only have had eyes for him.

"Gotta love those elephants," Connor chuckled in the car on the way home.

"I didn't mind the elephants. I just wasn't so keen on what came out of their backsides."

"It could only happen to you."

Well, of course it could. I was the world's biggest klutz. Nothing like that would ever happen to Connor. He sailed through life as if he was coated with Teflon.

"Thanks for pointing that out," I said, my mouth a tight line.

He reached over and squeezed my thigh. "Look on the funny side, babe. It'll be a great story to tell the grandkids."

I turned and stared at him.

"Just an expression," he said hurriedly. "How do you fancy going back to Linden Hollow tomorrow? Jenny sent me a message to say there's a dressage competition on Saturday. We could pick up where we left off with a few more lessons."

"I-I-I'm not sure." My most vivid memory of horses was lying on the damp earth while Folly stood dejectedly off to the side. My ribs had barely healed. Was it really a good idea to try riding again so soon?

Connor reached over for my hand. "You know what they say: If you fall off, it's best to get straight back on again."

"I bet the person who came up with that didn't end up in hospital."

"How about we just go and visit Jenny? If you don't feel up to riding, we can have a few days relaxing in the countryside instead."

Now, that was a good suggestion. I had to admit I missed Folly, and I could take her some carrots. "I'd love that."

"I'll give Jenny a call and fix it up."

CHAPTER 26

AS SOON AS Connor stopped the truck, I rushed over to the stables and flung my arms around Folly's neck. She looked a bit surprised but kept eating her hay anyway.

A chuckle came from the doorway. "Looks like you missed her," Jenny said.

"I did." I'd never had a pet before, or formed any sort of bond with an animal, so it surprised me how much of a soft spot I'd developed for the mare. And when Connor and I chatted on the way over, I'd decided to try riding again after all. "How have you been?"

She rolled her eyes. "Last week we had a pair that were even worse than Annabel and Felicity, but apart from that, everything's good."

"Ouch."

Connor sidled up behind her and put his hands over her eyes. "Guess who?"

It wasn't hard to tell—his low, smoky voice was a dead giveaway. She turned and smiled at him, and he kissed her on the cheek. I noticed that even she blushed. He had that effect on people.

"I've put the luggage in our room. You ready for your first lesson?"

I loved the way he said "our room." It made me go

all tingly. I hoped there would be many more of "our" things to come.

"Oh, Connor, the girl's just got here! At least let her have a cuppa first," Jenny said.

"Put the kettle on, then."

After tea, and maybe one or six biscuits, I surprised myself with how little I'd forgotten. Connor still made a tough teacher, but his commands were interspersed with smiles, and those were what made me get the wobbles. I made a mental note not to look at him during the competition because I'd most likely end up on the ground.

The next day, my lesson in the morning went well, and I'd learned the test for the following afternoon. Prelim 14 had plenty of circles to attempt plus the dreaded canter.

"You want to go on a hack this afternoon?" Connor asked afterwards.

"I'm not sure that's a good idea."

"It was a freak accident, babe. The best way to get on in life is by confronting what scares you."

"Okay," I said, but I wasn't feeling it.

He gave me a hug, wrapping me up in his strong arms and holding me close. "You're braver than you think."

"That's hard to believe."

"I believe it."

Once again, I wondered what I'd done to deserve this man. He had more faith in me than I had in myself.

A tear surprised me by rolling down my cheek, not due to sadness but as an outlet for the jumble of emotions in my head.

Connor's eyes widened. "What's wrong?"

Should I tell him I loved him? What if that sent him running? The words were on the tip of my tongue, but I bit them back. "Nothing, I'm just happy."

He raised an eyebrow. "Funny way of showing it."

I kissed him instead.

"Better," he said, when we finally broke apart.

When we got back from our hack, I was on a high. Folly had behaved perfectly, and we even cantered on the common, Connor loping alongside me on Captain, relaxed and gorgeous.

"Do you want to go to the pub for dinner?" Jenny asked, as I untacked Folly.

"Is there karaoke?"

She shook her head.

"Drag queens?"

"Nope."

"So it would just be a quiet evening out?"

"Er, there might be line dancing." Jenny gave me a sheepish smile.

Me and my three left feet were certainly not cut out for that. "Do you mind if we stay in? I'm really nervous about tomorrow, and I'm not sure having a hangover would help matters." Because copious amounts of alcohol was surely the only way to survive the embarrassment of tripping over my own toes.

"Sure. Fancy a takeaway?"

"My treat."

I was terribly nervous about the test the next day, but as I had no aspirations to do anything but not fall off, I didn't feel quite as stressed as the other competitors looked. I cringed as one girl on a pretty grey pony walloped it for the crime of spooking at the mounting block.

"There's no need for that," Jenny muttered. "Animals respond much better to kindness than cruelty."

Connor stood at the side of the warm-up ring and gave me a few hints, but he'd given me the biggest boost the night before. It turned out Jenny was right—a good shag really did open up your hips.

As I rode into the arena, the bell rang, and I turned down the centre line. Folly's ears pricked up at the sight of the judge in her car at the far end, and I swear she put an extra spring in her step. I'm not sure I breathed for the duration, but a few minutes later we walked out on a long rein at point A as specified, and I patted Folly's neck.

"It's done!" I slid off Folly into Connor's arms. "I didn't fall!"

"You were great, babe."

Jenny strode up, clutching her camera. "I got plenty of photos." She ran her finger down the lapel of her jacket, which I'd borrowed. "You looked really smart."

I felt joy mixed with relief. Another challenge done,

and not only that, I'd enjoyed it. "Can we come back some time and ride?" I asked Connor. "I mean, I know I don't have to, but I want to."

"I'm glad you've got the bug as well. And one day, I want to take you home with me so we can ride on the ranch."

My eyes widened. That was the first time he'd ever suggested I get involved in his life back in America. I reached over and took his hand. "I'd really like that."

He looked over my shoulder. "You've let go of Folly."

Oops. She was wandering off in the direction of the catering van, but a quick-thinking child in a show jacket studded with pink diamantés grabbed the reins and returned her.

"Thanks."

"You're supposed to keep hold of the rope," she said, before wandering off, ice cream in hand.

Connor stopped laughing long enough to help me load Folly onto the horsebox. We were just closing up the back when Jenny came running up, waving something.

"You came sixth!" she squealed, thrusting a purple rosette into my hands. "That's awesome!"

It was the first time I'd won any sort of prize, and I held it up, extraordinarily proud of myself. This one was for Edith.

We hung around at Linden Hollow for a few more days, and a part of me wished we could stay forever. I was learning to love the countryside, and I could see riding was in Connor's blood. But Monday came and Jenny had more guests coming in. It was time to go home.

"I've got six challenges left," I said to Connor in the car.

"Remind me what they are again."

"I have to go skiing on snow, try speed-dating, visit another country, have a go at scuba diving and throw a party. Oh, and drive a Ferrari, but I've got to learn to drive a normal car first, and that's probably going to take me the rest of the year."

I had more driving lessons booked for this week, and Grant reckoned we were going to work on my reversing skills. I wasn't so sure that was the best idea, seeing as I had enough trouble with going forwards.

Connor stared out the windscreen, deep in thought. "I reckon we could get the skiing done this week, and much as it hurts to think about it, the speed-dating."

"It's coming into summer. Isn't skiing a winter thing?"

"Edith's letter just said it had to be on snow, right? Nothing about having to go to a ski resort?"

I nodded.

"Then why don't we go to one of those indoor ski centres? They have snow."

I twisted to face him. "That's a brilliant idea! I can look for one on the internet when we get home."

"And let's get the speed-dating over with. I'll tell you now, I hate the idea of you sitting and talking to another man like that."

"I'm not so keen on it either," I admitted. "Are you coming? Will I have to beat the women away with a stick?"

"Too damn right I'm coming. I'll make sure I piss the women off, don't worry. Usually that happens effortlessly."

I thought back to when I'd first met him. If he brought that persona out to play, I could well believe it.

While I learned how to do a seventeen point turn and created chaos on the surrounding roads the next morning, Connor researched my next two challenges. He found a ski slope with real snow and a speed-dating event in a local bar on the coming Friday evening. We booked for both. That would be two more tasks done.

"Have you been skiing before?" I asked him as we walked out to the car on Wednesday morning.

"A couple of times," he admitted. "My dad's the skier in the family. Me and my brother used to spend more time having snowball fights."

"What's your brother called?"

"Scott."

"Is he older or younger?"

"A year older, and he's never let me forget it." He rolled his eyes.

"Do you get on okay?"

"Mostly. He's always been the responsible one, and we've had a few clashes over the years."

"I wish I could have had a proper family," I said, voicing something that I'd only ever told Edith.

Connor pulled me into a hug. "You can share mine. They're gonna love you."

He wanted me to meet his family! My heart did a

little jump. What were they like? Were they one of those close families that spent every holiday together? What did his parents do for a living? His brother?

Before I could ask any more questions, Connor handed me his phone. "Do me a favour and put the address in the SatNav, will you? We need to get going or we'll be late."

After a momentary hiccup where I tried to send us to the French Alps with a journey time of about three and a half weeks, I managed to sort out the postcode for the right place. I put the phone in the holder and looked over at Connor. He had that sweet look of concentration on his face, the one he always got as he drove.

My excitement turned to apprehension when we pulled into a parking space outside the ski centre, and that feeling only mounted as we tried on jackets and trousers to rent.

"I can hardly move," I said, once I was bundled up into all the gear. "And it's really hot."

"It's minus five out there," Connor said. "You'll be glad of it in a minute."

Our instructor came out to meet us. Well, my instructor. It was obvious Connor already knew what he was doing. We started off with a brief introduction on how to stand then shuffled off to the nursery slope. The instructor led us over to a travelator, a huge conveyor belt moving steadily skywards.

"You need to hop on that, and it'll take you to the top of the slope."

Fine for him to say. He might as well have asked me to tap dance on it, for all the hope I had.

Connor saw my worry. "It's easy, babe. All you need

to do is stand on it. I'll go up first and help you get off at the top."

I gulped as he stepped on and rose upwards. He made it look so easy. The instructor gave me a little nudge, indicating that I should do the same, and I lurched forward, a duck to Connor's gazelle. Then I was on and moving! Maybe this wasn't so bad after all.

I turned to give the instructor a thumbs up, and that was when I felt something click. Obviously, I hadn't done my boots up properly, because before I could process what was happening, they detached from the skis and I went tumbling downwards. I was tossed around at the bottom like a cork in a troubled sea, rolling over and over as my skis continued up the conveyor without me.

I caught a glimpse of Connor's face, looking down from the top of the slope in horror, then the instructor dragged me along by my arms to get me off the bloody thing. My knees cracked as I struggled to my feet, hitching up my trousers which had slipped down enough to border on indecent.

Connor ploughed expertly to a stop beside me, and although he said, "Fuck me, are you all right?" I could tell he was trying not to laugh.

A switched-on eight-year-old turned up seconds later with my skis. "You okay, lady?" he asked.

"I think so."

"You know you're supposed to stay on the skis, right?"

Thanks for that kid. "I'll try to do that next time."

He gave me a grin before skiing off gracefully.

Awesome. I'd just been bested by a child. Again.

"Do you think Edith would mind if I did the horse

riding part twice instead?" I asked Connor.

He held me by my hands. "Come on, have another go. You can do it."

Somehow, with Connor hanging onto one side of me, and the instructor helping on the other, I managed to ski down the slope upright by the end of the afternoon. The instructor roped in another member of staff to take a photo, and I practically ran out to the car.

"Thank goodness that's over," I said to Connor. "I think it was the worst one yet."

"Worse than the elephant shit?"

"Thanks for reminding me. Are you sure you want to be seen out in public with someone who's a complete klutz?"

He dragged me over into his arms, and the gear knob stuck painfully in my side as his lips brushed over mine. "I love you because you're a klutz, not in spite of it."

Time stopped, as did my heart. "You love me?"

"Of course I love you. Did you miss the part where I've spent every minute I could with you for the last two months?"

"Well, no, but..."

"But what?"

"I guess... I just didn't think anybody would ever love me."

"You're easy to love."

I burrowed into him, feeling the warmth of his body and the beat of his heart. "I love you too."

We must have stayed like that for five minutes, just being us, until the jabbing in my side became too much to take. Reluctantly, I wriggled back over to my seat.

"You ready to go?" he asked.

I nodded. "Could we stop for a snack on the way home? I'm starving." As if on cue, my stomach grumbled its agreement.

"Sure, babe."

A few minutes later, Connor pulled off the main road into a shopping centre with me still basking in the warmth of his recent declaration.

"This do?" he asked.

"As long as I can get a sandwich or something, it's perfect."

We held each other tight as we rode up the escalator from the car park. At least I didn't have skis on any more so I could stay upright. I tried to put the mess at the Snozone out of my mind. It was done now. I never had to ski again, and here I was with the most perfect man in the world.

At least, that was what I thought until the escalator rose to the next floor.

CHAPTER 27

THE SHOPPING MALL stretched away in front of us as the escalator reached the first floor. John Lewis on the left, Marks and Spencer on the right. But that wasn't what caught my attention.

Connor saw it at the same time as me. "Fuck." He closed his eyes and squeezed my hand tighter.

Smack bang in front of us, a huge billboard spanned the wall. It had to be twelve feet high and twice that wide. On the left-hand side, a blonde man reclined on white sheets, naked except for a pair of white boxer briefs, which covered a very generous package. A stunning blonde lady stood to the side looking down on him. Her floaty white negligee grazed his shoulder, and a halo glowed above her curly locks.

I couldn't fault him. Either the man was genetically blessed or a Photoshop wizard got involved somewhere along the line. Still, preferring my men with dark hair, my eyes soon slid to the other couple in the image.

The right-hand side mirrored the left, except devil horns peeped out of the woman's dark curls. Her black and red basque made the most of her assets as she trailed her riding crop along the man's side. He lay on black sheets, a hand resting on his toned abs just above a bulge that would make lesser men weep.

I knew that part of the picture wasn't

photoshopped.

How?

Because the man on the right was Connor.

Just in case I was in any doubt as to whether my eyes were deceiving me, the words "#TEAMBLAKE or #TEAMCONNOR - You decide!" were written underneath in foot-high letters. The small print helpfully gave a website address where people could go to vote.

I blinked a couple of times, but Connor's bits were still right there in front of me, several times larger than life. Just to be sure, I pinched myself but achieved nothing more than reddened skin. Finally, I dragged my eyes away and looked at Connor. His eyes were still closed. Denial was a wonderful thing.

Anger bubbling up inside me, I snatched my hand away from his and stared until he cracked a lid open. My mouth set in a hard line. "Did you not think it would be a good idea to mention this?"

He let out a long breath. "I wanted to. I tried... I didn't know what to say."

"You told me you worked in marketing."

He tried a grin. "Well, it kind of is."

I shoved him away. "Don't give me that look." My voice rose an octave. "I thought you meant you wrote advertising slogans or something, not fronted the latest Calvin Klein campaign!"

"Shit, I'm sorry, babe."

"Don't call me your babe. You didn't care about me enough to be honest. How many others have there been? How many other times have women seen what I thought was for my eyes only?"

"A few," he admitted.

I narrowed my eyes. "How many?"

"Hell, I can't remember them all. I lose track. Recently, Calvin Klein, Levi's, Diesel. I'm supposed to start shooting G Star Raw in a few weeks."

"What did you plan to tell me then? That you were busy preparing PowerPoint presentations?"

He rubbed the bridge of his nose and frowned. "I don't know. I hadn't thought that far ahead. I was just taking one day at a time."

Our raised voices had caused a small crowd to gather. As they stood staring, I wanted to sink into the ground and wither away. This was worse than the elephant poop, worse than the travelator, worse than everything.

Then a girl at the front looked at the billboard, stepped forward, and squinted at Connor.

"OMG!" she shrieked. "It's him! It's Connor Lowes!"

We both watched in horror as heads turned all over the shopping mall, and in slow motion, a stampede started. Women from Adidas to Zara stopped what they were doing and made a beeline for him.

He looked at me and I looked at him.

"Run," he said.

He grabbed my hand and pulled me towards the stairs. Even though I was furious, I had no choice but to go with him as the herd of girls snapped at our heels. I almost tripped over a rubbish bin as we sprinted for the exit, and they gained a few feet as Connor hoisted me up and half carried me with him. Across the car park we ran, and they were still on our tails as we reached Connor's truck and locked ourselves in.

He leaned back against the headrest for a second

and closed his eyes. "Fuck me, that was worse than Tescos."

"Just go, would you?"

He jammed the key in the ignition and peeled out of the car park, leaving a swarm of girls with camera phones in our wake.

Guts churning, I clicked my seatbelt on, keeping as far to the left of the car as possible. All I could see was Connor lying on that bed with that...that...dominatrix behind him. Women the world over would be staring at him in his underwear like that. The thought made me feel sick.

"Say something, babe."

"Asshole."

"I think I preferred it when you were quiet."

We lapsed into silence again, a painful chasm opening up between us. By the time we got back to Edith's the discomfort was a palpable thing, a pulsating energy filling the car with its bad vibes.

"Do you want me to stay in a hotel tonight?"

I nodded quickly. How could I face him? Sure, I knew we should talk but where did we start? I needed some time to process all this.

He tried to lay his hand on mine, but I pulled it away. If he touched me right now that would only add another layer to my confusion. One brush of his fingers could make me forget my own name.

He settled for shrugging. "I'll just come in and get a few things."

I paced the lounge while he went up to the bedroom, listening to his footsteps on the floor above. Something pounded in my chest, but it couldn't be my heart. That was scattered across the floor of a shopping mall somewhere on the outskirts of London.

Connor returned and dropped a bag next to the door before he came over to me. Face serious, he got in closer than was comfortable and locked his eyes on mine. I tried to step back but the wall blocked my way.

"Ella, I love you. That hasn't changed. It's never going to change. I've been in darkness for so long, and you're my light."

"I don't know you."

"Then get to know me. Ask me anything and I'll tell you." A note of desperation crept into his voice.

I shook my head. "I need a few days. Give me that. Please."

He picked up my hand and kissed it, and when he let go, it fell limply to my side.

"I love you," he whispered one more time before he went out the door.

The instant the lock clicked I dropped back onto the sofa, hugging a cushion to me. I thought I'd known Connor, but now it seemed I'd fallen for a smooth facade. Who was he, really? Did I want to find out? He said he wanted a future with me but was this the way our life would be? Me giving him everything and getting half-truths and evasions in return?

As I tried to get my thoughts straight, memories of the good times came flooding back. Connor at my side in hospital. Connor riding next to me in the fields. Connor holding my hair back as I vomited. Okay, so that wasn't exactly a good time but would a man do that if he didn't care at least a little?

I'm not sure how long I sat there before I heard a knock on the front door. Hours? Minutes? My heart jumped. Was it Connor? Had he come back? A shiver of a thrill ran through me at the mere possibility and I cursed myself. My damn body, betraying my brain like that.

A glance at my watch showed I'd been alone for over two hours, but I still didn't know what to say to him. Thoughts jumbled, I hurried to the door, not sure whether to be relieved or disappointed when I recognised the outline of Demi through the frosted glass.

I settled for relieved, because when I opened the door, she held out wine and cupcakes. I took the bag from her as she leaned on a crutch and limped over to the sofa.

"What's up?" I asked, nodding at her leg.

"Twisted my bloody ankle last night. It's all strapped up, and the doctor said I've got to take a couple of days off."

"Did you do it dancing?"

"Nope. Nothing that interesting. I tripped over Snowflake." Snowflake, Demi's black cat, adopted her a few months ago. After he'd mewed outside the door to her flat for three days, getting thinner and thinner, she'd given up and let him in. "Somehow that makes it worse."

"Is Marcus okay about it?" Marcus was her boss at Silk, a chain of gentlemen's clubs with a few branches in and around London. She'd gone up in the world since Edith went to see her at The Pink Panda.

"Marcus is always okay about things like that. He's a good guy. He sent me a bunch of flowers and told me to take as much time to heal as I needed."

That was certainly an improvement on Barry. Last time I took a day off sick, he'd questioned me over the phone until I excused myself to throw up.

Oh shoot. Throwing up. I thought of Connor again and eyed the bottle of wine Demi brought. "Do you want a cup of tea or do you want to open that?"

She looked at her watch. "It's four thirty. Isn't it a bit early for wine?"

"Nope," I said, and burst into tears.

She didn't miss a beat, just got up and threw her arms around me. "What is it?"

"Connor," I managed to get out.

"Oh, tell me he hasn't done the dirty on you?"

I couldn't speak. The words wouldn't get past the tears.

"Do you want me to tell everyone he's got a tiny dick like I did with Terry? I've got even more Facebook and Twitter followers than last time."

I shook my head. "Everyone knows he hasn't. That's the whole problem," I sobbed.

"Come again?"

Between slugs of wine, I managed to get out the whole sorry story. The further through it I got, the more Demi's mouth hung open.

"So let me get this straight," she said when I got to the end. "You mean to tell me you're dating Connor Lowes?"

"I guess. I mean, I don't know. I don't know what I'm doing with him anymore."

She shook her head, incredulous. "I didn't realise he was even out of rehab yet."

"Hang on. Rehab?"

"Holy shit, you didn't know that either?"

I closed my eyes. "I don't know anything."

Demi made a quick trip to the kitchen for another

bottle, then hauled out my laptop and typed Connor's name into a search engine. Millions of hits came up seconds later.

We looked at the pictures first. Only a few, the more recent ones, showed him as I knew him. In the older snaps he had bleached blonde hair, his face arranged in a perpetual sneer.

A few showed him with his brother. He'd done a bit of acting, Connor said. It turned out Scott Lowes was a card-carrying member of the A-list, starring in three Hollywood blockbusters in the last year alone. Not only that, but when we looked up his biography, Connor was also a movie star. He'd made a few films before he went off the rails.

Ah yes, that brought us to his fall from grace, documented in glorious technicolour by numerous gossip websites. If I'd ever read them, I would have known. There were pictures of Connor falling out of clubs with a different woman on his arm every time. There were pictures of him cavorting in swimming pools with scantily clad girls. There were pictures of him unconscious, lying in a pool of his own vomit. His pièce de résistance, the scandal before he went into rehab, involved the police finding him passed out at the wheel of his car, which sat parked on a lamppost with a pair of hookers in the backseat.

"I can't believe this," I whispered.

"It's fucking nuts."

Demi topped up my glass and passed me another cake, a chocolate one this time. I peeled the wrapper off without thinking and jammed it in my mouth.

After the lamppost episode, Connor disappeared. Nobody saw or heard from him in a year until he appeared back on the scene playing the bad boy for Calvin Klein.

Some rumours said he was in rehab, others reckoned he'd been playing hermit in the wilds of America, but I knew where he'd been for at least part of that time. Linden Hollow, with me. And Jenny. Did she know about his past? Surely she must have done? I couldn't help feeling betrayed by her as well.

"Bloody hell," said Demi, after we'd read the story of the time he got arrested for brawling in a nightclub. "What are you going to do?"

The tears came again. "I don't know." I'd never seen that side of him, not once, and I was still struggling to reconcile the Connor I gave my heart to with what was on the screen in front of me. "I just don't know."

CHAPTER 28

DEMI STAYED THE night, mainly because both of us were too drunk to call her a cab. We slumped over the breakfast bar in the morning, each hoping the other would get up and make the coffee.

Cheek going numb from the marble surface, I thought back to Connor and his smoothie. Now I understood his expertise with hangover cures. Maybe I should take advantage of his vast experience and try to make one myself? I glanced towards the fridge and my head pounded. Maybe not.

"I'm never drinking again," I groaned.

"Me neither," Demi said. "At least until this evening."

"You're not planning to go out, surely?"

"I can't work and you're, well, undecided. We should go out and have fun."

"No way."

"Oh, don't go all dull on me. Let your hair down for once."

"I do let my hair down. Before this mess happened, I was going to go speed-dating tomorrow."

She nearly choked on the water she was sipping. "What about Connor?"

"It's one of the challenges I have to complete. He promised to come with me to have a go as well. He was fun like that."

She shook her head in disbelief. "He'd have been eaten alive."

"I know that now. He must have known it then. But he was still going to come." For me. He was going to come for me. My heart lurched at that thought.

And maybe some of the things he'd done weren't that bad. I mean, here was I feeling sick as a dog this morning, and not for the first time. I could hardly judge him for drinking. And I hadn't seen him touch alcohol in all the time I'd known him. Maybe rehab really worked?

Had I been too hasty in my decision to walk away?

Maybe, but then I thought back to the nastier photos I'd seen, like the one of him clearly naked with some girl wrapped around his body. Would I ever get over that? After all, it wasn't just me who'd seen the pictures either. Half the world had.

I recalled the night we'd gone to see Indigo Rain, and that girl in the car park. Lori? Was that her name? How many more Loris lurked out there?

"You're still going," Demi said, pulling me away from my thoughts.

"What? Going where?"

"Speed-dating. I'll come with you. I said before I would, and I need to find a man, anyway."

"I'm not sure that's a good idea."

"It's a great idea. Don't be so boring."

I tried to resist, but Demi was a force of nature. I kind of pitied whatever man she ended up with, because he was certainly going to have his hands full, and with more than just her D-cups.

On Friday night, I stood by the front door waiting for a taxi while Demi made a last-ditch attempt to make me change my clothes.

"You look like a nun," she said.

"How many nuns have you seen in skinny jeans and a T-shirt with sequinned flowers on it?"

"That's not the point. You should show a little flesh."

"My arms are visible. That's all you're getting or I'm not going."

"Fine," she huffed. "Will you at least put a bit more make-up on?"

I gave her a look.

"Okay, okay. But don't be surprised if you don't get any phone numbers."

I didn't want any phone numbers—that was the whole point. I wanted to talk to as few people for as little time as possible, have Demi take a photo of me, then leg it back home and cry.

Everyone stared as we walked into the bar. Thankfully most of the eyes zeroed in on Demi, who'd taken her own advice to heart. Her top struggled to contain what God gave her, and her skirt was barely within shouting distance of her knees. At least we didn't have to buy any drinks. The queue of men offering was three deep as I hid in her shadow.

We'd been there about twenty minutes when I heard a familiar voice behind me.

"Buy you a drink?"

I spun to face him. "Connor?"

He was wearing a hat low over his eyes and a pair of glasses. "I'm not letting you go into this bear pit by yourself."

My heart started pounding. "I can't believe you're here."

"Believe it, babe. So, can I buy you a drink?"

"I'm on soft drinks."

"Sensible choice." He leaned over and ordered a couple of colas.

Demi picked that moment to turn around. "Who's your friend?" She peered more closely. "Is that Connor Lowes?" she asked me, her voice a squeak.

"Shh, not so loud."

"Bloody hell, Connor Lowes in a crappy bar in Reading." Then her eyes narrowed at him. "You're an asshole, you know that?"

"Someone's already told me." He glanced my way, smirking slightly.

She opened her mouth, no doubt to land another barb, when a woman with too much hair and a clipboard shouted for everyone to be quiet.

"Is everybody ready for the main event?" she asked, her voice sounding like she was off her head on happiness. A few murmurs of agreement broke the silence which she took to mean everyone was thrilled.

"Brilliant, amazing. Here's how it's going to work. Girls sit on one side of the tables, you lovely gentlemen on the other. Each time the bell rings, the men move down one seat. Do you all understand?"

I nodded half-heartedly and looked round to see others doing the same.

"You get five minutes to talk to each person," the

woman continued. "Everybody, take your seats!"

I counted nine places on each side. Forty-five minutes of hell until I could get out of there. I sat second from one end and Connor was on the other to begin with. I'd tried to grab the chair next to Demi, but the scary lady told me all the places were allocated and firmly pointed back to the seat she'd put me in, leaving a loud redhead in between us.

The first guy I spoke to seemed nice enough, and he'd gone to the effort of wearing a button-down shirt and slicking his hair back.

"So, what do you do for a living?" I asked, sticking to a safe question, and one I should have asked Connor right away.

"I deliver car parts. You know, to local garages?"

A nice, normal, down-to-earth job—pre-Connor, he was the type of guy I'd have loved to get to know better. But now? Who wanted Lambrini when they'd had Cristal?

The second guy sounded as if he'd learned his lines from the Dummies Guide to Speed-Dating. How was I today? What was I looking for in a man? What were my hobbies? Then I found out he was an accountant. Probably he *had* read a manual.

I glanced down the line at Connor. The bubbly blonde opposite him talked with her hands, her ample chest bouncing as she spoke. His eyes were firmly fixed on her face, and he looked bored. Score one for Connor.

I couldn't help checking my watch as the next guy talked about himself for his entire five minutes, a complete contrast to the one after who was so shy he barely uttered a word. I wanted to give him a hug, he looked so nervous.

The next idiot, I wanted to kick in the nuts. His first question was, "So darlin' what's your favourite position?" and he didn't mean on a football pitch. I breathed a sigh of relief when he moved to the other end of the table.

As I half-listened to the baby-faced guy who replaced him talk about the kind of girl his mother wanted him to meet, I was more interested in the conversation taking place two seats along. Demi laid into Connor, making sure he understood in no uncertain terms what a shit he was for hurting me. At times like this, I really found out who my friends were and Demi's protectiveness made me whisper a silent thank you to Terry for being such a twit.

The guy after momma's boy came across as a little creepy. He clearly didn't realise it was a social faux pas to ask a girl her dress size before going out for dinner, and the way he kept staring made me uncomfortable. If he wanted to get a date out of this, he needed to chat with guy number two and borrow his manual.

I found myself looking away as I gave him the brush off, my thoughts not on him but rather what I was going to say to Connor in a couple of minutes' time.

The moment came before I'd worked it out. For a few seconds we just looked at each other.

"So," I whispered, wanting to break the silence.

"So," he said back, his voice quiet. "Do you want me to start?"

I nodded.

"My name's Connor Lowes, I'm twenty-five, and I'm an alcoholic." He held my eyes, and I couldn't look away. He'd obviously thought through what to say a lot more thoroughly than me. "Before I met you, I spent six months in rehab and before that, I spent three years being a complete fucking idiot."

At least he was being honest now. "Why?" I asked, careful to keep my voice down. I didn't want the world hearing.

"Why what?"

"Why all of it? And why didn't you tell me?"

He leaned forward, chin in his hands, and sighed. "I'd just turned sixteen when I got scouted for modelling. The money was good, and the perks were better. I had the clothes, I had the car, I had the looks. That meant I got the girls and people turned a blind eye to my age when I showed up at parties." He paused while I absorbed his words. "My brother had landed a couple of big movie roles by then, and I started to get offers. Me being related to Scott Lowes would help sell a movie, regardless of whether or not I could act."

"But you can act," I said, thinking back to the time on set with the horses.

"I can hold my own, but that wasn't why I got cast. And I always ended up as the villain, the guy out to hurt everyone else, and that spilled over into my private life. The money kept rolling in, and I turned into an even bigger dick. It went out of control. I'd show up drunk on set, pick fights with everyone from the director to the wardrobe assistant. People hated working with me, and I hated working with myself, but I'd still get jobs because of who Scott was. I resented him for being the golden boy. Took me months of therapy to be able to say that." He let out a wry laugh.

"But you're not like that. Not really. Unless who you were with me was a lie?"

"When I met you, it was the first time in my life I

could be myself. You didn't know the old me, and better still, you didn't know my brother. I was just Connor, and you were just Ella." He shrugged. "And I loved that."

"I don't get it. Why were you even at Linden Hollow?"

"I like horses, always have. That was no lie." He closed his eyes for a second. "My brother paid for my rehab. Most of my money had gone up my nose or been pissed on walls by that point. I'd been out a week when he found out I'd gone to another party. At two in the morning, he hauled me out of there and told me if I didn't get my act together, my family didn't want to know me anymore. Then he called Jenny and begged her to babysit for six weeks to get me away from bad influences."

I processed what he'd just said. "You took drugs?"

He nodded slowly. "I won't ever lie to you again. I took them. I was stupid, and I'm not proud of it."

I absorbed that, pretty much numb by then after everything he'd said. "So what now?" I asked. "What are you planning to do in the future?"

The bell dinged, and we both groaned. The only thing worse than talking this through was not talking it through. I considered trying to get out of the whole stupid dating thing, but the clipboard lady gave me a withering glare and Connor's next "date" looked as if she wanted to shove me off my chair.

I couldn't tell you anything about the ninth and final guy. He talked, and I nodded in what I hoped were the right places. My mind was filled with Connor. He'd taken drugs, he said. One of my foster brothers took drugs, and I'd watched them turn him from a normal teenager into a monster. I hated them, and it was hard for me to accept Connor had been part of that world.

As soon as the bell rang, I grabbed my bag and got up. Connor stood by my side in an instant, and he guided me over to a quiet table in the corner.

"Where were we?" he asked.

"I wanted to know what you see in your future."

"You've changed me. More than rehab, or my parents, or my brother ever could. I haven't touched alcohol since I met you, or any of the hard stuff, although fuck knows it's been tempting the last couple of nights. As soon as I checked in to the hotel, I had to get them to clear out the minibar."

I gave him a smile I hoped was encouraging. He was doing better than me. "Are you going back to America? For work?"

"Not if you'll have me here. I'll need to fulfil the contracts I've signed, but I wouldn't take on more after that."

"What stuff do you have left?"

"Just what I told you about. Four modelling contracts signed. I've had a couple of movie offers, but I can knock them back."

That was crazy. He was offering to give up everything for me? "I need to think on this, okay?"

He gripped my hand. "Please, babe." His voice shook. "Don't end this."

The sound of a throat clearing broke the moment, and we looked up to see clipboard lady looming over us. "Oh, this is great! Somebody's found romance from one of our dating events! You look wonderful together, but I'll give you your slips anyway, just in case." She dropped a pile of papers on the table in front of each of us.

I couldn't help flicking through mine. One from the first guy, then the sex fiend, the creepy guy, and Connor.

"How many did you get?" I asked him.

He sorted through his pile. "Eleven."

"But there were only nine girls."

He shrugged. "It happens." We looked at each other and laughed then he took my hand again.

"Please," he said.

"Just give me a few days. I need to think things through. Please, can you give me that?"

Chapter 29

CONNOR HAD EVENTUALLY agreed to give me a week to think about things. I promised him I wouldn't write us off, but I did need some space.

"You've made the right decision," Demi said in the taxi on the way home. "He cares about you, that much is obvious, but he deserves to stew a bit."

"What did you say to him? You sounded like you gave him a roasting."

"I just made sure he understood if he ever pulled this shit on you again, he'd have me to deal with. I don't care if he's some hot shot model with Hollywood at his feet, he still can't treat you that way."

Tears pricked at my eyes as I gave her a hug. "You know, cheating on me was the best thing Terry ever did, because it meant I got you."

"You're right there. Terry and his tiny dick. Feck knows what we ever saw in him. Tell me Connor's got more to offer in that department?"

"You know that Calvin Klein advert?"

"Mmmm."

"There's nothing photoshopped in it."

"Holy hell, you're one lucky girl."

Yes, I was lucky, at least until the taxi got to Edith's and I went to pay my share of the fare.

"My wallet's missing. I know I put it in here," I said,

rummaging through my bag.

"Could you have left it at home?"

"No, I had it on the way because I got money out of it to pay for the first taxi. Somebody must have taken it in the bar." I'd been so distracted by Connor, it wouldn't have been difficult.

Demi gave me a hug. "That's shitty. It's been a hard enough day for you without that happening. Was there much in it?"

"Not a lot. Fifty quid and my credit card. Oh, and my provisional driver's licence, for all the good it's done me. I'll have to get another one of those little card things." Maybe I could have a better photo on it this time round. The last attempt looked more like a mugshot and half my chin got cut off.

"I'll pay for the taxi, but don't forget to cancel your card. If you do it straight away, they should give you any money the thief spent back."

I gave her a grateful smile. "I'll call you over the weekend."

As soon as I got inside, I rang the credit card company, and after five frustrating minutes fighting with the automated menu, a robotic-sounding lady informed me no money had been spent. At least that was one less headache. The mess with Connor gave me quite enough to deal with, thank you very much.

Ordinarily, something like the theft would have given me a sleepless night, but it was an unpredictable underwear model who kept me awake. What should I do about him?

Could I walk away? My heart told me no, but my head was still fighting it. The battle raged for the whole of Saturday as I scrubbed the house from top to bottom to try and keep myself occupied.

Connor had offered to give up everything for me, but I couldn't accept that. Not only would he start to resent his sacrifice, but I couldn't see him spending the rest of his life living on the outskirts of Reading, no matter what he might say. And I began to wonder whether I wanted to do that, either.

The trouble was, we'd lived in our little bubble at Linden Hollow without the paparazzi, his ex-girlfriends, random women who'd ogled him in his underwear, and all the illegal temptations California had to offer. What if Connor stumbled on his path? Was I strong enough to pick him up again? At twenty-two, I'd never been tested like that, never had to dig inside myself and find the strength to walk through hell and come out on the other side. Edith had been right about my sheltered life. The possibility of letting Connor, and myself, down terrified me.

I wandered around the house, thoughts tumbling through my mind. The garden, the bedrooms, the spacious kitchen—it was all very nice, but only special because it had once belonged to Edith. And I knew Edith would want me to be happy more than anything else. She wouldn't mind if I sold the house and moved elsewhere because my heart told me to.

But what about Jaz and Demi? They'd been there for me after Terry, and tonight Demi had demonstrated the value of our friendship once again. But I could always visit, right? With planes and cars and trains, the world was quite a small place nowadays.

The fight carried on in my head as I emptied a load of washing out of the machine and went outside to hang it up. Shadows danced in the twilight, that odd time of the evening where everything was a bit fuzzy, and you started to wonder whether you should pay a visit to the optician.

I put the basket on the ground and picked up the first piece of laundry, which happened to be a pair of Connor's underpants. Calvin Klein, of course. He probably got as many free pairs as he could wear, but although they looked nice on I preferred him out of them.

The thought of sliding them down his thighs helped me come to a decision. Could I go through life without that pleasure again? Or his sweet smile in the morning? Or his kind words? Or that thing he did with his finger when...? I didn't even have to finish the list, because the answer was no. I needed to call Connor and talk to him. Tell him my deepest fears about what a future with him could hold. Ultimately our discussions might end in tears, but at least we'd have tried. If I walked away, I'd always be left wondering "what if?"

I didn't need a week to think things over. Things were clear now as I picked out another pair of his undies and hung them up. I shivered with bliss at the very thought of seeing the package they normally contained again soon. Maybe even tonight? I considered leaving the laundry, but it would only take me another two minutes to hang out, and if I left it I'd end up with a crinkly mess.

Then I heard the quiet crunch of footsteps on gravel behind me and my heart soared as a pair of hands came over my eyes. Connor! He hadn't been able to wait a week either. He wanted to sort this out as much as me.

"Guess who?"

I froze, a cold finger of fear tracing down my spine

as I gasped for breath.

That wasn't Connor's voice.

CHAPTER 30

I ROLLED OVER, acutely aware of the burning sensation in my bladder. Why hadn't I peed before I went to bed? Now I'd have to get up, and I didn't want to. I felt tired, so tired.

My eyelids didn't want to open, but after a couple of attempts, I managed to lift one. Everything was dark. Strange... I was lying down, but not in my bed. Had I fallen asleep on the sofa again? And what was that around my ankle?

I tried to sit up, but the weariness in my muscles made it seem like I'd been walking for days without food and this was my first rest break. I tried again, and this time I managed to push myself upright. Rocks rattled around in my skull and my palms stung where I touched... What was I lying on? It felt like velvet, but Edith's sofas were leather.

A voice came out of the darkness, from somewhere on my right.

"You're awake."

I came awake in an instant, my senses fighting against the grey veil smothering them. Who the hell was that? Why was he in my house?

Only as I became aware of my surroundings, I realised it wasn't my house. I didn't know where I was, only that a man whose voice I didn't recognise was there with me.

With quaking fingers, I traced down my leg to my ankle. Whatever gripped around it felt cold, metallic. A handcuff? I traced the contours until I came to a chain.

My heart raced and blood whooshed in my ears, giving me a feeling of vertigo. The edge of a cliff beckoned. Already desperate to pee, I struggled to control my bladder.

"W-w-who are you?"

"I'm your new friend. We met last night."

Last night? What happened last night? My brain was a library, but each time I wanted to retrieve a thought, I had to wait for the ageing librarian to look up the reference and trundle off through the stacks.

Eventually it came to me. Speed-dating. "Are you from the bar?"

He flicked the light on, blinding me. I screwed my eyes up, blinking until they adjusted. Once I could see again, I recognised the guy I talked to before Connor. The creepy one.

And now he wore a sinister smile, a smile where his lips curved but his eyes sparkled with insanity.

"You didn't call me," he said. "And you forgot to tick my box, so I had to take things into my own hands."

Yeah, there was a reason I didn't tick his bloody box. He was quite clearly certifiable. I looked down at my shackled ankle, then back at him. "So what happens now?"

He smiled wider, but it was still at odds with his eyes. "You get some sleep, and tomorrow we go on our first date together." He clapped his hands in delight. "Isn't that exciting?"

That wasn't quite how I'd describe it, but at the

moment I had more pressing things on my mind.

"I need to use the bathroom."

"It's over there." He pointed at an open doorway.

I stood up, wobbly on my feet. As I got closer, I could see that the door wasn't just open, it was missing altogether. And he sat there, eyes unblinking as he watched me.

"Could you leave? It's not like I can go anywhere." The chain snaked along the floor to the far side of the room, where a padlock fastened it securely around a radiator pipe.

"We shouldn't have any secrets from each other, not if we're going to be together."

I had a feeling that pointing out the error in his logic wouldn't be welcomed. Instead I played along with his delusion.

"But we haven't even been on our first date." I resisted the temptation to use finger quotes around the word "date." Who only knew what he had planned for that? "Aren't you being a bit forward?"

He seemed to think that through. "You're right. I'll be back in five minutes."

The second the door to my prison closed, I leapt up. First I ran to the window, but there was only darkness. No streetlights, no other houses, nothing.

I looked around. The room contained the sofa and a matching armchair, a bed, and a wardrobe. I yanked open the door of that and found a rail full of women's clothing, cheap stuff, still with the labels on. This was why he'd wanted to know my bloody dress size?

None of it was any use, so I tried the bathroom next. It was little more than a cupboard, with a shower stall, a toilet and a tiny sink with a mirror above it. I tapped the mirror. Plastic.

Bottles of shampoo and conditioner and face wash were lined up neatly on the floor, as well as a hairbrush and some make-up. When I looked more closely, each item had been labelled with my name in black marker pen. I don't know why, but that freaked me out more than anything. My breathing quickened, and I struggled to control it. *Calm down, Ella. Panicking won't help.*

Breathe in.

Breathe out.

Breathe in.

Breathe out.

How long had he been gone? He said five minutes? How much time had I used up with my fruitless search? I still needed to pee, so I yanked my jeans down and got that over with as fast as I could. The last thing I wanted was for him to come back in the middle.

I'd almost finished washing my hands when the door clicked open, and the soap stung my palms as I rinsed them. Dirty and grazed, I also had a nasty cut running along one finger, and I took care not to dislodge the scab. What happened to me?

"Good girl. Proper hygiene is important." His voice came from my left.

"What do you want from me?"

"Isn't it obvious? What does a man usually want from a woman?"

Oh hell, not that. Please not that. I backed away, but there wasn't far to go before I hit the wall.

"Oh, don't look so worried. I'm not a monster. I like to do things properly. We need to get to know each other before we take such a big step. That's part of the fun."

Fun? *Fun*? The only fun thing would be to shove a spit up his ass and watch him roast.

He reached over for the light switch. "But we'll talk more about that tomorrow. It's time for you to get your beauty sleep."

Once he'd gone, I tried to turn the light back on again, but when I pressed the switch, nothing happened. He must have flipped the fuse. Left in darkness, I felt my way around, but in all my groping I didn't find anything else that might be useful to me.

After what seemed like an hour of pointless exploration—I didn't know exactly because he'd taken my watch—I decided he was right. I needed sleep. Without rest, I was nothing, and I needed my strength if I was going to escape before...before... I didn't even want to think about it.

The bed in the corner, a shabby-looking double, had old-fashioned woollen blankets tucked over its white sheets. It reminded me of a hospital, or worse, an asylum. No way was I going to lie on that. What if he'd slept on it before then? I didn't want to be anywhere associated with the sick bastard. Instead, I pulled off the top blanket and curled up under it on the sofa, my knees tucked tight against my chest.

To avoid the nightmare I was trapped in, I thought of Connor instead. What must he be thinking? Had he even noticed I was missing? Why would he when I'd made him promise to give me a week? I groaned softly to myself in the blackness. Why had I done that? A week—was I crazy? My heart knew all along what I wanted, and it had only taken my brain a day to catch up.

What if I never got out of here? What if, when Connor didn't hear from me, he just assumed I didn't want to be with him anymore? He might decide to go back home, and then who would look for me?

I forced myself to breathe properly again. I was on the verge of hyperventilating, and if I didn't calm down I'd end up having a heart attack and then it wouldn't matter whether anyone found me or not.

A heart attack... Like that stupid vajazzle that luckily Connor found so amusing. At least, he had until one of the diamantés came off and lodged in his throat. He'd ended up having a coughing fit while I thumped him on the back. What would my abductor think of that, huh? I wished he'd get something stuck in his throat and choke on it. Like a hand grenade.

Relax, just relax. I still had Demi and Jaz. Except I'd told Demi I'd call her over the weekend, which gave me until Sunday night. And Demi tended to be a bit scatter-brained, so it could be Tuesday before she realised something was wrong. A fog of hopelessness settled over me. Now that I'd left Payright, I didn't speak to Jaz so often. She tended to call towards the end of the week, but that was a lifetime away, maybe literally.

I tried to get some rest, but it didn't come easy. If I wasn't beating myself up over Connor, I was imagining the worst about the pervert. His eyes watched me in my dreams, staring from the edges of my consciousness.

I wondered if Edith was up there, looking down. She'd always told me to be more adventurous, and it would be hard to top getting kidnapped, wouldn't it? The only question was whether I'd live to tell the tale.

Finally, my brain wore itself out, and for better or

worse I drifted into a dark sleep, one ruled by monsters called guilt and stupidity.

CHAPTER 31

I DIDN'T KNOW how long I slept, but daylight filled the room when I woke up. The man sat opposite in the chair, face relaxed, gazing at me. How long had he been there? Any amount of time was too long, but the thought of him watching me sleep gave me the creeps.

"Rise and shine, my darling. It's a beautiful day."

I looked over to the window. Sure enough, the sun shone through the bars, but my mind was black. I made no move to obey his order. Under the quilt I felt cocooned, safe. Well, safer.

He clapped his hands. "Come on, I haven't got all day. It's breakfast time."

To my right, he'd set up a fold-out table and two dining chairs. The table was laid for two. Two slices of toast sat on each plate, with a tub of margarine and a jar of jam in the middle. A couple of glasses of disturbingly orange juice sat next to the plates.

Reluctantly, I sat up and unwrapped myself, and it didn't escape my attention that his eyes ran up and down my body as I did so. An involuntary shiver ran through me as I broke out in a cold sweat. Following his instructions, I walked to the table where he pulled out a chair for me—a bizarre gesture of chivalry considering he was holding me hostage. I sat and gingerly picked up the plastic knife from next to the plate.

Inwardly I cursed. I'd been hoping for metal.

As if reading my thoughts, he gave a high-pitched giggle. "Sorry about the cutlery. I used to give out metal, but there was a little incident a few months ago, and I had to change the policy."

I stiffened as his words penetrated. What did he mean, "a little incident"? *Was I not the first?*

And if I wasn't the first, what happened to whoever came before me?

Until then, I'd harboured some crazy belief that this was all a stupid misunderstanding, that he'd come to his senses and let me go. But he'd had practice at this, hadn't he? He knew exactly what he was doing. It was just me who didn't.

I may not have been hungry but I understood I needed to eat. If I weakened, he won. I tried to scrape up some butter, but the knife kept bending. He leaned over the table and closed his hand over mine.

"Here, let me help."

I didn't dare pull back. What if I angered him? I still had no idea what he was capable of, I only knew he was quite, quite mad. And bigger than me, much bigger, taller than Connor and heavier, although my captor's bulk consisted of fat rather than muscle. I let my arm go limp as he buttered my toast for me.

"Do you want jam?" he asked.

I shook my head. Not if it meant having his hand on mine a second longer.

My hand shook as I lifted the toast to my mouth and took a bite. Already cold, it tasted like cardboard as I chewed. I tried to swallow, but my mouth was so dry I ended up coughing. He looked up in alarm as I hurriedly reached for the juice and drank, but at least he didn't try to help. Yuck—it was warm, the cheap kind made from concentrate with sediment collecting at the bottom of the glass. And the bloody glass was plastic.

"Good?" he asked.

I nodded.

Once I'd pushed my plate away, he bustled around, clearing the remains of breakfast onto a tray and carrying the table and chairs out of the room.

"I have to go into town now, but I'll be back later. Just to save you a bit of trouble, the window's double-glazed and all the furniture's screwed down. Even if you could break the glass, the nearest house is three hundred yards away so there's nobody but me to hear you scream." He sounded matter of fact about it, but then his tone darkened. "But I'd appreciate if you didn't, because the noise annoys me."

With that, he closed the door and the lock clicked.

Despite what he'd said, I checked anyway. He wasn't lying. The bed, sofa and chair were screwed to the floor, and the wardrobe wouldn't budge from the wall. Not only was the window double-glazed, he'd nailed it shut as well. When I craned my neck to look, all I could see in any direction were high, evergreen hedges gone scraggly around the edges.

I checked again in the bathroom. Nothing useful, not even a nail file. The most dangerous thing in there was a toothbrush and while a trained assassin could no doubt think of some way to use it, I was at a loss for ideas. I gave up and did my teeth. I may be metaphorically screwed, but at least my mouth didn't taste disgusting any more.

With nothing better to do, I paced up and down the room, back and forth, back and forth. I had no way of telling the time apart from the sun, and it was high in the sky by the time my captor returned.

He'd brought me a knock-off Happy Meal. A fucking Merry Meal! What bloody planet did he live on? Or was he being cruel on purpose?

He handed it over to me, swinging the box by the handle. "I wasn't sure which toy you'd want, so I got you the fairy princess."

Was it possible, I wondered, to insert a fairy princess up his ass?

"Eat up. It's date night tonight, so I expect you to dress up. I've put a selection of clothes in the wardrobe."

"How do I get my jeans off? I've got a chain on my ankle."

"Just slide them along the chain," he said, in a tone that suggested I was creating problems where none existed.

I forced myself to eat a lukewarm burger served with a side order of cold fries, and washed it down with a tiny carton of orange squash. Fairy Princess sat on the arm of the sofa, mocking me with her smile. Bitch.

After that, I pulled open the wardrobe and took a proper look at the clothes. Mr. Freakshow sure had a thing for hooker chic. I took out a lime green mini skirt and a hot pink boob tube and held them up next to each other in all their nylon glory. They'd go beautifully with the yellow platform wedges. Traffic lights everywhere would lust after me.

One thing I noticed was that all the skirts were either wrap-around or had buttons the whole way down. Guess he didn't intend to take the chain off in a hurry.

Keeping an eye on the door in case he came back unexpectedly, I picked out the least revealing thing I could find—an unflattering polyester shirt-dress that scratched against my skin as I buttoned it up. As soon as he left for the night, I was putting my jeans back on.

The sun had set when he moved the table back into the room. My lovingly prepared dinner was an Indian takeaway. He spooned the curry out onto the plate himself, added rice, then offered me a piece of naan bread.

"No, thanks," I replied, gritting my teeth at the need to be polite.

"Suit yourself," he said, biting into it and chewing with his mouth open.

The sight of that alone made me want to gag, but I forced just over half of my food down. Normally I liked curry, but I wasn't sure I'd ever eat it again if I got out of here.

No, not if. When. When I got out of here. I tried to stay positive, but the situation seemed impossible. How could I escape when I was chained into a locked room? I had to hand it to him, he'd really thought this through. Tears prickled at my eyes, and I blinked them back, refusing to give him the satisfaction of seeing how much he was getting to me.

Meanwhile, he finished shovelling his own dinner in and wiped his mouth. "Delicious. Do you want dessert? I've got ice cream."

I shook my head. I didn't want that to be forever tainted as well.

After dinner he cleared the dishes away then, in a final act of meanness, cut my jeans off the chain and threw them out of the door. Before he left, he walked over and stood close up. The stink of garlic on his breath washed over me, and bile rose in my throat.

He ran his hand over my cheek. "I think we're going to have a lot of fun together, you and me."

Those words echoed in my ears as I huddled under the blanket again that night. Apart from the occasional clank of elderly pipework, the house lay silent, giving my imagination free rein to run wild. I wrapped my arms around myself, trying to imagine they were Connor's, that he was there with me, that I wasn't alone. Then my captor would invade my thoughts, and my pulse began racing as I imagined what he had in store for me.

I tried to shut off that part of my mind but it refused to be silenced, and six times I woke wide-eyed and sweating. The final time, I raced to the bathroom, groping for the toilet in the dim moonlight, and threw up what was left of the curry into the bowl. Then the tears came.

Breakfast the next morning was cereal, served in a flimsy plastic bowl with tepid milk.

"Sorry, I didn't have time to buy more bread. It's grocery day today though, so I'll go to the supermarket later. Do you want anything?"

Such a normal question in an abnormal situation. I had a feeling asking for a carving knife and a handcuff key wouldn't go down so well. "No, thanks." Whatever he brought would turn to poison in my mouth, anyway.

When he dumped a packet of sandwiches he'd picked up at a petrol station next to me at lunchtime, I felt nostalgia for the Merry Meal. I picked at the dry bread and sweaty cheese before giving up and leaving the sorry remains by the door.

The soft thunk of footsteps in the carpeted hallway heralded his return mid-afternoon, and a few seconds later the door swung open.

"I've brought you a present."

When I didn't put my hand out, he dropped a plastic bag in my lap then watched expectantly as I tipped out the contents. A gaudy red lipstick. How thoughtful. The garish shade was one that only supermodels and bawdy tarts could get away with, and of course, he'd be expecting me to wear it later.

When I didn't gush my thanks, his smile slipped. "Time for a shower, I think."

"Fine." I waited for him to leave, but he didn't. He dropped into the armchair to the side of me, and I realised he'd attached it in a place that gave him a perfect view into the bathroom.

"C-c-can you go?" I asked.

His face hardened. "I think we're past that now, don't you?" He pointed into the bathroom. "Now, get in the shower."

His pseudo-charming façade disappeared, and his eyes locked on mine. I looked away first, my skin tightening under a gaze that crawled over my flesh like a plague of ants. He didn't blink as I retreated slowly into the bathroom, turning my back on him when I unbuttoned the dress. As I caught sight of the ridiculous red heart, looking a bit ragged by now, I gulped down tears.

I jumped into the shower before it warmed up, just to get away from him, and scrubbed violently at my head with shampoo, the chain clinking away on the glass door I couldn't shut properly. When I picked up the conditioner, I glanced at the bottle. Instead of having "Ella" on it like all the rest, this one said "Melody." Who the fuck was Melody? The name rang a bell for some reason, but when I tried to remember why, the thought skittered away from me into a dark recess of my mind.

I'd left the towel, a threadbare off-white affair, by the shower door so I could wrap it around myself as soon as I stepped out. Anything to keep his eyes off me. There wasn't another towel for my hair, and water dripped down my face and back even though I'd tried to squeeze it out.

"Drop the towel," came the instruction from the other room.

Shaking, I did as he said, hurrying to get my clothes back on again. One thing he hadn't provided was clean underwear, and as I wondered whether to put my old stuff back on, he barked out another command. "Throw your knickers over here."

I tossed them over my shoulder, hoping they landed somewhere in the vicinity, then glanced back in time to see him sniff the crotch and put them in his pocket. Freak. But that wasn't news.

"I've cooked," he announced when I crept out of the

bathroom.

Was I supposed to be impressed or something?

When he said "cooked," he meant he'd taken one of those microwave-in-the-bag rice meals and heated it up. Only it was tepid now. I spooned it into my mouth, forcing myself to gulp it down as he cheerfully tucked into his. As he had the night before, he cleared away the table when we'd finished, and I expected him to leave.

But he didn't.

He popped into the hallway for a second then carried in a portable CD player, a chunky, old-fashioned one with dusty speakers.

"Time to dance, my darling."

Dance? Bloody hell. I closed my eyes and took a deep breath as I prepared to face one more indignity.

The freak held me close and shuffled me back and forth, hideously out of time to the music, occasionally treading on my feet. I tried to zone out of it. In my head, I was dancing with Connor, tucked against his chest, hearing him murmur that he loved me.

Would I ever hear those words from him again?

If I could have one wish, that would be it. Just those words.

I'd never ask for anything else.

Just those words.

CHAPTER 32

TUESDAY BROUGHT TOAST again. Toast and the freak running his greasy fingers along my bare thigh under the table.

"You should wax," he said. "It makes your legs smoother."

I'd had enough. "Have you even tried that? Having all your hair ripped out by the roots? Have you?"

He shook his head.

"Well, go to a salon and let a sadist in a smart white outfit torture you in the name of beauty, then see if you feel the same way. How about that?"

"There's no need to be grumpy."

I huffed. He was away with the fucking fairies.

"Any requests for lunch?" he asked before he left.

I smiled sweetly. "How about another Merry Meal?" I couldn't keep the sarcasm out of my voice, but he totally missed it.

"I'll see what I can do."

It must have been my lucky day because he turned up hours later with another box of happiness. Or at least I thought so until I opened it.

"What are these?" I held up a plastic bag.

"Apple sticks."

I couldn't believe it. The bastard chained me up and forced me to dance with him, then had the gall to bring me fruit instead of fries. "Is this some sort of joke?"

"You can't have fries every day, they're not healthy."

I laughed hysterically. He probably spent his days planning how to kill me, yet he was worried about my cholesterol? The man should be in an asylum.

When I dropped the apple back in the box in disgust, he cocked his head on one side and stared at me. "You know, Ella, sometimes you can be a bit strange."

I laughed harder.

Today I got Prince Charming, and I sat him next to Princess. They made such a merry couple, if you'll excuse the pun. That made my laughter turn to tears.

Before he left, the freak handed me another gaudy paper bag, and I put off opening it for hours until my curiosity got the better of me. Oh, how unoriginal—a bottle of nail varnish. If I drank it, would it poison me? Because that would be preferable to what was surely coming. I hadn't missed the signs. Every day, he stood a little closer, touched me a little more.

An hour later, as I scrubbed myself in the shower until my skin turned pink and raw, I looked through the steamed-up door and saw the blurred outline of my tormentor sitting in the chair, trousers open, touching himself. I doubled over and retched, what was left of my lunch swirling around in the water before it washed down the drain.

Please, let this be over soon.

The third "date" was the worst yet. The freak declared it pizza night, not even a takeaway, just a cheap cheese and tomato version from the supermarket freezer he'd burnt around the edges. I could barely stomach it, but since I'd lost my lunch and barely eaten any breakfast, I forced it down my throat.

A voice in my head told me to keep my strength up, but today I almost argued back. What was the point? He'd always be stronger than me. Maybe I could go on hunger strike? It was the only weapon I had left.

After we'd eaten, I wondered whether he'd force me to dance again, but he bypassed that and kissed me instead. His tongue was an alien invading my mouth, sucking, probing, making me heave. I was tempted to bite it, but I worried about the repercussions.

"I'll expect more enthusiasm tomorrow night, Ella."

I hoped I'd die in my sleep.

That night, as I lay on the sofa, I talked to Connor. I knew he couldn't hear me, but saying the words out loud made me feel better.

"I wish I could lie next to you for one more night, just to feel your arms around me. I wish I could tell you I loved you, and how proud I am of you for getting off the drugs and the drink. I should have said that before, but I was so busy worrying about the past that I forgot to think about the future.

"A future that I may not be a part of, but one that I hope you'll embrace and make the most of. And yeah, now I've had time to think about it, it would have been kind of fun to say I was dating a Calvin Klein model, knowing I had what every other woman wanted.

"I never got to complete my list, but I had more fun in three months with you than in my whole life before that. It'd be kind of cool if you completed it for me, but you've probably done all that stuff already. What's left? Driving—you can already do that, and I bet you've had a go in a Ferrari. Maybe you've even got one? I know you've visited another country, and you've thrown more parties than I could have ever hoped to go to. So that just leaves scuba diving. Have you done that? Maybe you could try it, if you haven't? For me?

"And if you stopped by every so often to give Folly a carrot, I'd be grateful. I miss her. Not as much as I miss you, but then, I could never miss anything as much as I miss you. I know what I've lost now, lying here. I love you, babe."

Tears were streaming down my face when I finished my monologue. I wished he could answer back, but that would only happen in my head now.

All I had left was myself and the freak, before I suffered whatever fate those before me had befallen. Melody was the only name I knew. Melody... Melody... Then it came to me—a news broadcast from a few months ago. Melody disappeared. Melody Swanson. She'd been living in Maidenhead, about fifteen miles away, when she vanished on her way home from work. The appeals dominated the news for days, but as far as I knew, nobody ever heard from her again.

And soon that would be me.

The freak was whistling when he brought the toast the next morning. He set down the plastic plate and handed me the plastic knife.

"Tonight's going to be the night, Ella, I've decided. I can't wait. I'm going to go out and get you a special outfit this morning, isn't that exciting?"

Fucking thrilling. I think I managed a grimace, but he barely noticed. He was too absorbed in his own thoughts, babbling away as if all the craziness had started leaking from his brain.

"We'll have candles and music and dancing and then I'll make love to you. I can't wait to see you writhing underneath me. How would you like to be a movie star? I'll bring my camera for something to add to my collection. I've been dreaming about it since the moment I met you, Caroline. I mean Melody. I mean Ella. Ooh, listen to me, I'm getting all my names mixed up."

He'd lost it. He'd fucking lost it.

I'd started pacing when he cleared breakfast away, kicking the door to my prison as I passed. I spat curses at the bars over the window and rattled them, but they didn't budge. Old me would have given up, but new me had the biggest incentive in the world to get out of the freak's clutches. Connor. Think, Ella, think. There must be a way to escape.

The house stayed silent as I scrabbled through the wardrobe and broke my nails trying to get the screws out of the hinges. I needed something, anything to use as a weapon.

Sofa springs? I ran over, only to find it was the cheap, unsprung kind. Nothing. I had nothing.

Tears threatened again as I flopped down onto the lopsided cushions and threw Prince Charming across the room, the smug bastard. Fairy Princess was up next, and I bent her arm until it snapped. Then I cried anyway—pointless, really, but what else could I do? Struggling to breathe, I looked through blurry eyes at the mangled mess in my lap.

And something glinted.

What was that?

I wiped my eyes with my stupid polyester sleeve and grabbed at Princess. A metal pin stuck out of where her arm used to be. Oh, hallelujah, praise sweatshops and their shoddily made children's toys!

What were the chances this would work? I didn't know, but I sure as hell intended to try.

I wiggled the pin until it came free, then gripped the end in my teeth and bent it over. Sitting cross-legged, I raised the handcuff lock and twisted the pin in it until it sprang open. I was free! Well, partly. The door was still locked, but I'd solved half the problem, and that gave me hope.

I started pacing again, my steps coming more easily now they were unencumbered by the length of chain, and formed a plan in my mind. Okay, so it was a pretty poor plan, but it was the only one I had.

One chance, one hope. One miracle was what I needed.

The freak came back in the afternoon with a hideous dress. Bright yellow, it was too short and slashed to my navel. If I'd ever had to set foot outside in it, I'd have only done so after taping myself into it to prevent wardrobe malfunctions. And also put a cardigan over the top and gone in the dark.

I sat down to dinner like an obedient little love slave and attempted small talk while I chewed on sausages and instant mashed potato. If this was his idea of showing a girl a good time, I hated to think what he'd do if he wasn't putting the effort in. Cheese and crackers? Ramen noodles?

Then the moment came. The moment that I dreaded, but at the same time, offered my only chance of escape.

"Strip," he ordered. He'd put some corny music on his crappy CD player and parked himself in the chair, watching.

I kicked off the hooker shoes he'd made me wear, but he held up his hand.

"Not like that. Do it slowly. I want sexy."

Shaking inside, I rolled my hips and swayed in time to the music. It wasn't easy, firstly because I was a terrible dancer and secondly, because he'd chosen a song more suitable for an aerobics routine. He didn't seem to care, though, because his pupils dilated and seconds later, his hand went to his zipper.

I couldn't watch as he started to pleasure himself. If I'd looked, I'd have flipped, I know I would. Instead, I closed my eyes and pretended it was Connor in the chair in front of me, that it was Connor with his eyes all over my body.

My dress lay on the floor when the music stopped. My stay of execution had ended.

"Lie on the bed," the freak ordered, his voice husky with excitement.

I hesitated.

"Do it." His words turned steel-edged.

Heart juddering, I walked over to the place I'd been avoiding for the past four days and laid on top of the covers. I kept my eyes firmly closed as he lowered his bulk over the top of me, a layer of his sweat rubbing off on my skin. The smell of body odour invaded my nostrils and caused me to gag.

As his hands fumbled down below, I bent my right leg up and snapped the handcuffs free. I'd opened the locks on both cuffs and stuck the ends shut with nail varnish so they were no longer locked but would pass a cursory inspection. As I felt him probing, I bundled both cuffs around my hand and whacked him on the temple as hard as I could.

I'd been hoping he'd go out cold, but I wasn't that lucky. He rolled off me with a grunt and landed on the floor. Free of his weight, I sprang up and walloped him again. This time he fell harder and lay still.

I ran for the door and slammed it. Where was the key? Where was the damned key? I'd planned to lock him in if I got this far, but it was missing.

Instead of wasting more time searching, I ran for the stairs and took them two at a time. The house was bigger than I thought it would be, and I ran through a large hallway to the front door. But the damn handle refused to turn. Choking back tears, I saw it needed a key, but he'd taken that one too.

There had to be another way out. There *had* to be. Where was the back door?

I ran down a passage, finding a row of doors leading into a darkened room. A gloomy lounge. A dining room. A study. A library. Finally, a kitchen. I ran to the door on the far side and rattled the door handle. Why wouldn't it open?

An anguished howl came from the other side of the house, followed by the sound of footsteps stumbling down the stairs. Where could I hide? I opened up the nearest cupboard, but it was stuffed to bursting with tinned carrots. The next one held ramen noodles—I hadn't been wrong there. I gave up on the kitchen and dashed out, hoping the next room would be kinder.

In the lounge, I cowered behind the sofa as he walked from one room to the next, but it was only prolonging the inevitable. Fury made his voice shake as he called my name, taunting.

"Ella, you bitch, you've had your fun, and I'm going to make you pay for that."

A door opened.

"Ella, come out, come out, wherever you are."

The sound of a light switch, close this time.

"Ella, if you come quietly, I promise I'll make your death quick."

My heart stuttered, and I knew this was the end. Giddiness overwhelmed me and the patterns on the freak's ugly carpet went all blurry.

BANG!

What was that? My mind didn't want to know. It gave up on me, and the last thing I saw was the desiccated rat lying beside me as everything went black.

CHAPTER 33

THE ROOM CAME back into focus as somebody called my name.

"Ella? Ella Goodman? Are you here?"

Was it him? Had he missed me the first time round? I pressed myself harder against the sofa, but it came almost to the floor so there was no chance of me crawling underneath it.

"Ella, it's the police. Are you here?"

The police? The police were in the house? Was it really them, or was he just playing a trick on me?

A tiny bud of hope formed in my chest as I listened, trying to figure out the sounds emanating from a couple of rooms away. A bump. A squeak. A door closing.

Then I heard the most beautiful noise in the world. Beside it, birds singing in the morning, the dash of rain on a glass roof, the pumped-up tunes of Indigo Rain— they all paled into insignificance. The whoop of a siren sounded from just outside. The bud blossomed, and relief overwhelmed me as I dragged myself up off the floor.

"I'm here," I called, but it came out as a croak and I tried again. "I'm in here."

My legs gave way as I tried to stand, and I fell to my knees, the pain making my vision go black again for a second. Torches shone in the doorway, and an officer wearing black ran over to me, the white "POLICE" logo stencilled across his chest visible through the gloom.

"She's in here," he yelled, and more footsteps sounded, running this time.

Figures swarmed around me, and my arms were pinned to my sides as I was wrapped up in a blanket. I tried to get free, but someone else, a lady in a green uniform, held me still.

"It's okay, Miss Goodman, we're trying to help you."

Despite the warmth, I started shaking uncontrollably, my teeth chattering while shivers racked my body. Maybe the blanket wasn't such a bad idea after all.

"She's going into shock," a voice said, and then I rose in the air as they lifted me onto a stretcher and strapped me down.

"He was here," I mumbled at the nearest figure. "There was a man. He was here."

One of the men in black loomed over me, but his face was kind, his expression sympathetic. "We've got him. It's okay. He's under arrest."

Thank goodness. Thank goodness. They had him. There would be no more showers, no more trashy clothes and no more cold toast. When I got home, I planned to throw out every slice of bread in the fridge. With those obscure thoughts swimming through my mind, I drifted off to sleep.

An irritating beeping woke me, and I flapped my arm

around, trying to find the source to shut it off.

"Babe?" a voice came from next to me. "Are you awake?"

The heaviness in my eyelids lifted and my eyes popped open. "Connor?"

He was sitting in a chair next to the bed, slumped across the blankets. As he turned his head, I saw he hadn't shaved in days, and if he were to do a photoshoot right now his haggard looks would require a lot of retouching. I reached out until my fingers touched his. "Are you real? Or am I dreaming again?"

He smiled at me, a tired smile, but a proper Connor smile nonetheless. "I'm here. Not going anywhere else."

I couldn't help it. I burst into tears. Connor climbed onto the bed and pulled me tight against him, and I freed my other arm from the blanket and wrapped myself around his torso.

"Fuck, babe, you had me scared."

"I had me scared, too," I said in a small voice. The shakes came back, and the vibrations travelled through Connor as well as I tried to make them stop. "He said he was going to kill me, right before the police came." The freak's words still echoed in my head, telling me my death would be quick.

"He's not gonna touch you now, I promise. I promise."

He kissed me, the scratch of his beard and the sweetness of his tongue helping to momentarily erase the horrors of...when? This evening?

"What day is it?"

"Thursday. Lunchtime. You've been out all night, and the morning."

My breath quickened, and I willed myself to calm

down. I breathed in Connor's scent and filled my lungs, my veins, and my mind with him, using his presence to force the freak out of my consciousness.

Connor was my drug. I didn't need another. I murmured what I'm sure were incoherent ramblings to him, telling him I loved him, that I wanted him, that I needed him. Exhaustion overcame me and I drifted off again, my head tucked into his chest, except this time when I closed my eyes, my heart was whole and my sleep was deep.

I'd had my test of strength, and I'd damn well passed it. After what the freak did to me, I knew I could handle anything Connor threw at me. We'd have our future.

Someone gently shook my shoulder and I tried to bat the hand away, but it came again. Why wouldn't they leave me alone? Couldn't they see how tired I was?

"Miss Goodman, we need to examine you, and the police are waiting outside." It was a lady's voice, and I opened my eyes to find a white-coated doctor peering down at me.

I mumbled something I'm sure wasn't very pleasant and tried to turn over, but Connor sat up, taking me with him. "Babe, they have to do their job."

"Will you stay?" I asked him.

He looked at the doctor, who shrugged.

"Of course I'll stay."

A nurse came in to assist, and they stripped me out of my paper gown. Their eyes widened at the horrific sight of the Heart Attack.

"Did he do this?" the doctor asked, clearly unable to believe that someone would inflict that on themselves.

I felt myself colour up. "No, that was a beautician."

She did a little eye roll, which I couldn't really blame her for, then carried on poking and prodding. I stared at the ceiling, trying to imagine I was somewhere else. A tropical island, maybe, relaxing on a sun lounger amid the smooth white sand. The hum of the air conditioner became the gentle whoosh of the sea, and if I closed my eyes tight enough, I could turn the heart monitor into the chirp of birds.

Connor's hand tightened on mine, and I reluctantly opened my eyes. The two staff whispered to each other, and I caught the words "rape kit."

I glimpsed the fear in Connor's eyes and shook my head violently. "No, no, he didn't."

"Are you sure?" the doctor asked.

"Yes." My shake switched to a nod. "He was about to, but the police came just in time."

The breath escaped Connor's body, and I squeezed his hand to try and reassure him. Nobody had been there. I was still his.

The doctor backed off with a small smile. "That's good news, then. Do you feel up to talking to the police? They've been waiting outside since last night."

It was the last thing I wanted to do, but I nodded. "Send them in."

They grudgingly agreed Connor could stay while they questioned me, probably because I refused to talk without him there. I had no desire to speak about it at all, and I certainly didn't want to rehash it twice.

One of them set up a portable recorder, and I

started at the beginning with what I could remember. "I felt his hands over my eyes, and I thought it was Connor. He did it to me once before, and Jenny, but then the man spoke, and it wasn't him." Connor went white, and I knew he'd never play that game again.

"What happened next?" asked the policeman.

"I don't remember. I woke up on the sofa at his house."

"We found a syringe in the bushes in your garden. We think he injected you with something, but the lab's still running tests."

I shuddered. That could have been anything.

With the policeman's probing, I told him about my nightmare in the house, and how the freak became more unhinged with every passing day.

"That's often how it works. These people can function in society, appear relatively normal, and in private, they're unravelling. We're just glad we got to you in time."

"How did you find me?" It was something I'd been trying to fathom out.

"You've got your young man to thank for that." He jerked his head at Connor. "Ruffled a few feathers, he did."

He shrugged as if to say, "What's new?" then took up the story.

"I missed you," he said simply. "I know what I said, but I couldn't stay away from you for a week, and I went round on Saturday night to tell you that. Only you weren't there. The back door was swinging open then I found a basket of laundry scattered all over the ground, so I called the police."

"I'm surprised they took you seriously." I thought

back to when I'd reported Mike's unwanted attention. They wouldn't give me the time of day. "No offence," I said to the policeman.

"They didn't." Connor glared at him.

"We had to follow our procedures."

"Your procedures are shit."

I put my hand on Connor's arm. "Down, boy."

He gave me a dirty grin. "That'll have to wait until later, babe."

How could he say that in front of a policeman? I blushed again, although parts of me heated in a very different way.

"So what did you do?" I asked Connor, desperately trying to get the conversation back on track.

"I called my own press conference." He looked ever so pleased with himself.

"Caused us no end of problems," the policeman said.

"You deserved them," Connor snapped, and I squeezed his arm again.

"Not helping," I muttered.

"We found blood on the patio when the sun came up," Connor said. "Then they started to take things more seriously."

That must have been from my hands. The grazes were healing but still sore.

"So how did that lead to the freak?" They both stared at me. "It's what I've been calling him, in my head."

"About right, that is," said the policeman. "That type does seem attracted to you."

I thought Connor was going to swing for him, and I held his arm down. Whatever school this copper went to, he'd skipped the lessons in tact.

The cop continued, "First there was that one living in your shed, but he had an alibi. He spent the evening snoring on his mate's sofa. Him and his girlfriend got upset by the noise and shaved the man's eyebrows off for a joke."

I couldn't help but snort at that.

"Then he gave us the details of the other bloke who was bothering you. He's a few olives short of a martini, but when we brought him in he screamed his innocence. Said it couldn't have been him because he'd met his soulmate, and she was the only girl for him. Apparently she's an anthropologist, specialises in the mating rituals of raccoons. We had to let him out on bail in the end."

I'd almost forgotten the bloody raccoons. Now I'd have to try and block them from my mind again. Did the anthropologist know she was his soulmate? Or was she merely the recipient of some dodgy flowers and a multitude of rambling text messages about his musical?

"I only met the freak the day before. How on earth did you find him?"

"You've got your friend the stripper to thank for that."

"She's got a name," I snapped. If he kept this up, my patience was going to wear as thin as Connor's.

"I know: Miss Demeanor. She's got a lot of fans down at the station. Anyway, she picked up some strange vibes from your man as well, but while he was talking to her, he kept looking at you. Then she remembered your driving licence got stolen and realised if he took it then he'd have your address."

"I couldn't even remember his name. I wasn't

concentrating that evening."

"It wouldn't matter if you had. Miss D did and it was false. His phone number turned out to be a dead end too. It was unregistered and switched off."

"So what did you do?"

"That's where your boyfriend came in. And his brother. They had the world's media flocking after them, press conferences and appeals on every channel. I only wish we had that kind of reach."

His brother? The Hollywood megastar? No wonder the press paid attention.

Connor took up the story again. "We put out an appeal for information with a sketch Demi and the police artist put together, and another girl recognised him and phoned in."

A chill ran through me. "Was she another one of his victims?"

The policeman shook his head. "The thinking is she was going to be, but he was still refining his methods up until then and things didn't go as smoothly as he planned. He met her in a bar and invited her back to his place. She'd been drinking, but on the drive over she sobered up, and by the time they arrived she was having second thoughts. When he stopped to open his gates, she legged it."

A narrow escape indeed. "So she was able to tell you where he lived?"

"Exactly. We broke in within an hour of her coming forward." He said that with a bit of pride. Finally, the police had managed to get something right.

I let out a long breath. Thank goodness she'd called when she did, because if the police had arrived five minutes later the outcome would have been very different.

The nurse bustled in with food and told the policeman I'd had enough for now. Thank you. I noticed she didn't try to throw Connor out—far from it, she even brought him a cup of tea.

By the afternoon, I felt a little better. I'd been allowed to have a shower and put my own pyjamas on. Demi had brought me in a bag of my things. The nurses wouldn't let her stay long, but it was enough time for her to give me a hug and promise she'd steer clear of speed-dating for the rest of her life.

"I owe you so much," I said into her hair.

"Just get better, that's all you owe me."

The rest of the police interviews took another two days, endless questions dredging up every last second I spent in that place. When I came to the bit about Fairy Princess, both cops in the room looked at each other before laughing.

"I thought the prince was supposed to swoop in and save the girl?"

"He didn't do such a hot job of things, did he?"

The worst part came at the end of the week, when we got the news that they'd dug up the grounds of the freak's house and found Melody. And Caroline. And two more bodies that they had yet to identify.

"That could have been me," I whispered to Connor.

"But it wasn't."

"But—"

"No buts, babe. It wasn't."

When they released me from hospital, I didn't go back to Edith's. I couldn't. That house held so many good memories, but the freak ruined them all with his final act.

"Where do you want to go?" Connor asked. "I'll take you anywhere."

I thought on it for a few minutes. I'd never called anywhere but Edith's home, but the place I'd felt most comfortable over the last few months was a little further west. "Could we go to Linden Hollow?"

Chapter 34

CONNOR MADE A quick phone call and came back smiling.

"I've fixed it," he said. "But you gotta promise you won't be mad at Jenny. She told me loads of times to tell you about my past, but I didn't know how to."

All that paled into insignificance in light of recent events. Besides, I remembered my ramblings while I was stuck in the house of horrors—I had to look to the future. "I won't be mad at her, I promise. Life's too short. I know that now."

I felt a bit guilty about running off, but my friends wouldn't hear of it. Demi and Jaz came to visit every day, and before I left, they piled me high with gifts to take on my trip. Make-up from Demi, chocolate from Jaz. She drooled as she handed the box over.

"How's the diet going?"

She sighed. "Painfully."

I pulled them into a group hug. "I'm going to miss you guys."

"You take all the time you need," Jaz said. "We'll see you when you feel better. Barry sends his regards, by the way. He's been telling everyone he knows you used to work for him."

I suppose I'd have to get used to that if I was going to be with Connor.

Demi held me tight, and I felt dampness on my shoulder as she pretended she wasn't crying. "Look after yourself," she sniffed.

"I'll be back soon," I promised. "Or you could come and visit?"

"Really?" She brightened a bit.

"Of course. You two are my best friends."

Even Grant and Todd stopped by, with homemade muffins and ready smiles. It wasn't visiting time, but the nurse took one look at Grant and waved them through.

Todd dropped into the chair next to my bed and gripped my hand. "Thank goodness you're all right. We were so worried."

"I bet Grant's car wasn't."

That got a laugh.

"It's dent-free now. All fixed."

Thank goodness. "I should introduce you to Connor."

They shook hands all round, and I noticed Grant held on a bit longer than usual. And possibly a little tighter if Connor's pained expression was anything to go by. Grant looked him straight in the eye. "Look after her. You promise?"

"I promise."

Grant broke into a smile. "Then we'll get on fine."

Demi and Jaz packed up my suitcases, and as soon as I got released from hospital Connor helped me into his truck, and we started the trip west.

The motorway was clear this time, and as we sped along, I couldn't help hoping this would be a fresh start. Just me, Connor, the horses and a bit of recovery time.

Then Connor scuppered that plan. "My brother's gonna stop by for a few days. He's a friend of Jenny's as well."

His brother? Sure, Connor was famous, but he was, well, Connor. Scott, on the other hand... "Stop! Go back."

"What? What's wrong?"

Demi had packed my make-up, but that hardly cut it. "I need to get my hair done and buy more clothes." And look up articles on the internet on what to do when you meet a Hollywood megastar. Did I need to curtsey? So much for a relaxing break.

"For Scott?"

"He's practically royalty."

"He's my brother. He still looks like shit in the mornings and farts while he watches TV. He won't care if you're not ready for the red carpet."

A bubble of laughter escaped. "Are you sure?"

"Positive."

One of the holiday cottages was free, so rather than bunking in with Jenny and her husband we had our own little place. It was there that Connor took away the final demon the freak left me with.

He hadn't made any kind of move the night before, just held me in his arms as we drifted off to sleep. But when we woke in the morning, I felt something digging in my hip and knew what was on his mind. After everything that had happened, I'd thought I might worry, but when Connor looked down at me, all I remembered were the good times.

"You sure you're ready for this?" he asked.

"I need it. I need you."

He slid inside me with a tenderness I'd never experienced before. Love flowed through the connection between us, and the act healed the jagged hole that had been ripped in my soul.

He fixed me.

And just in case the repair hadn't done the trick, he had another go in the afternoon. And the evening.

The next morning, I felt a little bowlegged as I stumbled down the stairs to make us both coffee. We'd been up half the night, and I desperately needed caffeine before the shower Connor promised me.

So focused was I on the kettle, I barely noticed the man sitting at the kitchen table. And when I did, all I could do was sprint from the room.

Halfway up the stairs, I ran smack into Connor, and he caught me before we both tumbled to the bottom.

"Babe? What's up?"

I pointed back in the direction I'd come. "Man," I gasped. "In the kitchen."

His face hardened. "Like a burglar?"

"No. Like your brother."

He turned me round and herded me back towards the kitchen. "Why were you shooting up the stairs? I thought something was wrong."

"I haven't brushed my hair."

Connor burst out laughing. "Like that matters."

So I had to get through my first meeting with a living god with my hair sticking in thirty-seven directions and gunk in the corners of my eyes. At least my morning breath covered up the smell of sex.

"This is Ella," Connor told his brother.

"Good to meet you, Ella." OMG! He sounded exactly like he did in the movies.

I stuck out my hand, but Scott bypassed it and kissed me on the cheek, ignoring Connor's glare. I clutched at the back of a chair to stay upright. When Scott turned away to clap Connor on the back, I sank gratefully into it.

Connor took over the coffee, and I got the opportunity to study the pair of them. Connor's looks were dark and brooding, whereas Scott had lighter hair and a softer jaw. Classic heartthrob. Or in my case, heart-pound-like-it-was-trying-to-escape-my-ribcage.

But Scott didn't seem to hear it as he chatted with Connor about their parents, work, and horses. "You want to ride this morning? We'll have to go out the back way, though. The vultures are camped at the end of the drive."

"What do you want to do, babe?"

I wasn't sure. Mainly because I was too busy gawping at Scott.

"Babe?"

"Uh, yeah, riding. That's good."

Jenny joined us as well, and together we rode through the countryside, enjoying the peace and quiet. At least until someone with a camera spotted us and we had to go for an impromptu canter.

In the afternoon, Connor and Jenny went to jump Captain, and I got a few minutes alone with Scott. At least I'd sorted out my hair. Looks aside, he turned out to be a normal guy, and as long as I didn't look straight at him, I found I could hold a reasonably coherent conversation.

"You've changed Connor, you know," he said.

"Have I? He doesn't seem that different to when I first met him." A little less cocky, perhaps, but still just as hot.

"That was when he changed. I have to thank you. So many people wrote him off, but you saw the good in him."

"So did you. You pushed him into doing what he needed."

He laughed. "And I suffered for it at the time, believe me. We came to blows over it at one point."

"You fought?"

"He's got a mean right hook."

"I can't imagine him being violent."

"I don't think he would be now. Like I said, he's changed. Now we have Connor 2.0."

"He's perfect."

Over dinner that night, Jenny's husband got out a bottle of champagne. "We've been saving it for a special occasion, and this definitely is one." He popped the cork and poured a glass for everyone. "To the pair of you. I never thought anyone would tame young Connor."

"Does this count as a party?" Jenny asked. "You know, for your list?"

I'd forgotten all about the bloody list. Life had taken over. How many things did I have left? Apart from the party I needed to travel abroad, learn to drive a Ferrari, and go scuba diving. It seemed impossible from where I was sitting. Maybe I should just give up and enjoy what I had?

"What list?" Scott asked.

Connor explained it to him with a bit of assistance from Jenny. I barely got a word in edgeways.

"We can do a better party than this. And I know a great scuba instructor."

"Uh, okay."

Scott carried on. "And you'll be coming to visit us in the States, right? That'll count as travelling."

"I know a guy with a Ferrari," said Connor. "That only leaves passing your driving test." Four faces looked at me.

"Okay, I'll take more lessons." When they made it sound so straightforward, it seemed silly to give up now. Grant would no doubt be thrilled at the news.

Scott and Connor both started talking, telling me more about San Francisco, and their enthusiasm was infectious. Maybe, with the help of my new friends, and against all the odds, I'd manage to complete Edith's list.

CHAPTER 35

I STOOD IN the middle of the deserted airfield and looked around. There was nothing in any direction but smooth tarmac. Well, apart from three things.

One could be forgiven for thinking I was at a photoshoot, seeing as those things were Connor, his friend Blake Hunter of #TEAMBLAKE fame, and a shiny red Ferrari, but the only camera was in Todd's hand. It was just the latest instalment of Challenge Edith—the dreaded driving part.

I'd passed my test on only my fourth attempt, and I liked to think I'd shown some improvement. At least I didn't accidentally cut up a police car like I managed to on my first try. When I came back finally waving my pass slip, Grant cheered louder than I did, although he pointed out that his income would halve now I didn't need any more lessons.

When it came to my twelfth task, Connor had thought of Blake, who, it turned out, only moonlighted as a model. He drove racing cars for his day job, and the Ferrari was his latest toy. Plus Connor reckoned he had nerves of steel, which face it, he would certainly need.

"Are you sure this is a good idea?" I asked Connor as we stood by the car.

"You'll be fine."

I bit my lip. "You think?"

"Look around, babe. There's nothing out here. What could you possibly hit?"

I don't know. I kept expecting a pillar to materialise from somewhere. Or a wall. I'd already made a slight miscalculation and reversed Connor's truck into the gatepost at home.

Our new home, at least until we decided where we wanted to live permanently. Seeing as Jenny needed the cottage at Linden Hollow back for guests, Connor had suggested a visit to the local estate agent. We were now the proud tenants of a four-bedroom country house, complete with a tennis court and swimming pool.

I'd had a go at playing tennis, but after I'd gone through two rackets and eighteen furry yellow balls, I decided I was better off sticking with Connor's. I hadn't managed to damage those yet, although he did end up with carpet burn last week.

"You ready to go for a ride?" Blake asked me.

Connor glared at him.

"I'm talking about in the car, you idiot. Bloody hell, you never used to get like that over women."

I squeezed Connor's hand, and he pulled me in for a kiss. He liked to mark his territory, and as long as he didn't start peeing on my leg, I found it sweet.

Blake made a gagging noise. "You done?"

"Live with it. It'll happen to you one day."

"Yeah, right." Blake opened up the passenger door and motioned me inside.

Before I sat down, I waved at Grant and Todd, who were standing at what Grant determined to be "a safe distance." I could only just make out his hand as he gave me a thumbs up. Todd jumped up and down and waved his camera.

I slid into the seat, which felt ever so low compared to Connor's truck. Even when I sat up straight I could barely see over the dashboard. Blake checked my seatbelt was done up before hopping in behind the wheel then we took off.

I couldn't help screaming as he floored it, but he only laughed. "Just thought I'd show you what she can do."

Tarmac flew past in a blur as I opened one eye and looked at the speedometer. We broke a hundred and fifty miles an hour before we got to the grass at the end, and sweat prickled my skin.

Blake reached over and patted my knee, and I said a silent thank you Connor wasn't around to see that. "Don't worry, I'm good at this."

"Do you think you could go a teeny bit slower?"

"Okay."

That time we hit a hundred and forty-nine.

After a couple of laps and a thousand mini heart attacks, Blake slammed on the brakes and pulled over in front of Connor. "You ready to try?"

I shook my head. I felt like I was glued to the seat. Blake unpeeled one of my hands from the edge, and Connor reached in and did the other.

"Can you give me a minute?" I asked as I waited for my legs to stop shaking.

Both of them sniggered. Bloody men!

When my nerves returned, Connor helped me into the driver's seat and Blake showed me how to adjust the seat. I checked I could reach the pedals then took a deep breath. "Okay, I think I'm ready now."

The engine purred to life and the sporty exhaust burbled behind me. This was quite unlike anything I'd driven before, not that I had vast amounts of experience, and my hands trembled as I put the car in gear and gently released the clutch. Here goes nothing.

Out of the corner of my eye, I caught Blake's look of surprise as we shot off backwards. Oops. I tried again, stalled, then had another go. That was better. This time, we trundled off in the right direction, topping out at twenty miles an hour.

After we'd gone a couple of hundred yards, Blake cleared his throat. "You can go faster if you want."

I gripped the wheel, my knuckles white. "No, this is fine."

I was doing it. I was driving a Ferrari! I wanted to wave at Todd but I didn't dare move my hand. Still, inside I was shrieking.

We'd got almost halfway down the airfield when the car went all bumpy.

"What's that? Is it supposed to be doing that?" Had I broken it?

Blake was silent for a second then he burst out laughing. I took my foot off the accelerator, and we ground to a halt.

"What's so funny?"

"Connor said you were a disaster on wheels, but I didn't believe it. Guess he was right."

"What? What did I do?"

"You've got a puncture. In the middle of acres of nothingness, you've managed to get a puncture."

Blake turned the car around, and we crawled back to the others.

"Bad luck, buddy." Connor patted him on the back.

"You got off lightly there," put in Grant.

"Did you get photos?" I asked Todd. That was the only thing I cared about.

"At least fifty." He grinned and held the camera up in triumph.

Thank goodness. I sagged against Connor, relief flowing out of every pore at the news I'd completed another challenge.

Even better was Todd's offer to cook for us that evening when we got home.

"It's very kind of you," I said, as we followed Connor and Blake towards the house.

"Oh please, I'd have to be dead from the waist down if I passed up the chance to stare at that gorgeous man candy for an evening. I mean, would you look at that?"

"He's got a point," Grant said.

Three pairs of eyes dropped as the pair climbed the steps in front of us, and Todd started fanning himself. "How do you like the idea of a live-in chef?"

I only had three challenges left, and thanks to Connor's brother, help arrived for one of them the weekend after Blake's visit.

"I'm Gabe," he said.

"I'm, uh..." What was my name again? "Er, Ella."

Beside me, Connor chuckled. Odd, because usually he gave any man who got within three feet of me a death stare.

He saw me looking at him. "Relax. Scott's already told me I'm the one that should be worried. And put your tongue back in."

Ohhhh. What a waste.

There was nothing in Edith's letter saying where I needed to make my scuba diving attempt, and Gabe reckoned the pool at our rented house would be perfect. The end with the diving board measured twelve feet deep, which was quite enough for me.

We helped Gabe unload all sorts of equipment from his car then he sat down to give us a briefing. When he started talking about ruptured lungs and perforated eardrums, I began to wonder what could possibly possess anybody to do this for fun.

"Are you sure this is safe?" I asked.

"I'll be right next to you. All you need to remember to do is breathe and equalise." He showed me again how to pinch my nose and breathe out to stop my ears from hurting. "Any problems, if you feel any discomfort, signal to me and we'll come up."

Connor went first, and when he didn't drown, that gave me some confidence. He had a big red ring around his eyes when he took his mask off, but he was smiling.

"That's cool. It'd be even cooler if there were real fish down there instead of tiled ones."

I'd stick with the mosaics, thanks. At least if there were no fish, there were also no sharks and no stingrays.

I sat on the bench at the edge of the pool while Gabe strapped me into a waistcoat thing, or BCD as he called it, with an air tank attached to the back. Altogether, it weighed a tonne.

"Good to go."

I tried to stand up, got halfway, and fell backwards. "Uh..."

"Not to worry. Plan B."

Gabe and Connor carried me over to the pool and lowered me gently into the shallow end. My heroes. Once I'd steadied myself against the side, Gabe held the air thing up in front of me.

"Put the regulator in your mouth and close your lips round it. Just breathe normally."

All very well for him to say. He was probably a merman in disguise.

I dipped my head under the surface and quickly brought it up again. What if the regulator didn't work? What if I got a lungful of water?

Gabe popped out his own regulator. "It's okay, take a few deep breaths and try again."

Connor sat on the edge of the pool, his feet dangling in the water. "You'll do good, babe."

With his confidence and Gabe at my side, I took the plunge. Well, what do you know? It really was just like normal breathing except a bit wetter. Gabe let air in and out of my BCD as we floated around the pool a few feet under the surface. When we got to the deep end, he gave me the "OK" signal by forming a circle with his thumb and forefinger, then let go of me and took a few photos with an underwater camera.

A minute later, it was all over.

With Connor pulling and Gabe pushing, I managed to get out of the pool, then Gabe took the equipment off me. Even though I'd only worn it for a short time, my shoulders ached.

"Hoorah!" I panted. Tired or not, I still felt elated because I only had two challenges left. House or no house, I wanted to complete the list for the sense of achievement alone.

Gabe stayed the night, and we pigged out on pizza. "You sure you don't want to hang around for a few extra days?" I asked. He was great fun and easy to talk to, and I loved hearing his stories, especially about his time in Egypt.

"My family is expecting me tomorrow, but thanks for the offer."

"Where does your family live?"

"Switzerland."

Ooh, cuckoo clocks. "Scott said you're living in the States at the moment?"

"Only for a few more weeks, then I'm off to the Caribbean to work on another movie."

I sighed. That sounded so glamorous. Would Connor ever get another movie role? I knew agents were talking to him, but I had a feeling he was turning things down because of me. Sometime soon, we needed to have a proper talk about our future.

A couple of nights ago, I'd made him show me one of his films. We'd snuggled up with a bowl of popcorn, and he'd cringed while I watched, captivated, as he played the villain in a comic book adaptation, creepy, cool, and hot at the same time.

While he washed the truck the following day, I looked the movie up on the internet. He'd got rave reviews for that role, and there was even talk of a sequel. It would be such a waste if he quit that world for my benefit. I spent the rest of the day thinking, and then slept on my thoughts for a night. When I woke my decision was made.

"Where do you want to live?" I asked him. "I mean permanently."

He smiled at me. "Wherever you are."

I gripped one of his hands in mine and voiced what had been on my mind. "How about America?"

CHAPTER 36

CONNOR LOOKED ACROSS at me, eyes wide. "America? Do you mean it?"

I bit my lip and nodded. The thought was terrifying, but Connor's star was on the rise, and it wouldn't get very high if it was tethered to Reading. "As long as I can still come back to visit my friends."

"Any time you like, babe. It's only a plane ride away."

Two months before the lease on the country house ended, we made our first trip overseas. That achieved two important things—it knocked another challenge off my list with six weeks to spare, and it meant I got to meet Connor's family.

On the flight over, I must have looked a bit nervous because the air hostess crouched next to me with a friendly smile. "First time on a plane?"

I nodded, reluctant to unwrap my fingers from Connor's arm.

"There's nothing to be worried about."

Easy for you to say, lady. I could hardly tell her I didn't care a hoot about the flying part, it was the fact Connor's parents were picking us up from San Francisco International that had me peeing my pants.

"What if they hate me?" I asked him.

He leaned over and gave me a hug. "They haven't

had to bail me out, or scrape me off the pavement, or hang their heads in shame in front of the neighbours for almost a year now, and that's mostly thanks to you. Believe me, they're gonna love you."

"I'm still nervous."

"Here, have chocolate."

It turned out Connor was right. The second we walked out of the "Arrivals" door, I found myself enveloped by a sniffling lady in a lilac pantsuit. As she squeezed harder, I tried not to throw up the two boxes of chocolate I'd troughed down.

"Ella?"

It was a bit late if I wasn't. "That's me."

"I can't believe you're finally here! We've been waiting for months to meet you. Connor's told us so much."

His father stepped forward, and it was like looking at an older version of Connor. At least he was going to age well. "Let her go, Helen. The poor girl looks terrified."

She patted me on the arm. "Oh, you poor dear. Didn't you like flying?"

I quickly shook my head and saw Connor smirk behind her.

His father stuck out his hand and clasped mine. "David. It's a pleasure to meet the lady who's turned our son into a human being."

"Uh, thank you. I think."

He laughed and put an arm round my shoulders,

ignoring his son's glare as he led us towards a waiting SUV. "I brought the big car. Thought it'd be more comfortable."

Helen insisted on sitting in the back with me so she could "get to know me better" on the drive to their place. Only I barely got the chance to speak. She chattered away the whole time, first telling me about herself and David, then starting on stories of all the trouble Connor and Scott got into when they were younger. I could see Connor's eyes reflected in the wing mirror, and he looked like he wanted to gag her.

As soon as we pulled up in front of their lovely ranch home, he snatched me out of the car and tugged me away from the clutches of his family.

"In a hurry to christen the bed, eh son?" his father asked, chuckling.

I went beet red, but Connor shook his head. "No, I just want to keep her away from Mom and the photo albums."

"Ooh, I hadn't thought of that." She squeezed my arm. "You have fun this afternoon, dear, and I'll get them out for you after dinner."

"I like your Mom," I said as Connor dragged me towards the guest cottage at the back.

"Good. I, on the other hand, am rapidly changing my opinion."

"Shouldn't we stay and talk to your parents?"

"My father was absolutely right. I've gone fourteen hours without seeing you naked, and I'm suffering withdrawal symptoms."

"I wouldn't want to be responsible for any kind of discomfort."

He picked me up and flung me over his shoulder.

"That's my girl."

After we'd survived the family dinner, we spent a few days playing tourist, but after that it was time to get down to the serious business of finding somewhere to live.

"Rent or buy?" the realtor asked, her eyes lighting up as she realised who her new client was.

I narrowed my eyes as hers dropped below his belt buckle, but Connor ignored her puffed-out chest and kept his gaze firmly fixed on her face.

"For the short term, either would do, but long term we'll be looking to buy."

Hearing him say that made this all the more real, and a funny fluttery feeling started in my chest. This was actually happening! I still pinched myself some mornings when I woke up, and I had the bruises to show for it.

"I've got a few fabulous properties on the books. Would it suit you to view tomorrow?"

Connor made the arrangements while I stood there in a daze. This was a huge step, but after all the things I'd done in the last year, I no longer feared the unknown. Unless, of course, it involved talking to strangers in pubs.

Moving to San Francisco was just one more adventure, and if Edith was up there watching me I hoped she'd be proud.

Connor and I fell in love with the third place we saw. More of a small ranch than a house, it had a couple of hundred acres surrounding a beautiful single story home. Both our eyes lit up when we saw the block of stables to the side.

"We could have horses," I said.

He nodded. "This is a family home."

"You want a family?" My chest tightened. This was new. We hadn't talked about children.

He nodded again, jerkily, then looked away.

I pulled him to me and hugged him as tightly as I could. "This probably isn't a conversation to be having in front of the realtor," I whispered. She was walking towards us, having finished the phone call she'd been on. "But I think I do too."

Unless the kid turned out like Stevie. Then all bets were off.

The inside of the house could best be described as having potential. The rooms were huge and empty, shards of sunlight glinting off the swirling dust patterns in the air.

"It was owned by an old couple," the realtor said. "They decided to move to Florida to be near their grandkids."

We wandered through the house, taking in the four bedrooms, the three bathrooms, the massive kitchen.

"It's a big project, babe, and I'm gonna be working a lot, at least for the next year."

He'd just signed up for two movies—a modern western, and another about a band. I couldn't make my mind up which one I was looking forward to most—Connor the cowboy or Connor the rock star. It was a good thing I got both of them.

"It'll give me something to do before I look for a job."

"A job?"

"I can't keep living off you for the rest of my life."

"At the moment I get paid six figures a month for standing around shirtless. That's plenty for the both of us, and I'd rather have you around to kiss."

To make his point he brought his lips down on mine, causing the realtor to swoon a little bit.

"Are you sure?"

"That I want to spend every possible moment of my life with you? Positive."

I smiled, and I smiled big. "So are we getting the house then?"

It had a "Sold" sign outside by the end of the day.

"You've got one challenge left," said Connor as he slid out of me that night.

"What?" I was still dazed from the mind-blowing sex we'd just had.

He stroked my hair off my face. "This deserves a celebration. We need to have a party."

"For multiple orgasms?"

He choked back laughter. "No. Well, yes, but a private party. I was thinking of one to celebrate the move."

My faculties were gradually coming back. "We should have two, really. A leaving party in England and a housewarming party when we move in to the new place."

He leaned down and kissed me on the nose. "Deal."

CHAPTER 37

IT TURNED OUT that not only could Todd cook, he was also a party planner extraordinaire. The instant I mentioned the word, he'd jumped all over it.

"I've got a great selection of party games, and I can do the food, and my friend Manuel makes fabulous cakes, and..."

"Do you want me to stop him?" Grant asked.

I looked at over at Todd, already thumbing through his phone with a gleam in his eyes. What did I know about organising parties? "No, let him go ahead."

A week before we were due to leave, the rental house in the Cotswolds was transformed into a rainbow of glitter and sparkles.

"What's with all the pink?" Connor asked, wide-eyed.

"Todd got a little carried away."

He'd even done his hair to match—pink streaks and silver sparkles. Connor had threatened him with bodily harm when he'd approached with the can of glitter spray.

"How many people are coming?"

"Not that many. I think everybody's going to be taking leftovers home."

First to turn up were Jaz and Amir. Demi had hitched a lift with them and unfortunately they'd been forced to bring Stevie after another babysitter quit.

"He'll be okay, though," Jaz said, sounding as if she was trying to convince herself more than me. "We've got him a new bed. It's got walls and a roof."

"Isn't that a dog crate?" I asked as Amir unloaded it from the back of the car.

"It's multipurpose. And if we padlock the door, he can't get out."

Demi gave me a hug. "How are you feeling?"

I took a deep breath. "Okay, I think. Sad, but happy at the same time, you know?"

She nodded. "We're gonna miss you."

"You're coming to visit. How have you been, anyway? I haven't seen you in what, three weeks?"

She gave me a small smile, but there was tension behind it. "Not too bad." She sighed. "Well, I might have a teensy problem but that's another story. I'll tell you about it later."

I wanted to hear about it right away, but another car stole my attention as it crunched over the gravel outside, and I hurried to the front door.

"Albert! You made it!"

He leaned on his walking stick as he shuffled up the drive with his girlfriend on his arm. He'd proudly introduced his "young lady" to me a few weeks ago. She must have been at least seventy, but she was wearing a leopard print dress and a feather boa. If Edith had been alive they'd have got on famously.

"Wasn't going to miss your final challenge, lass. Reckon Edith's up there having a party of her own at the sight of you like this."

"It's certainly been an experience." And a good one, I had to admit, apart from the kidnapping. I still suffered from flashbacks, and even now the sight of toast made me want to throw up. But I also had Connor, and he was determined to drive out the bad memories and replace them with happy ones.

And so far he'd done a brilliant job. I blushed, thinking back to this morning's episode in the shower, then forced my mind back to the task at hand.

"Come on in. Everybody's gathered in the kitchen."

Following the party, Edith's house would be transferred over to me, as well as her estate. Albert assured me the paperwork was all in hand. We'd spent three hours going over everything last week, and I'd been gobsmacked to find out she had over half a million in the bank. No wonder she liked to party. Now that and the house would become my nest egg, something to give me the financial security I'd always craved.

Ah, the house. I couldn't live in it, so I'd hired a local agent to rent it out. With that income, I'd be able to contribute something to our new life whether Connor liked it or not. Part of me would be sad to leave the only real home I'd ever known, but the bigger part looked forward to the future and whatever it may bring.

A knock at the door heralded the arrival of Jenny and her husband, plus Lenny, Marion and a few other stable staff we'd become friends with over the past months. Grant brought Tony the climbing instructor, who was a friend of his, and Sue from Payright came along as well. Soon the place was buzzing, and the pop of champagne corks echoed through the house.

The roar of a Ferrari signalled Blake's arrival. At least he hadn't got a puncture this time. He strode in the front door with a voluptuous blonde in tow. Wow. Her smile could be seen from space, surely?

"This is Lexi," he said. "My sister."

She gave me a hug, squashing her impressive assets against me as she raved about the decorations. I'd never met her before, but as she was carrying a bottle of champagne in each hand, I could see us becoming fast friends.

She squealed when she saw Connor and threw herself into his arms. I wasn't sure whether I should be jealous or not, but when he'd unravelled himself, Connor whispered, "Don't worry, she does that to everyone."

"Do you know her well?"

"Well enough. Not in that way," he hurried to add. "Blake would have killed me. But if she offers to mix the cocktails, it's a good idea to go easy on them."

Last to arrive were Connor's brother and his wife. I'd met her a few weeks ago, and she'd already invited me to hang out with her when the boys were busy. I'd expected a typical movie star's girl, all plucked eyebrows and Botox, but she was anything but. In fact, she'd grown up not too far from me, and we had loads in common.

The party may have been small, but it made up for its size with energy. Todd had hired a DJ, who'd ensconced himself in a corner of the lounge, and once the food had gone down and we didn't feel like being sick, we all shoved the sofas out of the way and danced.

At least until Stevie wandered in, dragging the sorry remains of a pillow. He passed something to his mother. "Balloon broken," he said, then burst into tears.

Jaz held up the remains of the condom he'd found and raised an eyebrow at me. From where I stood, I could see it was one of the strawberry-flavoured ones, ribbed for extra pleasure, and I wanted to sink gracefully into the floor and disappear.

It was Scott's wife who saved me. "Do you like those ones? I thought they tasted really synthetic," she said, then clapped her hand over her mouth, looking horrified.

The room erupted into laughter, and Demi gave us a rundown brand-by-brand of the best ones to try. I committed her advice to memory. Probably it would have looked weird if I'd got my phone out to take notes.

All in all, it certainly was an evening to remember, and I wasn't going to forget the night, either.

As I lay awake in Connor's arms, listening for any sign that Stevie might have escaped again, I let out a long sigh. "I feel like a new person."

He paused for a few seconds, staring at the wall behind me before dropping a soft kiss on my cheek. "How would you feel about having a new name?"

"Sorry, what?"

He smiled his secret smile, the one I'd only ever seen in the bedroom. "I'd quite like you to have mine."

It took me a few seconds to process that then bells went off in my head. Not alarm bells. Wedding bells. "Did you just ask me to marry you?"

"Yeah. Shit, I didn't think this through. I haven't even got a ring."

"I don't care."

"So will you?"

"Of course I will, you idiot." All my birthdays, Christmases, Easters, and Valentine's days had just come at once. Oh, and seeing as we were moving to America, I needed to add Thanksgiving to that list.

He beamed at me, the full, dazzling effect. "Love you, babe."

"I love you too."

I didn't love the next day's headache quite so much, as I stumbled downstairs and found Scott cooking breakfast. Everyone had been informed of the "no toast" rule, so he offered me a bowl of fruit.

"Have you got any paracetamol to go with that?"

He fished a packet out of his pocket and slid it over. His wife obviously had him well trained.

"I don't suppose you guys want to go riding, do you?" he asked.

"Can't this morning. We're going shopping," Connor's voice came from behind me. He pressed against me and wrapped his arms around my waist.

"You? Shopping?"

"Yeah, it's important."

Scott looked up at the smile on his brother's face. "Jewellery store?"

"Yeah."

Scott broke into a grin as well. If they kept this up, I'd have to go and get my sunglasses. "Shit, bro, I never thought I'd see the day."

"You're not the only one." He gazed down at me, eyes filled with love and just a little hint of naughtiness. "You're not the only one."

EPILOGUE

I STOOD ON the back deck and watched the morning sunrise. For the last month, I'd woken with butterflies in my stomach each day before the builders arrived. They'd got behind on everything from plastering the walls to re-fitting the bathrooms, but yesterday they'd packed up their tools for the final time. And no sooner had their van disappeared off down the drive, Nica and Jewel, two frightfully efficient ladies recommended by Scott, arrived.

And today, I didn't have butterflies any more. No, they'd turned into pterodactyls instead, because today was my wedding day.

"Tell me again why we thought having the wedding at home was a good idea?" Connor slunk up beside me. As the orange glow rose over the horizon, men were already hard at work, hauling chairs around and putting together framework for the marquee.

"Go away! You're not supposed to see me before the wedding."

"Why not? I see you every morning."

"It's bad luck."

He leaned over and nuzzled the side of my neck. "Somewhere in the world it's still yesterday."

"Okay, fair enough. Ten minutes, and then you really do have to go."

He dragged me back to the bedroom and took fifteen, but I lost track of time. The sound of the front door slamming made him sit up and groan, but I was still plastered to the mattress.

"Hey, bro." Scott's voice drifted up the stairs.

"Two minutes," Connor yelled back.

"You couldn't wait half a day?"

"That's rich, coming from the dude that didn't last out the reception."

"Just hurry up, okay?"

The door opened and closed again, and more voices floated in. I recognised Jaz's unmistakable screech right away. "Stevie! Stop that."

Connor leapt out of bed in an instant. "See you later, babe." Stevie struck fear into his heart, same as the little blighter did with everyone else.

As the echo of Connor's feet on the stairs faded, it was replaced by a stampede in the other direction. I hurried to do up my robe before the gang burst into my bedroom.

Jaz got through the door first and nearly took me down with a ninja hug. Demi followed close behind.

"We missed you," Jaz squealed. "Barry's toupee got stolen by a Yorkshire terrier last week—you'd have loved it."

"I bet." I leaned back a little. "You've lost weight."

"Nope. I just discovered Spanx. Two pairs make a hell of a difference."

Demi flung her arms round me as well. "And Terry's latest victim stuck posters of his boy-bits on every lamppost in Reading town centre."

I smothered a laugh. "What did he say?"

"He's been telling everyone she photoshopped it

smaller, but nobody believes him."

And with good reason. I spied Jenny behind them. "How are the horses?"

"All good. Folly sends her thanks for the care package." The local farm shop delivered, so I sent treats every month. "And I could ask you the same question?"

The smartly refurbished stables behind our house had two new inhabitants, and my quarter horse, Ralph, would be taking a starring role in the wedding this afternoon. At least, that was the plan. At the rehearsal he'd shat halfway down the aisle then refused to go any further. Of course, Connor's Andalusian, Sonajero, behaved impeccably.

"Ralph ate a couple of the ribbons off his bridle, but the vet said he'd be okay."

Jenny laughed. "That nag's going to be the death of everybody."

I couldn't deny he was a little quirky, but when I saw the story of his rescue on the local news, I felt compelled to offer him a home. The poor thing had been a walking skeleton back then. The lady who'd starved him was serving six months in jail for cruelty, and I firmly believed it should be much longer.

"He's stopped running away from me in the paddock now. Bribery works."

"That's a start." She laid a hand on my arm. "You've done a good job with him."

More footsteps came up the stairs, and Nica appeared at the door, complete with clipboard. Scott said she and Jewel had "organised the shit" out of his wedding, and we'd hired them to do the same for ours, even if Nica did scare me a little.

"The hairstylist's just arrived and the makeup

artist's on her way." She pressed her earpiece. "Ten minutes out."

I sighed, and the pterodactyls flapped again. "Guess I'd better take a shower."

Two hours later, I'd been groomed to within an inch of my life, and I began to understand why Ralph objected when I primped him. At least it wasn't as bad as the time Demi took me to the beautician, although Connor said he wouldn't object if I got another vajazzle, purely for the comedic value.

Demi, Jaz and Jenny had also been subjected to the same treatment, and Jenny looked about as happy as I did. "It'll be over soon," I whispered.

"I can't remember the last time I wore a dress."

Jaz leaned over. "Look on the bright side, at least they're pretty. I had to be bridesmaid at my cousin's wedding last year and the outfit looked like it was made from tinfoil."

Beside us, Jewel suddenly went white and clutched at her ear.

"What's happened?" Nica asked.

"Ralph just escaped. He chewed through his rope and took off across the pasture."

Two minutes later, we watched from the deck as Taff gave chase on Sonajero, lasso in hand. "Don't worry," Jenny said. "He was stunt double on a cowboy film last year. He's done this loads of times."

It wasn't long before Ralph galloped back into view, only it was a very different Ralph.

"Oh shit! He's orange," Demi said.

Grant and Todd had arrived by then, and Todd's gasp eclipsed my groan. "He'll clash with the dresses."

I closed my eyes, hoping if I squeezed them tight enough orange Ralph would turn white again. "There's this patch of mud he likes. Last time he escaped he went there as well." And by the time I'd finished cleaning him, I was orange too.

At least this time he got caught faster. When I was responsible, it took me half a day of waving carrots and wandering around behind him while he ambled just fast enough to stay out of reach. Taff roped him within minutes and coaxed him back home, both of them looking far from impressed.

Jenny appeared beside me, dressed in a pair of jeans. "You go back inside. Me and Taff'll sort it. Don't worry."

Nica sucked in a breath, then another. "Yes, we need to finish getting you ready."

Friends. I'd be lost without them.

The moment had arrived. Nica pronounced me ready, and the guests were seated outside, facing the spot under the old maple tree Connor and I had chosen for our vows.

"Is Ralph fixed?" I asked Jenny. She'd just kicked her jeans off and tugged on her dress, and the hairstylist was attempting a last minute up-do with a whole can of hairspray.

"Uh, mostly."

"Mostly?"

Before she could answer, Nica grabbed my hand and pulled me outside, where Ralph sulked next to the veranda.

My eyes bugged out of my head. "He's... He's..."

Jaz and Demi both dissolved into giggles. "He's fluffy," Demi spluttered.

Taff held out the reins apologetically. "He wasn't drying fast enough so we had to get the blow drier out."

And that was why I rode down the aisle on the equine equivalent of an angora sweater. The vows got delayed a bit while Connor, Scott and the official stopped laughing. Sonajero, who Connor was seated on, had of course recovered from his shenanigans and stood perfectly, while Taff fed Ralph apple slices to keep him quiet.

Thankfully, the ceremony itself ran smoothly, and soon we were man and wife. Ella Lowes. I could definitely get used to that.

"Now it's time for a proper party," squealed Todd, clapping his hands in glee.

We'd decided to combine our housewarming party with the reception, and two hours later, the huge marquee next to the house was filled with half of Hollywood.

"I still can't believe you got Indigo Rain to play at our wedding," I whispered to Connor.

"Me and Travis go way back. He said he wouldn't miss it for the world."

Security was tight, with uniformed guards checking

people in and out. We didn't want any photos appearing in the press, and thankfully the guests shared our sentiments. The only person not drunk by the end of the night was Connor.

"Don't you miss it?" I asked, motioning at his glass of water.

"Nope. Not when I've got you instead."

I snuggled back into him. "You know what you said about your brother not lasting the reception?"

He grinned at me. "Yeah?"

"What if that's genetic?"

I didn't get another word out before he swept me into his arms and carried me out of the tent.

"You think the guests will notice?" I asked as he hurried towards the house.

"Probably. Do you care?"

I only cared about one person that night, and I was about to get him. All of him. And hopefully more than once. "Can you walk any faster?"

What's next?

The Trouble series continues with *24 Hours of Trouble*. Are you #TEAMBLAKE or #TEAMCONNOR?

Amelia Stanbrook is the golden girl, competing on the international show jumping circuit with the world at her feet and handsome millionaire Antonio by her side. Or so everyone thinks.

Behind closed doors, it's a different story, and Amelia dreams of escape. But that's not easy with two horses in tow. When she makes a break for it and bumps into Blake Hunter, he makes her an offer she can't refuse—pretend to be his girlfriend for two weeks to get him out of a sticky situation and he'll write off the money Amelia owes him.

Two weeks. All she has to do is keep her head and she's free to start a new life. But can she keep her heart as well?

Find out more here:
www.elise-noble.com/24hours

If you're in the mood for some darker humour, why not try my Blackwood Security series, starting with *Pitch Black*?

After the owner of a security company is murdered, his sharp-edged wife goes on the run. Forced to abandon everything she holds dear—her home, her friends, her job in special ops—assassin Diamond builds a new life for herself in England. As Ashlyn Hale, she meets Luke, a handsome local who makes her realise just how lonely she is.

Yet, even in the sleepy village of Lower Foxford, the dark side of life dogs Diamond's trail when the unthinkable strikes. Forced out of hiding, she races against time to save those she cares about.

Pitch Black is currently available for FREE:
www.elise-noble.com/pitch-black

If you enjoyed *Nothing but Trouble*, please consider leaving a review.

For an author, every review is incredibly important. Not only do they make us feel warm and fuzzy inside, readers consider them when making their decision whether or not to buy a book. Even a line saying you enjoyed the book or what your favourite part was helps a lot.

WANT TO STALK ME?

For updates on my new releases, giveaways, and other random stuff, you can sign up for my newsletter on my website:
www.elise-noble.com

Facebook:
www.facebook.com/EliseNobleAuthor

Twitter: @EliseANoble

Instagram: @elise_noble

If you're on Facebook, you may also like to join Team Blackwood for exclusive giveaways, sneak previews, and book-related chat. Be the first to find out about new stories, and you might even see your name or one of your ideas make it into print!

And if you'd like to read my books for FREE, you can also find details of how to join my advance review team.

Would you like to join Team Blackwood?

www.elise-noble.com/team-blackwood

END OF BOOK STUFF

I think we've all got a little bit of Ella in us—I know I have. Some days I like nothing more than to curl up on the sofa and pretend the world doesn't exist, but every so often I have to venture outside and talk to people. Dammit.

As with Trouble in Paradise, Nothing but Trouble contains a few real-life stories, although I won't say which ones ;) I will confess to taking off the passenger side wing mirror in my first driving lesson, though. At first I felt a bit guilty, but let's just say my instructor was no Grant so the feeling soon wore off.

And I haven't met a Connor during my years of equestrian antics, although I have come across a few polo players who look nice from the back.

Ella taught me a few important lessons while writing this book—that good things come to those who get off their backsides, that no matter how bleak things seem you've got a strength hidden inside you that will help you get through them, and that it's important to look past people's faults. Oh, and never get a vajazzle.

I also need to thank a few people for inspiration— my un-named colleague who really did fall off her skis on a travelator, my horse for keeping me on my toes, and the many, many Calvin Klein models whose attributes I researched thoroughly. My editor, Amanda, and Team Blackwood, for being endlessly supportive. And finally, you, the reader, for taking a chance on my book :)

OTHER BOOKS BY ELISE NOBLE

The Blackwood Security Series
For the Love of Animals (Nate & Carmen - prequel)
Black is my Heart (Diamond & Snow - prequel)
Pitch Black
Into the Black
Forever Black
Gold Rush
Gray is my Heart
Neon (novella)
Out of the Blue
Ultraviolet
Glitter (novella)
Red Alert
White Hot
Sphere (novella)
The Scarlet Affair
Spirit (novella) (2020)
Quicksilver
The Girl with the Emerald Ring (2020)
Red After Dark (2020)
When the Shadows Fall (2020)

The Blackwood Elements Series
Oxygen
Lithium

Carbon
Rhodium
Platinum
Lead
Copper
Bronze
Nickel
Hydrogen (TBA)

The Blackwood UK Series
Joker in the Pack
Cherry on Top (novella)
Roses are Dead
Shallow Graves
Indigo Rain
Pass the Parcel (TBA)

Blackwood Casefiles
Stolen Hearts

Blackstone House
Hard Lines (2021)
Hard Tide (TBA)

The Electi Series
Cursed
Spooked
Possessed
Demented
Judged (2021)

The Trouble Series
Trouble in Paradise

Nothing but Trouble
24 Hours of Trouble

Standalone
Life
Coco du Ciel (TBA)
Twisted (short stories)
A Very Happy Christmas (novella)

Books with clean versions available (no swearing and no on-the-page sex)
Pitch Black
Into the Black
Forever Black
Gold Rush
Gray is my Heart

Audiobooks
Black is my Heart (Diamond & Snow - prequel)
Pitch Black
Into the Black
Forever Black
Gold Rush

Printed in Great Britain
by Amazon